WE'RE GOING IN, BOYS

Damage Analysis

€20 Billi

Residential   Industrial   Infrastructure
Agricultural   Recreational   Areas of Flooding
■ 1 - 2 Metres
■ 3 - 5 Metres

Donegal
Galway
Milford Haven
Bristol
Portsmouth
Brest
Nantes
Bilbao
La Coruna
Porto

8/01/15

UK to commence 60% Carbon Rations

Government sets date

n an historic parliamentary speech, the Prime Minister today announced the date of full UK entry nto a nationwide carbon rationing system. As of January 8th, 2015, the UK will be the first nation ate within the EU to implement the system. It's an emotive date, exactly 63 years to the day the ation last endured food and petrol rationing in WW2.

WHAT DOES IT MEAN?

COMPULSORY CARBON CARD FOR ALL CITIZENS
200 POINT LIMIT PER MONTH
NEW Minister for Carbon Department

Environmental leaders from around the world have acted with joy, hailing today's events as a major leap orward in the ongoing political deadlock over mplementation of the EU Co2 Rationing Accord of 012. It was, of course, hammered out in response o the apocryphal Great Storm of December, 2010. An unprecedented environmental disaster, the week-ng storm is estimated to have caused 8,000 deaths nd destroyed 2.5 billion hectares of agricultural land. 6 million homes and 40,000 businesses. Lloyds of ondon have placed a €200 billion price tag on the long erm damage sustained to the European economy over

At the heart of the the legislation is a commitment to ensuring levels of CO2 in the atmosphere do not rise above 450 parts per million, the level environmentalists have set as the upper limit before irreversible global climate change happens.

The Carbon Card system will be nothing short of a total grassroots' fuel revolution for every citizen and it will be enforced by a new department of carbon emissions.

Former vice-president and environmental campaigner Al Gore has given an immediate positive reaction to the announcement. 'Finally the so-called Big Three of Europe have taken a lead. It is now imperative that all of Europe follow.'

Gore, who has been a leading figure in the Emergency Carbon Committee set up by the European Parliament in the wake disaster, is reported to have become increasingly fru

Coming soon . . .

The Carbon Diaries 2017

January

Thurs, Jan 1st

Exhausted. The whole family looks like death after an all-day meeting. The last time we were all in one place together for more than 3 hours was when my sister, Kim, locked us in a holiday cottage in France for the whole of Millennium night by mistake. Happy times. Today she locked just herself in her bedroom and sulked until Dad got her to come out. Typical. Mum is Being Very Positive – ranting about when she did voluntary work in the 80s on a kibbutz in Israel, knitting lentil ponchos and *it being the best days of her life*.

Dad muttered that we shouldn't just focus on it being difficult, but think up a New Year's wish list. He typed our answers into his laptop. Ever since he got made Head of Travel and Tourism at Greenham College he zaps everything into Excel and files it as evidence. Mum says The System's got him by the Balls.

Brown Family New Year's Luxury Item List. 01/01/15			
Nick Brown	**Julia Brown**	**Laura Brown**	**Kim Brown**
One hour of quiet time in study per evening	The car (Saab hydro-hybrid 9-50 Convertible)	Keep the dirty angels up and running	Her life back
Archer's Omnibus on Sundays	Shiseido face and body range	24/7 access to e-pod	
	Inner Growth	Ravi Datta to notice me (did not write this down)	

She just rolled her eyes when she saw Dad's list. She said, 'God, Nick, I didn't know we were so *polarised*.'

Fri, Jan 2nd

My parents are in deep denial; they've spent the day on the sofa, staring blindly at the TV like amoebas. So far they've back-to-back watched *Dumbo*, *Mary Poppins* and *Judy Garland: a Tribute in Song*.

I saw Kim for a total of 5.2 seconds when I answered the front door to a pizza deliveryman. She stormed out of her room and snatched the pizza box off me with dead eyes before marching back into her room again. She's so using my parents' death state to get her boyfriend, Paul, round and blaze in her room. I caught a real blast when she opened her door.

I wanted to watch the news and check out the

2

countdown to rationing, but fat chance of that in this house of drugs and musicals, so I sneaked out next door but one to Kieran's. When I got there he was unblocking his kitchen sink – which is kind of funny because Kieran is a single, gay hairdresser in his 30s and if anyone should be wiped out on the sofa and drooling over musicals after an all-nighter it should be him, really. But that's why I love him. He's actually not predictable and ground down to dust, the *total opposite* of most adults. I reckon if he can get away with it then maybe I can too, when my time comes.

'Hold this,' he groaned, handing me a bit of sink before ducking his head under again and poking upward viciously with a coat hanger. The plumbing let out a totally brutal gurgle and evil gunk exploded out of the plughole.

Kieran screamed, 'Oh Jesus!' and sprang backward, shards of meat and grease and carrots streaming down his face. Gross.

He dived under the power shower and stayed there for one long time, so I flicked on Channel 4 News. They've got this big countdown clock in the studio with massive Day-Glo carbon symbols instead of numbers on its face. It was kind of like kid's TV cept it's so real. Messed up.

Anyway, today's symbol was about food miles. The presenter stood in front of a split video screen and waved his arm towards the left-side screen, where there was a South African farmer holding out a ripe mango. On the other side there was a farmer in Kent holding a wrinkled apple. Basically a 12,000-air-mile mango versus a 40-minutes-in-the-back-of-a-dirty-old-truck apple. The carbon maths is a no-brainer, but life is definitely going to be a lot less glamorous.

This 60% reduction is way over the top. We were supposed to get there by 2030, but after the Great Storm everything changed and it all became more hectic. Even so, why is the UK going first? I know we were hit the hardest in the storm – that was one messed-up time; houses literally ripped out of the ground, thousands of people homeless over the whole winter, no petrol for a month. I guess something really happened to people then. It was like everyone went *That's enough. Stop now.* Europe's going to follow – I mean, they've got to in the end – but right now it's like they're happy for someone else to do it first. So looks like we're the stupid guinea-pig freaks, giving up everything while the rest sit back and watch.

11 p.m. In bed now. *Jeeesus*, Kieran's got himself in a real state over rationing.

'I'm all washed up. Finished,' he kept moaning. 'It's the

hunter-gatherer, macho, sink-unblocker's world now. What'll become of a little skinny hairdresser guy like me?'

Kieran goes to the gym about six times a week, so I told him he had gorgeous pecs, which usually sorts him out.

'Yeah, yeah, but what's the use when there'll be no clubs, no weekenders in Ibiza, no chilled Laurent-Perrier, no Versace? A male hairdresser can't be taken seriously without a lifestyle!'

'Like you do any of that stuff, anyway,' I snorted. 'You're always moaning about those scene queens.'

'I know, I know – but they're taking my right to choose away!'

I checked he wasn't being ironic, but his mouth was all drawn down like a little boy.

When I got home, my parents were asleep in front of the TV screen, every single light in the house was blazing and Kim was in the bath with the stereo and her bedroom HD on. I don't know what's gonna happen to this family once rationing really kicks in.

Sat, Jan 3rd

Dad sat us all down again tonight and took us thru a disgusting government online form to work out what our family CO allowance actually is. It's heavy. Basically we've got a carbon allowance of 200 Carbon Points per month to spend on travel, heat and food. All other stuff like clothes and technology and books have already got the Carbon Points built into the price, so say you wanna buy a PC but it's been shipped over from China and built using dirty fossil fuel then you're gonna pay a lot more for it in Euros – cos you're paying for all the energy that's gone into making it.

At first they set up a free trading system so that if you were rich you could just buy up carbon in cash and live how you wanted – but after the riots last September the Gov backed down and changed the rules so that no one's allowed to buy more than 50 extra points a month.

And the worst thing is, on top of all this, me and Kim have to give up loads of our points for the family energy allowance, which leaves us some pathetic amount for travel, college, going out . . . The car's gonna be cut way back, all of us get access to the PC, TV, HD, stereo for only 2 hours a day, heating is down to 16°C in the living room and 1 hour a day for the rest of the house, showers max 5 minutes, baths only at weekend. We've got to choose – hairdryer, toaster, microwave, smartphone, de-ioniser (Mum), kettle, lights, PDA, e-pod, fridge or freezer and on and on. Flights are a real no-no and shopping, travelling and going out not much better. It's all kind of a *choice*.

I sat there and thought about my band, the *dirty angels*.

We've just got back together after a break for *musical differences* after Claire got heavily into hardcore Straight Edge. She was so militant. You couldn't even unwrap a Snickers around her without a lecture on skinny cocoa-bean farmers. Anyway, she blew it by getting back with her snotty boyfriend *and* eating a bacon sandwich – all on the same day – and so we're together again and sounding *sooooo* good right now. It's my dream.

And all the time everyone was saying stuff like, *Well, I'm not selling the car, I worked hard for it,* and, *I just want to go on my gap year and get away from your selfish messed-up generation,* and *I insist that one of the daily TV-hours is spent watching a current affairs programme.*

Mon, Jan 5th

Carbon cards came today . . .

They've got these little blocks down one side going from green to red and as you use up your year's ration they fade away one by one till you're down to the last red and then you're all alone, sobbing in the dark. Kim won't unwrap her card, she says if she touches it then that's all her youth gone. I felt pretty shaky unwrapping mine, not that I really have a youth in my family. My sister's got it.

Tues, Jan 6th

The whole of London exploded tonight. It was all pretty normal round ours till about 9. Friends of my parents had come for supper. They were talking all the usual shite, then Marcia Hamilton, head of hardback non-fiction at Penguin, suddenly crawled under the table and started pawing at my dad's leg, like a little lost poodle, *yelping:* 'I can't cope!' Dad clutched his knife and fork really tight and tried to pretend it wasn't happening. Then Mum slammed her hand on the table and went: 'Damn right – let it out, Marcia!' before pouring half a bottle of wine down her throat. She turned to Phil Hamilton and said, 'Will you dance with me to the passing of an era?' *Phil Hamilton*, who is 5 foot 5, bald, with a woman's bottom and acne at 47 years of age!

I thought I was going to puke. I got myself out on the street – and breathed deep. Please God, let me die before their genes kick-start in me.

Anyway, once I was there, a sudden movement caught my eye – and I turned to see Ravi Datta leaning against his front door. His family moved in next door a few months ago, he goes to the same college as me and is in my Design Tech class. And he is fully gorgeous. He was silhouetted by a street-lamp, smoking a totally illegal cigarette and staring up at the rockets the Leaders were setting off over the estate. The lamp kept flickering on and off, lighting up his face and jet-black hair. And the best thing of all is he doesn't *know* he's fit. And the worst thing of all is he makes me so nervous and I say stuuupid things when I'm around him like pointing at his smoke and saying, 'That's gonna kill you.' He turned and grinned: 'So?' before taking in a last vicious pull and flicking the butt into the sky in a shower of sparks. Then he went back inside the house. He hardly ever says anything. It makes me mad when gorgeous people won't talk because boring people never shut up.

I hung out for a while, just looking up at the stars, and then suddenly a rocket fizzed right over me and smashed into Kieran's upstairs-flat window. Kieran stormed out on to his balcony and started screaming at the estate about them all being homophobic pigs and hunter-gatherers. Then the whole Leader family came out on to the estate balconies and started wolf-whistling him.

There are about a hundred Leaders, but never at the same time because they're always in and out of prison or young offenders. The top dog Leader is Tracey because she's too smart to get put inside. Tracey Leader has got arms like tree trunks. She's got a tweety bird tattoo on her collar bone and is dead scary. When she laughs she throws her head back and her gold tooth *glistens* but her brother, Karl Leader, is totally fit. I don't know how because the rest of the Leaders look like a horror film. He has got Bambi eyelashes and a chiselled jawbone.

Anyway it could have been really bad for Kieran, but Tracey was in a gold-tooth mood and sent over her cousin, Desiree Leader, with a bottle of Cava to say sorry. And so me and Kieran wandered the streets, all the way up to Blackheath, swigging from the bottle. Bringing in the new era in style. The roads were full of crazy people and there was smoke and explosions and screaming and singing and fights and madness everywhere.

I'm excited.

Weds, Jan 7th
Midnight. This is it. Let loose da dogs o' war!

Thurs, Jan 8th

Rationing.

Back to college, and I got in late cos I had to take Mum to her bus stop. Her eyes filled up with tears as we walked past the Saab. She whispered, 'It's not for ever,' and stroked the bonnet. I pretended not to see – it's better than her being positive.

We missed the first bus cos her high heels were rubbing, so we had to wait 15 minutes in the drizzle till the next one. When it finally came I leapt on, swiped my card and was scooting upstairs, only to see Mum behind me going thru her purse, bag and pockets, throwing fluff and Conran receipts everywhere. She looked up at me.

'Laura, darling, I can't find my card. Can you lend me some . . .'

The driver shook his head. 'No carbon card, no ride, love.'

'But, please . . .'

A woman out in the rain shouted: 'Get off, yer stoopid cow! You're holding us up.'

And then Mum started to cry. I went back down and walked her off the bus. 'We'll have to go home and get your card, Mum.'

'Found it! In the lining! Bastards!' Mum shook the green plastic at the bus, now rumbling off into the traffic.

'Oh, I shouldn't get so upset. Sweetie, let's pop into Alfredo's for a cup of tea.'

'I'm so sorry, Laura.' Mum stirred her dodgy brown tea. 'I know I should be strong, but I feel so responsible for my generation – we're the ones who've messed it all up for you.' She tapped my hand. 'Don't bite your nails, sweetie. I mean, what's going to become of you young things? Woodstock, freedom, women's rights, the Magic Bus . . . that's what it was all about – but you'll never know . . . Don't forget, I'm your mother and I'm always here if you need to talk.'

I kept quiet. I once worked out that if Mum had actually been to Woodstock, she'd be about 70 by now, but there's no point saying anything.

'Ah well, that's better!' She drained her mug. 'Isn't this fun, a greasy spoon? I haven't been in one of these since I was supporting the miners in Bradford in the eighties.'

I stood up and put my jacket on. I will blow my brains out if I'm forced to hear this story one more time.

When I finally got to college there was a huge queue at the entrance cos everyone had to swipe their CO cards at the turnstile and the swipe machine kept breaking down and setting off the alarm. I don't know what we were swiping for anyway – the building was freezing cold.

'Welcome to the future,' muttered Adisa. 'They're

ripping us off already.'

Adi's my best mate. He's so deep.

When I finally made it to my tutor group, they were shivering in the drama studio and everyone's breath was all frosty. We've got a replacement form tutor for our old one, Katy Willis, who's gone off sick with some invisible, *Guardian*-reader disease like lentil fatigue. The new one's called Gwen Parry-Jones, who boomed 'Welcome!' when I walked in and shook my hand like a man. She looked over my re-enrolment subjects form. 'Good – Design Technology. Finally, someone doing something useful.'

I spent the rest of the day in queues and being given bits of official paper. It was weirdly quiet like nobody really wanted to talk to each other. Same at home. We ate dinner like zombies and stared at the Prime Minister being positive on the TV. I feel really sorry for Prime Ministers when the country's in the shit. They know they're never going to sound as good as Churchill.

Sun, Jan 11th

2 a.m. I woke up in a cold sweat again. The second time this week. Maybe it's the beginning of madness . . .

Mon, Jan 12th

Everybody's looking really *bad* at college. Claire, Adi and me couldn't even be arsed to bitch about anyone. And that's when you know it's bad.

We had a totally weird assembly in the main hall. All the teachers were lined up around the edges and had so been told to look *positive*. You could see it was killing them, specially the frizzy-haired women teachers. They looked on the edge of a nervous breakdown.

Bob Jenkins, the principal, got up on stage and talked a load of crap about new horizons but he looked the shakiest of the lot if you ask me (I saw him come in by bus this morning – where's your leather-seated Volvo now, Bobby boy?). Beads of sweat kept dropping off his forehead on to his notes about our new heating and lighting allowance. He finished up by telling us we're all being reprogrammed with a compulsory Environmental Energy Saver A-level. Gwen Parry-Jones is going to teach it.

When we were leaving they gave each student an Energy Saver Pack envelope, stuffed full of leaflets, pens, paperclips and pathetic post-it notes with *Making Charlton Green* on them. Talk about hopeless – it's like how they give you a whistle on your aeroplane lifejacket for when you go down in a fiery ball in the middle of shark-infested Pacific waters.

Tues, Jan 13th

My family has disappeared. Dad spends all night in his study on his laptop, Mum is always lost on a bus somewhere and Kim basically lives in her room – an evil ball of silent sulk. I actually feel sick being in the same atmosphere, she's radiating so much wicked energy. She's definitely got the TV going 24/7 in her room, I can hear it thru the wall. I had another really bad nightmare last night where she was strangling me and every time I tried to escape she grew more and more arms. I woke up, gasping for breath. And then I had an idea – I grabbed a

pen and started to draw. It's the only way to get the poison out my system. The only paper I could find was those stupid Charlton post-it notes.

It worked, too. After I'd finished I lay back and fell asleep.

Weds, Jan 14th

I woke up this morning and it was freezing, freezing cold. I'm only allowed heat on in my room between 7 and 8. I went and looked at the Smart Meter in the hall. It's this thing that tells you everything that's going on with energy in the house. Even for our one hour of heat Dad's locked the bedroom temp at 15°C. What a joke – it's not even enough to melt the frost on the windows.

Thurs, Jan 15th

There's heavy snowstorms all over southern Europe.

Fri, Jan 16th

I've been given an essay to write by next Friday for AS Critical Thinking: *Write an informal personal review of an aspect of your home-life environment in the light of the new carbon rationing system.*

Whoever thinks this stuff up (Crit Thinking teacher, Lisa Bell) definitely needs more sex. She's got to be frustrated. Otherwise why would she want to punish innocent teenagers so badly?

Mon, Jan 19th

The blizzards in Europe are getting worse – and spreading north. Italy has just lost all its electricity. The news showed this footage of the Vatican going black, window after window. Later they started up emergency generators so they could power up the Pope saying something into a microphone in Latin to a bunch of cardinals. Whatever.

Tues, Jan 20th

We had a powercut in the night. The house is so cold now, it feels like 200 years of evil chill creeping into my bones. Reminds me of the Great Storm. Cuts give me the creeps – you know when you go to switch the light on and it's dead? It was so freezing I went shopping to Waitrose with Mum and Dad just to keep my blood moving.

Super-strange experience. It was all dark in there cos they'd switched off loads of lights and the aircon and those fans that waft baking-bread smells around. It was just like a big warehouse. It was pretty funny, all the nice middle-class people pretending they weren't panic buying and that it was completely normal for them to be pushing six trolleys around, totally bulging with stuff. The staff kept making people put things back at the checkout cos they'd gone over their CO points.

My mother nearly had a fight with this other woman over a multi-pack of garlic and basil passata.

They both put their hands on the box at the same time and gave a little jerky tug and then went *Excuse me*, followed by another tug and an *Aha, ha, ha*, knuckles starting to whiten around the cardboard edges. Then my mother really went for it.

'I wouldn't insist normally, but this is one of the few foods my daughter' (stroking my hair) 'can eat – she has an acid deficiency. Her skin comes out in boils if she gets low.'

The other woman backed off like a defeated animal in a nature programme.

Thurs, Jan 22nd

Italy has only just got its power back. They've found out the cause of the blackout – a tree fell on a live cable on the Swiss border. A bloody *plant* wiped out a whole country for 60 hours. Loads of old people have died. So strange. I never knew that cold could kill people like that. France is under deep snow now, and it's coming our way.

We had a Sunday roast, the first one ever. Mum is *so*

desperate for everything to be normal, and even Dad joined in. He came into the kitchen rubbing his hands going, 'Mmm, that smells good,' like he was a dad in a happy-family sitcom.

Kim refused to come out of her room and eat with us, even though my father begged her. This is unusual cos normally she softens up for him, if a crocodile *can* soften. Finally Mum lost it. She shouted from the kitchen:

'I've spent the whole afternoon cooking this dinner for you, so you can at least have the manners to come and eat it.'

Kim's door opened for a second. 'Don't pretend you did it for me. You did it for *you*. You make me sick!' Slam!

The really annoying thing about Kim is although she's a total bitch, she is also the most honest person I've ever met. She's raised her game to a whole new level right now, though – basically used the cancellation of her gap year to New York to start a war against my parents. They're doomed.

As a special Sunday treat we watched separate movies in separate rooms. That was *so* the best thing about unrestricted carbon. The freedom.

I don't know if our family can survive being *together*.

Fri, Jan 23rd

I woke up to bright sun glinting off snow. I had a stab of fear when I first saw it, but then it was just so *pretty*. We had a wicked snowball fight out in the Yard at break. Claire got stuck in a lift in John Lewis cos of a powercut last night. Serves her right for being middle class! She had a group of people gathered round her in AS Energy Saver.

'Yeah, I was trapped for three hours. Felt like a lifetime.'

'Din't you shout an' all?' this kid, Nathan asked. 'Man, I'd be screaming like a girl if I was boxed in like that.'

Everyone laughed cept Claire.

'Nate, don't stereotype *me*. Course I shouted to begin with, but my throat just gave out, my knuckles were bleeding from knocking . . . nothing worked.'

'So what you do?'

'I had my smartphone, remember?'

'Yeah, but you say before you got no signal in there.'

Claire raised an eyebrow. 'But I still had battery. So I took it off my wrist and held it up against the speakerphone in the lift – and played my ringtone again and again . . . and finally, *finally*, this security guard heard it and rescued me.'

Nathan whistled. 'Nice work, girl.'

Claire glanced at her mobile. 'Maybe. But I can't ever

hear that tune again. I've killed it dead.'

Then Gwen Parry-Jones walked in and the room went quiet. She is dead thin, like those women who run marathons for fun. The lesson began and she was striding about the front of the room when who came slinking in 20 minutes late but Ravi Datta. My ears buzzed. Is that normal?

GPJ made us get into pairs and colour in and fill in the numbers on a diagram about the Gulf Stream cooling down. Ravi did his with some random girl on the other side of the room. Lucky cow. I did mine with Zafran, who's got, like, 3 brain cells in his entire being. He did the colouring in.

Another powercut. What's going on? When I got home, Dad was listening to the news on a wind-up radio Mum gave him 4 Xmases ago that's never come out of its box before. The bulletin was about emergency power-saving measures the Government's going to bring in. Basically they're going to make businesses cut back to a 4-day week to save power. Dad flicked the radio off.

'Christ, they haven't done that since the miners' strikes in the eighties.'

I ran out of the room. *Both* parents going on about the miners! If they don't watch out I'll be a damaged child.

Mon, Jan 26th

Massive snowstorm last night. It's knocked out loads of power lines across the country. I never knew cold could be this bad. It *hurt* to get out of bed this morning. The news is full of the powercuts, they are saying the electricity grid is old and completely messed up cos the private companies have been bleeding it dry since for ever. No one's got any answers. Just arguing – nuclear this, renewable that. Blah, blah.

I only just made it out of the house. Dad had to shovel snow away from the door so I could get my bike out.

He frowned. 'Are you going to be OK?'

I looked down the road. 'Yeah, as long as I follow the car tracks.'

I wobbled off, trying to look cool cos I could feel him watching. It was all going good until I hit the corner of the high road. I braked for a dog, skidded right across a junction and came off hard on the pavement. I got straight back on though, it's like I need to be with the others in college right now. No bunking off for me. On some back roads I had to get off my bike and clear a path thru the snow drifts.

My Design Tech class is packed out. Last term there was only 6 of us. The reason I took DT in the first place was so I could fix my bass amp, but now everyone's doing it – dropping stuff like Philosophy, Sociology, Art – and picking up more practical stuff. Dave Beard, the DT teacher, looked like he was going to cry.

It was dark by 3. I pressed my face up against the window to see thick snow falling out of a grey sky. When I pulled back I saw all of us reflected – we looked dead little. And when the lesson was over you could see no one really wanted to go home.

I put on my jacket slowly so I could listen to Ravi talking to Dave Beard.

'I measured the power voltage at home last night. It's at 150/160 volts instead of 220. They are cutting us so deep.'

Dave shrugged. 'But what can they do? There's not enough gas to fire up the power stations. The Danish are still piping it to us under the North Sea, but the French aren't letting any under the Channel. They're under a metre of snow themselves.'

'What happened to our own gas off Scotland?'

'All gone . . . We import it all now – and our storage facilities are tiny. The UK only keeps about eleven days' supply for the whole country. Some European countries keep as much as fifty, sixty days.'

Ravi swept his fringe back. 'But, if they knew this was going to happen – why didn't they do something?'

'Good question. The new nuclear stations are delayed because of all the protests; offshore wind's only giving us thirty per cent, hydrogen's still a nice dream for the future. We're addicted to oil and gas, Ravi. And the drug's running out.'

'Then let's all go to Ibiza,' Nathan cut in. 'Everybody having a nice time there.'

Dave laughed. 'Yes, but how long d'you think the Spanish are going to let a bunch of lazy British carbon-clubbing rebels stay?'

'For as long as they paying in cash.'

'Ah, but I've heard that the Government is going to freeze their bank accounts. All UK citizens are on rations.'

Nathan flipped his fingers. 'Heavy.'

'There's no escape, Nathan.' Dave sighed. 'For good or for bad, we're all in this together.'

Finally did something normal tonight. We had our first band practice of the new world order in Adisa's garage. On fire – wrote a monster new tune, real old skool, Minor Threat style. I got on this hooked-up bass riff and then Claire totally screamed over the top.

```
I ain't got no energy
for your messed-up world
```

24

```
I ain't got no energy
for your stupid mi-i-nd games
I only got
syn-ergy
un-predictability
ex-plosivity
so don't you dare mess with me!
```

God, I wanted to sing so badly, but there's no way Claire's gonna hand over that mic. Sometimes I write lyrics and give them to her and she goes, 'Cool' and puts them into her back pocket, which is like a black hole for rhymes cos no line I've ever written comes out alive again.

It all got a bit hectic in the end though and Stacey, the drummer, hurled her sticks at the garage door – but instead of bouncing off metal they bounced off Adisa's mum's chest, who'd just come in with Coke and crisps. His mum is Nigerian and she's got presence, if you know what I mean. She breathed deeply and muttered something about white people's music.

At the end everyone made a vow to give up 10 points a week to power up the band. I felt dead emotional when I said my vow. This band's my lifeline. I don't know how we're going to keep going, though – a screaming, Straight X punk band isn't anybody's idea of important right now.

I've just had a strange thing happen. I was on my way home from practice, walking down icy Blackheath High Street when everything just died all around me. All the street lamps, the shop lights. It's the first time I've been outside when it's happened. I was by an internet zone and the monitors went black. The strange thing is nobody reacted for ages. It felt like I'd dropped into a dream.

The cut went all the way across South London. Before, it's only been in a few small neighbourhoods. The power's back on now, but I still feel kind of shaky, like something's changed underneath.

Tues, Jan 27th

Mum flung open my bedroom door this morning.

'Darling, the Met Office are saying the worst is over!'

I lifted my head from the pillow. Her eyes were full of tears. 'It's going to start clearing up from tomorrow! Can you believe it?'

In a word, no. When's the weatherman ever been right? I didn't share these black thoughts with my mother. She can't cope.

5.30 p.m. I'm really struggling with this Crit Thinking bollocks and it's got to be in tomorrow.

11 p.m. Done!

The 1970s age-bracket of parents was very selfish. For example, they invented mood lighting instead of mending stockings under one forty-watt bulb like our grandparents. They were heavily influenced by lifestyle magazines such as the Daily Mail on Sunday and this led to Rampant Consumerism. My parents are ex-hippies from the seventies generation, their wedding photo kills me. They've both got so much hair, like it's a competition. They look like Eastern European immigrants but my father is from Axminster, Devon and is Head of Travel and Tourism at a college and my mum is from Upstate New York and works in publishing. In my opinion ex-hippies are the most dangerous kind because they really believe their lives are worthwhile.

I showed it to Dad. He tore his eyes away from his laptop screen, scanned my page and sighed. Heavily.

I think he might be going thru the male menopause. His neck and face keep going flushed and then he blows his breath out really sharply – like the time when he stayed underwater for too long in the Red Sea and had to be rescued by 3 gorgeous Swedish babes who were floating, topless, nearby. He told us later that he'd been following a beautiful shoal of angelfish and dived down too deep. Uh-huh.

Weds, Jan 28th
I was at Adi's this afternoon when the power went again.

One power station's gone down and the others are running at half speed cos there's not enough fuel. It's amazing how quick you get used to stuff. 2 weeks ago it would've been freaky, but this time we just sat around and jammed for a bit and then, when it was too dark to see any more, we wrapped ourselves up in blankets and sat out on Adi's porch and watched the stars, all glittering, imagining ourselves back in the day, surrounded by forest and wild animals.

On the way home I knocked on Kieran's door but no answer, even though I could hear his cat Gary purring on the other side of the door. Gary only purrs when Kieran's home – he's a very co-dependent animal. I was about to turn away, when something made me knock again. I heard a groan from inside. I pushed the door open. Kieran was sitting in the gloom, with his feet in a washing-up bowl.

'Look at them,' he whimpered. 'Blisters the size of saucers.'

'Kier, what happened?'

'Got caught in the powercut, darling, on the top floor at Foyles on Charing Cross Road. The whole of the West End went out, like someone'd thrown a tin of black paint over us all.'

I perched on the edge of his sofa. 'Why didn't you

stay in the shop?'

'Well, at first it was kind of panicky and everyone wanted to get out of the building – you know, like it was a terrorist attack. But once I'd groped my way down to the street everyone was going no, no it's just a blackout.'

'But how did they know?'

Kieran shrugged. 'Dunno, cos there was no TV or radio. It was weird, Laura. After the first shock wore off, things went kind of really peaceful. No one was yelling or screaming, just swarms of people in the streets, all moving like lemmings to the bridges. I crossed the river at Westminster with thousands all around me. It was complete gridlock until I got well south, cos the traffic lights were out.'

I glanced down at his red feet. 'You walked all the way home?'

'No-o – I hitched a ride once I got to Lambeth, but only as far as Camberwell cos the guy ran out of petrol and all the pumps were down. I tell you, I just wanted to get home so badly.'

'It's going to be all right, isn't it?' I said. 'I mean, this isn't the—'

Kieran took my hand. 'Come on, it's going to be fine. It's just a few powercuts. But can I let you in on a secret?'

I nodded.

'I think that was the most beautiful I've ever seen London. The moon was massive, the stars were so clear . . .' Kieran's face twisted into a strange smile. 'And it was so magnificently *quiet*.'

Thurs, Jan 29th

I'm starting to get scared. There was a queue outside Tesco's for bread, like in the war. It's still bitter cold. I can't remember what it's like to be warm.

February

Sun, Feb 1st

Stacey came round to mine for a wash. She lives on the 12th floor and they're not getting any water cos there's not enough power to pump it up there. The Government's holding it back for priority places like Queen Elizabeth Hospital in Greenwich.

'Man, if this carries on I'm gonna mess up a kidney or something so I can get on to the ward,' Stace muttered, teeth chattering as she threw freezing cold water over her face.

Mon, Feb 2nd

I've just found out that *the hydrogen* are releasing early tickets at Shepherds Bush Empire on Tuesday. I am so going – they're basically the coolest band in London. They've taken over a gigantic warehouse in South London and hooked it all up to hydrogen fuel cells. They don't tour so the only way to see them is to go down to the warehouse.

I'm gonna ask Adi if he wants to come and get the tickets with me. I'm not going to tell my parents I'm going across town though, they'll freak, with all the cuts.

Tues, Feb 3rd

All the local shops have run out of candles, so everyone's going to All Saints Catholic Church on the edge of the Heath to buy them. If someone is old or sick, the priests give them candles for free. I went down there for Mum this evening after college and it was so surreal – the giant arches flickering in the dim candlelight and all the people huddled together at the altar for their candle ration. Hypocrites. When did we all last go to church?

Another weird thing I'm noticing is people walking around just talking to themselves. Coming back from the church I saw 3 or 4 old women wandering down the road or standing in their doors, chatting away to no one.

Weds, Feb 4th

11 p.m. Oh God. Oh God. Me and Adi got trapped on the tube in rush hour.

We'd jumped on the train in such a good mood cos we'd got the *hydro* tickets and then it happened – just after Marble Arch. We were squeezed up right against the doors and the train was going dead fast, rattling and shaking along, and then suddenly vooom! Blackout and engine dead. The train didn't stop, though – we rumbled on down the tunnel, like the brakes were messed up too. Everyone was screaming and trying to get on the ground, but there wasn't enough space. I was going *please make it stop* over and over in my head but we just kept on and on. I thought we were gonna die. And then, finally, a massive screech of brakes, sparks and a burning smell filled the carriage – and we screeched to a stop.

For a moment it was silent, except for people breathing. And then someone cried: 'We've got to get out of here!' The screaming started again and there was a massive push towards the doors. I thought my lungs were gonna burst, so much pressure on me. A voice, shouting: 'All right, everyone, the way to get out of here is to keep calm. People by the doors – can you open them?'

I felt this guy next to me take the door seal in both hands and strain against it with all his strength. He pulled away in pain. 'No, man. No way.'

'What about the windows? Where's the bloody emergency hammer?'

Someone next to me went: 'We need a light . . . who's got a torch?'

'I've got a lighter!'

'No!' the first voice answered. 'No naked flame – we

don't know what's down here.'

I made a vow to myself to carry a torch if I got out. Always.

'It's a bomb!' A woman's voice. Breaking.

'Keep calm. We're all going to get out of here. We have to believe that. Can anyone see where we are?'

I peered thru the grimy window. Nothing out there, just dirty tunnel. Shit. I could feel the panic rising again around me.

And then another voice. Somebody was shouting from the next carriage. 'The driver's sent a message along the train. We've had a powercut – but we're all right cos the front carriage is in Bond Street Station. He says we've got to make our way slowly from carriage to carriage till we reach the front. But you've got to stay where you are till the people in front move forward. Pass it on.'

Adi squeezed my hand. 'Oh, Jesus.'

The big guy next to me began to cry softly.

And then we stood in the dark for the longest time till it was our turn to move. You could feel everyone trying to control the fear. Trapped underground, pressed tight, heat rising, pitch black. Suddenly a beam of light flickered across the carriage. A sea of pale, scared faces.

'All right, people. I'm a police officer. Is anyone hurt?'

34

Nobody answered. 'Then let's get you out of here. Step away from the connecting door so I can open it. And when you do move, *please*, do it slowly and calmly.'

Me and Adi held hands as we stumbled down the endless black carriages. On and on and on until finally we got to the front and stepped on to the platform. There were some kind of dull back-up lights there. I peered forward into the gloom. The platform was packed full of people slowly shuffling forwards, like souls risen from the dead. We joined them, step after step, stair after stair, tunnel after tunnel. At one point a load of people fell. It was too packed. I went down, bodies around me. People screaming, others shouting, 'Keep calm, it's OK,' and shit like that. Then Adi's hand on my arm, pulling me up. 'Come on. We're nearly there.' And then the best part of all – air, fresh air on my face. I never knew how good that could feel.

When we got on to the street, there were thousands of people crushed into the cordoned-off area around the exit. There were police and ambulances around the front. The streets were gridlocked. Me and Adi stood there, gasping. A fireman waved us over.

'Are you all right?'

I couldn't find any words, I just felt cold.

He frowned. 'Can you hear me OK, love?'

Adi nodded. 'She's fine. We just want to get home.' He took out his mobile.

'There's no network. Emergency Services only. Where's home?'

'Charlton.'

The officer glanced around, uneasy. 'Look, the official line is that people should stay here until the power comes on, but . . . well, my feeling is you'd be better off away from the West End. Are you fit to walk for a bit?'

'All the way to Charlton? It's miles, man.'

'I know, but nothing's moving here – and it's just going to get more and more packed. D'you know the way across the river at least? I reckon once you get clear of the centre there'll be buses running, and maybe the phone network will be back up by then too.'

'But why? What's happening in the West End?' I asked.

He hesitated. 'There's some reports of looting. I don't want to scare you, it's probably on a small scale – and normally I'd never advise two kids like you to go alone . . . but look at the amount of people we've got here – we can't protect you properly. It's best to get out of the area.'

Adi nodded. 'All right. Thanks.'

The fireman touched my hand. 'Take the back routes and if you see any trouble, run.'

We pushed through the crowd and slipped under the

cordon at the top of South Molton Street. We only went 50 metres before it was pitch black. I turned and looked back at the crowd.

'You sure about this, Adi?'

'Come on, girl, things are gonna turn ugly here soon. You know it. We're gotta get home.'

Even as we watched, a fight broke out on the edge of the crowd and police officers closed in. We slipped away into the darkness.

That boy has got a mean sense of direction. We took the blackest, tiniest back roads and traced a route down behind Piccadilly and then cut east, towards the City and the river. For 30 minutes, we saw no one, just rats and rubbish spilling into the road. By the time we got down behind the Strand, my foot was killing me. I leaned against a railing. 'Wait, these new trainers are messed up.'

Adi looked around us. 'We're doing good. Maybe we can sneak out on to the main roads and check out the buses now. I reckon that fireman was freaking out. We ain't seen nothing, huh?'

I winced with pain as I peeled my sock back. A massive blister. It popped, sending a gush of slime over my hand. 'Urggh!' Adi, have you got a tissue or something—'

'Sshh.'

'But it hurts—'

'Laura . . . Can you hear that?'

'What?'

We both stood still for a moment, and then there it was – a dull, roaring sound. A siren cutting across it. Coming towards us. We looked at each other.

'Get your sneaker back on.'

I crouched down on the corner of the road, tying up my lace, when suddenly a man hurtled round the corner, carrying a massive TV.

'Move!' he snarled, jumping over my outstretched leg.

'Laur, get up now. We've got to hide.'

Heart racing, me and Adi running down a crazy maze of city streets, trying to get over a railing or into a basement area, but there was nowhere to hide. By now there were sirens all around us. Then we took a sharp turn and ran straight on to the Strand. We stopped dead. It was a massive standoff. At least a thousand people in a silent mass outside Somerset House. Facing them, a line of police in riot gear. It looked like a photograph, like they'd been there for ever. Then without warning the police fired 3 gas grenades into the people. The crowd fell back, screaming. Thru the smoke I could see the police moving forward, beating on their shields with their sticks. Suddenly I heard Adi screaming in my ear. 'What you doing? Move! Move!'

And then we ran and ran and ran. Across the bridge, along the Embankment, till we couldn't run any more.

The feeling of opening my front door – and walking into my *home*. I can't describe it. Not that anyone noticed I'd been gone. Dad was the only one up. He looked up from his book. 'Had fun?'

I nodded.

I can't write any more tonight.

Thurs, Feb 5th

And the funniest thing of all is the power was only out for 2 hours. All that for 2 lousy hours. 30,000 passengers trapped till midnight, 8 million euros' worth of damage in the City, 2 buildings burnt down, 4 separate riots, looters fired on with gas and water cannons, 6 people dead, 260 injured, 800 arrests.

And the cause? A circuit went in the 275,000-volt system that goes around London. One stupid tiny transmission circuit blew in a substation in Kent.

I can't believe how naive I was before. I'm so down. Our first test and we failed it so bad. Looting? What's that about? It's just greed, stupid greed – same thing that got us into this mess in the first place. Sometimes I really hate people. What's going to happen when something *really* bad happens?

It's got to end soon. The blizzards are finished in Europe, but now the snow's melting so fast that it's all flooding like crazy. Denmark has increased our gas supply to 75% but the bloody French are still holding theirs back. There's just not enough fuel to keep our power stations running.

Sat, Feb 7th

Timewarp factor 10. Mum decided we needed to do something *fun to cheer us up* so our big happy family went for a drive this afternoon like it was such a big deal, like we were going to the moon.

I squeezed into the back of the car with Kim (dragged out of her room) but I made her boyfriend Paul sit between us to soak up her radioactive rays. What he sees in her is a total mystery. I guess she must be hot at the old you-know-what. Urggh.

'I'm not sure about this, Julia,' Dad muttered from the passenger seat.

'Well, I am. We haven't used the car in over a month and I, for one, need some goddamn normality.'

'All right, but we should really think about trading this car in for a full electric.'

Mum shivered. 'I'm not driving around in a milk float, Nick, and that's final.'

Dad sighed and looked out the window.

She's kind of right though, this Loud Dad guy who lives 4 doors down has just got an electric and it takes him to the end of the street to get up to 10 kph.

Mum drove us to Virginia Water and we had a freezing picnic by the side of the lake. And then a strange thing happened. Mum kept trying to force the last bit of quiche/cake/Kettle chip on to Paul – 'Come along, growing boy like you! Blah blah' – and he was saying 'No, no, thank you very much, Mrs Brown, blah, blah' – when suddenly Dad bounced up off the grass like a hot coal. 'Why don't you ever bloody listen? The boy said no!' Then he hurled his Scotch egg on to the ground and stormed off into a wood. We all stared at him in silence. Our dad, all angry. Kim began to laugh. 'Finally, we're starting to crack.'

Mon, Feb 9th

Yes! France has finally, finally lifted its ban on exporting gas. No more powercuts! Or at least until the next snow. Everyone is so happy. Bob Jenkins twirled Lisa Bell down the link in some hideous back-in-the-day dance move. But the bad news is the Gov's hooking up all the Smart Meters in our homes to the energy grid so they can control people and cut them off if they get out of line. Disgusting.

Tues, Feb 10th

I had the house to myself this morning so I hooked my e-pod up to the speakers and cranked it way up. Green Day, Peaches, New York Dolls – all the old classics – and I pogoed my little arse off all over the lounge. God I love those bands – so much strut, so much style. Claire's always trying to get me into the whole Straight X scene, but I dunno – no drugs, no meat, issues, it's so heavy. I mean, I care about stuff, but I want a life, too.

After a bit, I sneaked into Kim's room with my bass to practise some moves in her full-length mirror. I tried lowering the strap, but then I couldn't hit the high notes on *death to the capitalist scum*. There was a load of junk in front of the mirror so I moved a pile of papers to one side. The top ones slid off – and underneath was a ton of mags and brochures about Ibiza. What the hell was Kim doing with all these? I felt the back of my neck prickle. I had to look – all those UK people partying and burning up fuel like crazy traitors. I was jealous and dead angry with them all at the same time.

Suddenly I heard the front door slam and I legged it big time.

I hate Kim so much it makes me feel sick. The thing that's so bad about it is that until 2 years ago we used to really watch each other's backs. Kim's always been kind of nuts, but she was cool too – she'd teach me how not to take shit from anyone; I'd hang out in her room all the time, doing make-up, chilling out, playing tunes – and then when she started going to fashion college, she flipped and dropped me like I was the biggest loser.

Weds, Feb 11th

6.30 a.m. Postman just woke me up.

'Sign here, please . . .' he said, handing me a red envelope with a Carbon Department official stamp on it. 'That's a red.' He raised an eyebrow. 'They only send them to the real over-spenders. Ta ta.'

I didn't even open it, just hid it under the recycling bin. There's so many wine bottles in there, they'll never lift it. I can't stand the trauma.

I almost feel like a standard teenager on a Friday night tonight. We had a popping band practice – rationing's made us go dead focused. After an hour or so we took a break. Claire looked across at me.

'So, you're finally getting radical, Laur?'

'What d'you mean?'

'I hear you're going to the *hydro* gig. They're out there. They don't say it, but they're behind the SUP action.'

'The what?'

'Y'know, Scratch Up Petrol – any car on the streets that burns dirty fuel. Kids everywhere are scratching the Hydro logo on them with keys.'

'Oh what, that anarchy symbol that's got an H instead of an A?' asked Stace. 'My dad's dentist got a fat one right on the hood of his Porsche the other day. My dad said he was so mad he nearly drilled thru Dad's cheek.'

I shook my head. 'Look, I don't know – I just like the music. Why does everything have to be political with you, Claire?'

She twirled the mic around her arm. 'Cos it is, Laura.'

After practice we all went to watch *Icebreaker*, which was this 3-D thriller about New York freezing over. It was kind of weird watching it though; it was meant to be all tear-jerky – this family and all the shit they were going thru – but every time they cried or whatever, everyone in the cinema laughed. The family just seemed so spoilt, like children. In the end scene the dad hero guy was trying to outrun a glacier in a Jeep and Adi shouted 'Bullshit!' and a whole bunch of people in our row cheered.

Bloody Claire. I don't want everything to be political. I want everything to be normal.

Sat, Feb 14th

Happy Valentine's Day to me. How am I going to get RD to notice me? I'm in 2 very bad non-sexy categories – the girl next door and the girl he solders circuit boards with on Monday mornings and Thursday afternoons. I kind of want to tell people, but the last time I liked a boy (Scott Harris) everyone got so angry with me obsessing and not making any moves that they fly-posted the college with a blown-up photo of Scott with Call Me! and my mobile number all over it.

I dropped in on Kieran this afternoon. He hasn't picked up his scissors for weeks. Instead he's been pacing up and down his living room, talking to himself. I tried to calm him down, but his eyes were all mad and he kept going: 'What am I gonna do, what am I gonna do?' like a parrot.

Like I know. I'm *sixteen*.

When I got home Dad was out in the back, pretending to sweep the yard, but in reality chatting to Mr Datta. It's the first time I've heard him speak more than 4 words in weeks, so I listened in.

Jesus, grown-up men are so boring. 30 minutes of

conversation for this:

1) Mr Datta came over to Britain in 1987 to go into business with his brother and everyone has disappointed him since.

2) My dad went into teaching in 1986 and everyone has disappointed *him* since.

They only stopped cos Ravi came out to tell his dad he had a call. When Mr Datta had gone past him into the house, I saw Ravi spit on the ground just where he'd stepped. Ooh-er. I tried to catch his eye, but he just turned on his heel and disappeared indoors.

Dad went back to bed again – so much for that burst of life. I took the chance and sneaked into his office to log on. Every time I use electricity now I feel like a criminal. I wanted to look up some background on *the hydrogen*, but I couldn't remember the address of this underground music site, so I went into *history* – and guess what I saw? A load of hits on *Ibiza.com*. Kim *can't* be that crazy. I went to the BA site to find out the CO points for air travel. Man, it's heavy – 100 points for a return to Ibiza. That'd leave you with hardly nothing to survive on for the rest of the month. It's impossible. I also found this printout in a drawer.

That man's got no idea what he's up against.

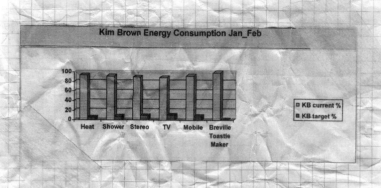

100
80
60
40
20
0

Heat   Shower Stereo   TV   Mobile Breville
                                        Toastie
                                        Maker

□ KB current %
■ KB target %

Mon, Feb 16th

So much for the carbon white market. There's a total black market in the Yard now. There was nearly a riot today when this kid got rushed cos he'd got a box of jacked batteries and was selling them with no CO swipe. It's not about money any more, it's about keeping your card low. This kid's set up a business on the bike-shed roof where you take him your backpack in the morning and he charges up the solar panels and then you pick it up at the end of the day for a chiller. It's a pretty good deal, you can run your smartphone for a day off it. I've finally got the carbon points in my head. 1 point is a cooler, 10 is a chiller and 100 is a cube. I think.

I think I might have found out what's wrong with Dad. I was walking down the D-Block corridor with Claire to her Travel and Tourism lesson, but when we got to the room there was a notice stuck on the door saying the course'd been cancelled. The *whole course*. Everybody's dropped it, and you can't blame them. What's the point in studying something you'll never do? I got a really sick feeling reading it. All the places I'm never gonna see.

Claire kicked the door. 'Brilliant! Let's go home and cook and sew and have babies and freeze our arses off and never go anywhere or do anything exciting and die in a storm and live with our parents for ever.'

I feel dead sorry for Dad. I mean Travel & Tourism is a really stupid department to be head of, but what was he supposed to do after cruising around the world in a VW camper van with a head full of weed in the 80s? Mum got pregnant with Kim and he went into teaching and now it's 18 years later. He's like a dinosaur, one of those big, soft, leaf-eaters, a brontosaurus maybe, who one day looks up at this strange cold stuff falling out of the sky and goes, 'Ooh, pretty snow!' and the next thing is kids are sticking gum on the back of his skull in the British Museum.

I know for a fact he hasn't always been bottled up like this. I saw an old photo of when he was working on a summer camp in Africa. You can hardly tell it's him, he looks so . . . happy.

We all had to complete this Energy Spot Check with GPJ this afternoon.

At the end, she talked to us about helping others in this time of crisis. She wants us to come up with a *Care Energy* presentation. It really affected me – I'm going to find a needy person and look after them.

Who, though?

Tues, Feb 17th

I watched the news tonight. A group of world leaders have come to London for the run-up to Kyoto 3. They bussed them thru town in a hydro coach. You could see them looking at us on the streets like we were rats in a lab. The *rationers*. They know they're next and they want to see how miserable we really are. And the weird thing is it makes us all act really casual, like nothing's happening

– that we've never seen a mango, or flown abroad, or driven a car, or had a warm house before. I think it's the only way to keep your head up, to act like it's *completely normal*. Especially in front of *the others*.

They've got this new section at the end of the news. Now a really stupid positive woman journalist drops in on people up and down the country to see how they're getting on with their lives.

Tonight she went to see this random couple from Bradford who run dog kennels. They are getting their dogs to sled them around the moors. The report opened with a long shot of the couple 'mushing' 4 Alsatians up a hill on a shaky sledge covered with shopping. And then, just when they'd got to the top, the sledge hit a bump and all the stuff flew off on to the snow and there were boxes of tampons and Kellogg's Cornflakes everywhere. The man dragged himself off the sled, got down on his knees and started picking everything up. The camera zoomed in on his tear-stained, frostbitten face.

'Fantastic, you can do it!' cried the reporter from her climate-controlled Jeep.

Is this supposed to make us feel better?

Went to my room and felt dead deep.

Fog drifts at three a.m. and
my mind, like a takeaway, stays open. My
    window is opacity
on to streets where street lamps used to
    flicker and burn.
Dark now.

In my hand the batteries die; acid burns
    the flesh and
the pain falls, laughing, to the ground.
The cars are dead, their souls are stolen
by the trains that smash thru the silent
    breath.
Ra ka da ra.

The city breathes. It gasps. It dies and
in my room I hear its fading beat.
Fog settles and chills my bone like an
    abuser completing
the cycle of abuse.

Another one for Claire's coat pockets.

Weds, Feb 18th

I smacked my alarm across the room and dived under the covers for an extra hour. Rhymes are so draining. It was after 11 by the time I got my shit together, and when I stepped out thru the front door I saw a weird thing – Brains Fitzsimmons and a couple of college IT/engineering geeks hanging around the Leaders' stairwell. Why? Do they want to get their heads kicked in?

On my way up the road I passed old Arthur, our next door neighbour on the left side. He was struggling along with some shopping and looking dead creaky. And then it hit me – he's perfect for my needy person for the Care Energy presentation! I'll go and see him tomorrow.

Thurs, Feb 19th

Massive storm today. I couldn't face going in to college on my bike so I sat in my bedroom, forced to listen to Kim row with Paul. I heard him say, 'But it'll bankrupt us, Kimmy.' And her screaming, 'I hate you! It's over!'

I threw on my jacket and knocked on Arthur's door. There was no answer from the front, but I could smell frying bacon thru the letter box so I went round the back, climbed over the fence and peered into his kitchen window. Thru the cigarette-smoke haze I could just about see Arthur, reading the paper. After about 50 million knocks at the door, he lifted his eyes from the sports pages, clocked me and stepped over to the door.

'Ye-es?' he boomed. I told him about the new Care

Energy presentation and me needing a *Needy Person*.

'Splendid, but no thank you.' He started to shut the door.

'But, it's me, Laura, from next door.'

He waved his ciggy at me. 'Oh, in that case, splendid, marvellous! Come in!'

Arthur Stoat-Wilson is the poshest and happiest man I've ever met. He says this is the richest he's been since the 15th of September, 1952, when his house was taken off him after his brother drank the estate away. He's a carbon creditor now, which means that he gives off less CO_2 than he uses and can trade the rest. He is totally happy with sitting in front of his 1-bar electric heater in 3 overcoats, he says they make him look big for robbers. He is spending his extra points on horse gambling and stout. I took a sip of it, it tastes like rust.

I asked him if he had anything he needed doing and he chuckled, unfolded the sports pages, and asked me to pick a winner for the 3.45 at Aintree. I'm going back again next week – he's just putting on a happy face for me. I know for a fact that stories like this come up in the local newspaper all the time and it'll turn out that the food packets on his shelves are empty, and that really he's only got one tin of tuna left and a jar of sleeping pills he's built up since 1973 for The Final Moment.

Fri, Feb 20th

I went into my Design Tech class a few minutes early today, and my heart went all fluttery cos it was just Ravi in there.

'Hey.' (I'm so cool.)

He looked up. 'Hey.'

'Are you all sorted out next door?'

'Uh?'

'You know – getting to know the place? If you need anything . . .'

'Oh, right.'

Suddenly the door swung open – and in walked Thanzila Amar, the prettiest, hottest, sexiest girl in college. She fixed Ravi with her bambina eyes.

'Are you Ravi Datta?'

'Yeah.'

'Oh, good, cuz I got a proposition for you.' She smiled, resting her beautiful arse on Dave Beard's desk. 'Hey, Laur.' She flicked a glance at me. 'Not interrupting anything am I?'

I smiled right back, but it was wasted on Thanzila; her eyes were only for Ravi. What happened to her boyfriend, Samad?

'I hear you can fix stuff?'

He nodded.

'Like my vid phone?'

He nodded again.

'Really?' breathed Thanzila, leaning towards him. 'Cuz if you could sort it I'd be sooooo grateful.' She reached into her pocket and pulled out the mobile. 'Waddya think? The vid keeps pixellating . . . and y'know, I can't just upgrade it any more.'

He took it and turned it over in his hands. 'Yeah, probably the graphix card. Leave it with me.'

'Truly? That is sooo cool. What can I give you back?'

'Don't worry about it.'

She slipped off the desk, centimetres away from him. 'Thank you so much . . . By the way . . .' she touched his hand with her manicured nails, 'you've got totally gorgeous hands. Has anyone ever told you that?' She slung her bag over her shoulder and smiled into his face before walking out the room.

Ravi turned back to me with an effort. 'So, uh, yeah. Thanks for the offer, but I'm all cool at home.'

I nodded and smiled so much my teeth hurt.

I don't care anyway, if he doesn't like me for who I am then he can get lost.

Woke up in the middle of the night and stared at my ugly hands by candlelight.

Sat, Feb 21st

The Carbon Department engineers came to our street and hooked up all our Smart Meters to the national grid today. When it came to our turn I made the man a cup of tea and asked him how it worked.

'S'easy, darlin'.' He tapped the meter screen. 'You got yer two hundred carbon ration points for the month, yeah?'

I nodded.

'Well, this little meter is so you can check on yer progress. Makes sure you ain't overspendin'. Want to give it a spin?'

'What, now?'

'Yeah, I'm all done.' He pointed to a slot at the top. 'What it is, yer just swipe your carbon card thru this section, 'ere . . .'

I took out my card and swiped it across the slot. The machine lit up and chattered and grockled to itself for a few seconds before spitting out a paper printout. I reached for it with shaky hands.

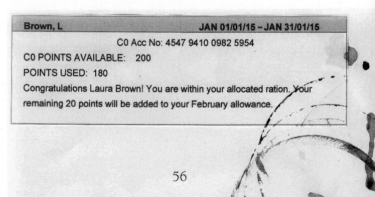

Brown, L	JAN 01/01/15 – JAN 31/01/15
C0 Acc No: 4547 9410 0982 5954	

C0 POINTS AVAILABLE: 200
POINTS USED: 180
Congratulations Laura Brown! You are within your allocated ration. Your remaining 20 points will be added to your February allowance.

'There yer go,' said the electrician, smiling. 'No bother.'

'What happens if you go over?'

'Well, that's the thing. Basically the meter takes over and manages your energy use – it'll even start shuttin' things off in the 'ouse if you're really bad.'

Super-tense dinner with Mum and Dad. Dad finally finished eating, put his knife and fork down and then turned oh so casually in his chair towards the meter.

'Ah, of course, our new toy, shall we give it a go?' He glanced at Mum's carbon card on the sideboard. 'Is this yours here, darling? D'you mind?'

Mum turned dead pale. 'Mind? Why would I mind?'

And then everything went into slo-mo as Dad picked up her card, stepped across to the meter and swiped the card thru the slot. There was a moment's silence, then the machine whirred, the earth turned – and a slip of white printout slid into Dad's waiting fingers. He stared at the paper in silence for a few moments, frowning.

'This can't be right. You can't have gone over by fifty points!'

Mum clip-clopped across the room and snatched it off him.

Brown, J	JAN 01/01/15 – JAN 31/01/15

CO Acc No: 4548 9460 0489 0589

CO POINTS AVAILABLE: 200

POINTS USED: 250

Warning! You have exceeded your allocated ration. The extra 50 points have been charged at the Super50 rate.

'Oh, it's all some mistake. Look, press the *Further Details* button on the meter . . .'

Dad bent over the machine, pressed a yellow button and a few seconds later it spat out a longer piece of printout.

Mum reached for it, but Nicky boy was there first. As he read it, his face went all blotchy. He switched to his super-dangerous quiet voice. 'The gym? Hours and hours at the pigging gym?'

Mum threw her hands up in the air. 'So what, Nick? I need space to get away from you and your goddamn misery!'

'Did it ever occur to you to get off your arse and actually run somewhere? Look how much they've charged you for the Super50 rate. Twenty chillers and a hundred euros!'

'Oh, blow the system! When did you get so much goddamn faith in the goddamn system, Nick? Where've you gone?' (Mum was born in New York – and even though her family moved to Washington when she was

10 and she's lived in London for 20 years, when she rows her New Yoik comes back strong.) 'I work so hard. I need this!'

He just looked at her really cold. 'You don't need it. You just *want* it.'

I went into my room and rubbed Mum's Shiseido Hand Revitaliser cream into my ugly hands, like an old spinster. Rationing is turning out to be like a spotlight, searching out all our escape plans and little secrets. What's my parents' little secret? They are terrified they don't like each other any more.

Kim's gone away for the weekend. Says she's staying over with mates in North London. I can feel a huuuge row building. It's always been like this – Kim, Kim, Kim and her problems. Everyone running around after her.

Sun, Feb 22nd
6 p.m. Dad has just spent the last 10 minutes in my room, perched on the edge of the bed and repeating himself/ sighing a lot. He kept saying stuff like 'We all need time to adjust' and 'We'll get through this, as a family' and 'Is there anything you need?'

Got a new bike out of him. Score!

10 p.m. Mum has just spent ages sitting cross-legged on my bed and sighing/justifying herself/sighing a lot. She kept saying things like 'The world is only complicated if you make it so' and 'We need to value the needs of *all* the family members' and 'You are becoming a woman now, with your own needs.'

On the way out, she stooped and picked up my old CSS shirt off the floor and murmured, 'I'm sorry. I'll watch my points in future.'

This is the killer about Mum. Just when I want to plunge a knife into her guts, she goes and picks up my shirt and makes my heart go all soft.

Anyway, got a new bass case out of her. Score!

Mon, Feb 23rd

It has rained and stormed for almost a week now; I nearly got my bass blown away on the way to band practice. The weird thing about weather now is that it's gone so big. So like today you're thinking is this just a normal winter storm . . . or is this going to destroy us? Everyone's dead tense, in case the powercuts come back.

Anyway, I got up the nerve to tell everyone about liking Ravi. They listened for about 30 seconds and then they all screamed and started playing until Adi's E-string broke and twanged across the room. He was playing that guitar pretty vicious.

'Mmm,' said Stacey, doubtful, 'he's a bit gorgeous . . .'

'Yeah, and that's the problem – he's too good-looking for me,' I wailed.

'Huh. *Too* gorgeous, if you ask me. There's something a bit *too* perfect about him,' Claire muttered.

'No-o . . .' Stace frowned. 'Not perfect – more a loner type . . . a bit . . .'

'Weird!' cried Stace and Claire together.

'Well, thanks for the support, guys. So far he's a creepy nerd, and no one said no he isn't when I said he was too good-looking for me.'

Everyone burst out laughing.

After practice I stayed at Adi's and played old skool Monopoly with his family. They're so normal, it's fantastic. When I was leaving Adi went: 'D'you really like him, Laur?'

I nodded.

He sighed. 'Then we need a plan. You're hopeless with boys.'

p.s. I smacked everyone at Monopoly – 10 hotels, all the way down the Strand, Piccadilly and Mayfair. Invincible!

Tues, Feb 24th

There's heavy snow across Europe again. A bunch of us went to the media suite at college to watch Sky. It's so surreal seeing white people crying and huddling in shelters in places where you used to go on holiday.

'Er, what happened to global warming?' muttered Adi.

'No, man, it's gonna get colder and colder. The Gulf Stream's shutting down, we've already dropped a degree in the last 10 years,' said Nathan Giles.

'So? What's a degree gonna do?'

'You know the diff between us and the last ice age? 5 lousy little degrees, man. That's all that's standing between us and the mammoth, my friend.'

'Which mammoth?'

Nathan sucked his teeth. 'The woolly one. Fool.'

It's like some ice-giant's taken Europe in its frozen grip. Traffic paralysed everywhere – 20,000 people stuck in their cars overnight around Budapest in –33°C; 35,000 trapped on a motorway near Heidelberg in Germany; 18,000 snowed in in Vienna. Practically every airport's closed in central Europe.

On the way home I saw Arthur Stoat-Wilson on the street and walked with him to Ladbrokes and then on to pick up a 6-pack of ale. He's not acting very needy, but I ain't giving up. When we got back to his house, I pretended I needed to use the bathroom upstairs and sneaked into his bedroom to check for sleeping pills. Couldn't see any but there was a real dead stuffed leopard leaning against the wall. I went downstairs and asked Arthur if he'd shot that beautiful creature. Arthur's really deaf if you ask me, cos whatever I say to him, he just laughs and says: 'Yes! Marvellous, isn't it?' which clearly isn't the right answer to everything.

Weds, Feb 25th

The Smart Meter cut off Kim's hot water in the shower, blasted her with ice-cold H_2O, like she was a football hooligan. Heh, heh.

I've been given a new Crit Thinking essay today.

> *Imagine a) Your family OR b) A fictitious family*
> *– is from a different era. Reconstruct a mealtime conversation, with particular reference to social norms and idiomatic use of language.*

Mick Thomas asked Lisa Bell why she was setting such a pointless essay. Lisa Bell then made us stay after lesson for 20 minutes while she sat cross-legged on her desk and led a discussion on group values, owned rules and the rights

& responsibilities of the student body. Lisa Bell sure knows how to crush a rebel.

Fri, Feb 27th

We're definitely in CO trouble at home. The Smart Meter switched the toaster off at breakfast. Dad looked up and frowned. 'Has the power gone off again?'

I nodded.

'Hmm, there must be some mistake! We can't be overspending that badly. I'll get in touch with the Carbon Department today.'

It's finally stopped raining, though – I went out with Claire at lunch and we gazed into the sky for the sun. For a second I thought I saw a bright smudge within the grey, but it turned out to be coming from the canteen security light. I was dead disappointed, and had a real flash of insight into how ancient tribes/modern Scandinavian people go bonkers and kill each other in the winter time.

Spring.
March

Sun, March 1st

The Smart Meter cut off the oven in the middle of macaroni cheese and we had to sieve out the hard pasta chunks and suck up the cheesy sauce on its own. Dad drummed his fingers on the table.

'I don't understand this, Julia – I've been trying all week to get through to the Carbon Department, but I keep getting put on hold. You've no idea how much *Greensleeves* I've been subjected to.'

Mum shrugged. 'That's what happens when the system takes over, Nick.'

Mon, March 2nd

A recorded delivery letter came at 8.30 this morning.

28/02/15

Nicholas Brown,

Despite repeated written warnings your family has failed to stay within the parameters of its carbon quota. You are, therefore, in breach of Ration Directive Clauses 1, 3 and 4 in regard to your legitimate allowance.

Immediate action will be taken on behalf of the Borough of Greenwich to enforce C0 compliance. In accordance with our policy of Open and Transparent Management, we enclose the following evidence of extreme individual over-expenditure for your information.

Date	Item	Payment	C0 Pts
06/02/15	AirTours Flight: F569 IBZ	Visa €455-82	40
09/02/15	AirTours Flight: F439 LSTND	Visa €389-50	40
23/02/15	RyanAir Flight: SL239 IBZ	Visa €640-60	40
26/02/15	RyanAir Flight: SL334 LSTND	Visa €485-28	40

Yours sincerely,

Kim Brown. Unbelievable. She even tried to get a job out there, working in a club. She don't give a shit about the rest of us. I just escaped, went to Adi's.

'What, she went to Ibiza, *twice*?' Adi clicked his tongue. 'You gotta hand it to her, she's got some style, your sister. But I don't understand how nobody knew . . .'

I shook my head. 'Nobody asks any questions in our family. They're too scared of what they'll find out.'

After that we listened to tunes and didn't say anything all afternoon. Adi's the same – when he's got stuff going on, he doesn't want to talk, either.

And just to finish off the day, later on I picked up a message from my cousin Amy from Washington.

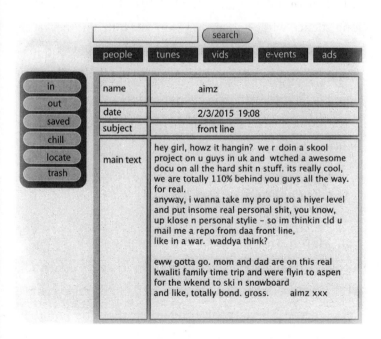

	search
people	tunes	vids	e-vents	ads

in	**name**	aimz
out	**date**	2/3/2015 19:08
saved	**subject**	front line
chill		
locate	**main text**	hey girl, howz it hangin? we r doin a skool project on u guys in uk and wtched a awesome docu on all the hard shit n stuff. its really cool, we are totally 110% behind you guys all the way. for real.
trash		anyway, i wanna take my pro up to a hiyer level and put insome real personal shit, you know, up klose n personal stylie – so im thinkin cld u mail me a repo from daa front line, like in a war. waddya think?
		eww gotta go. mom and dad are on this real kwaliti family time trip and were flyin to aspen for the wkend to ski n snowboard and like, totally bond. gross. aimz xxx

Adi took one look at it. 'Print it out so we can burn it!' he snarled, reaching for a lighter. We watched the flames lick up the page into a big ball of carbon. I love that boy; he's so totally on my side.

Tues, March 3rd

Elise Penatata phoned from the Carbon Department. She is coming round next Friday to start our *Carbon Offenders Recovery Programme*. I heard Mum going, 'Once you meet us, I'm sure everything will be fine . . . I mean, we're not criminals or anything, ha, ha, ha!' And then there was a long silence while she went 'Umm, uh-huh' and her face turned bright red. She put the phone down and stood for a minute drawing a squiggle on the phone pad – before filling her lungs with oxygen and shouting:

'*I am really, really angry with you right now, Kimberley Brown! This is not just your life.*'

Then Kim's voice. '*I am really, really angry with you right now, Julia Brown! Cos of you I don't have a life.*'

Fri, March 6th

Kim's been shut in her room in carbon cold turkey all week. Even though I hate her I took her in a cheese and onion toastie. She was shivering in foetal position on the top of the duvet, her eyes all glazed like a wild animal that's been run over by a car.

Even the Leaders are behaving better than us. Two of them, Delaney and Conrad, have actually started going to college. They hang out with a load of IT and engineering nerds like Brains Fitzsimmons and that crew. Maybe they needed a crisis to make them get serious. Doubt it though.

At 6.30 Mum got all of us in the sitting room to wait for the carbon pigs. Since that letter she's been in manic-control-superdrive, but when the doorbell rang, she looked terrified. That's the trouble with people who *need* control; when it starts to slip away, they've got nothing left.

Dad let Elise Penatata in. She talked at us for an hour. Blah, blah, the UK is achieving its targets; blah, massive reduction in CO_2 emissions in the atmosphere; blah, blah, setting an example to the world; blah, the personal is political; blah, blah. She kept putting her head on one side and doing this weird smile, sort of peeling her lips back over her pointy teeth, like a weasel on drugs.

Dad's eyelids started to close.

'And this brings us rather neatly to your daughter. The Carbon Department can, of course, work with a certain level of overspending, but this is a flagrant breach of the rationing rules. Kim has spent nearly all of her month's two hundred points on flights alone and is now a hundred and fifty points in deficit due to her energy use in London. We cannot allow you to use cash to buy your way out of carbon debt. You must pay back the energy.' Elise snapped her little teeth. 'It is not for me to presume to interfere in the private affairs of a family, but . . .' (Huh. Whenever anyone says *but* like this you better watch out big time) and then she basically told my parents how crap they were – about how out of control Kim was, how they were setting a bad example, how they had to get their act together. It was harsh. She shamed them big style and they just sat there and took it, Mum's face all white and Dad staring at his shoes.

Suddenly Kim jumped up from the sofa. 'Back off my parents, you bitch. I'm the problem, not them . . . and I want to try again!' She burst into tears and then Mum burst into tears. Even Elise squeezed out a few drops – and then they turned and looked at me super evil because I was *not* crying. Kim's up to something, I know it.

Anyway, the deal is the whole family is on CO Death Row for a month till we get our emissions right down again. The only cool thing is that Kim's gonna be reprogrammed at the *Carbon Offenders Rehabilitation Outreach Centre* on Lee Road.

As she was leaving, Elise turned to us. 'It's not so bad –

this could be a really positive thing, y'know, bring you together as a family . . . You might even enjoy it!' There was dead silence while she clipped her metal pencil back on to her clipboard. 'Well, I shall see you in a month's time then,' she said stiffly.

Sat, March 7th

So much for family togetherness. March is going to be the month of a thousand nights. Day 1 and I'm already going crazy. Every one of us is sitting in the dark in our own separate freezing rooms. Our ancestors couldn't have had it this bad – at least they had candles and corsets and cards and lutes and shit. Oh yeah, and servants too.

The *hydro* gig's coming up next week. There's nothing going to stop me going, even if I have to walk there. I had to get off the bus today cos I didn't have enough credit to get me all the way to college. I am a carbon leper.

Mon, March 9th

The Smart Meter's gone like a military dictator. It cut the cooker *and* the fridge off, so tonight we sat around the table in coats and gloves, eating cold beans and ice cream.

'Oh, by the way, I'm joining a Women's Skills Group.' Mum scraped the inside of her carton.

Dad forked a bean. 'Uh-huh?'

'Nothing formal, just a few women from publishing sort of clubbing together to share tips, darling.'

Dad rolled his eyes ever so slightly, but got busted anyway.

'I saw that,' she muttered. 'Anyway, it sure beats moping around here like a wet hen.'

The front door slammed. Kim stood there in the doorway. We all looked down at our plates.

Tues, March 10th

Cool afternoon. I finished up my fuzz pedal case in Design Tech. I gave it one last layer of gunmetal-grey paint and scratched *dirty angels* on the lid and it looked pretty good. Even Dave Beard lisped, 'Very original, Laura.'

Anyway, I was packing away my tools at the end of class when Adisa strolled in.

'Hey, let me see!' he cried in a weird happy voice, picking up the pedal case. He turned to Ravi.

'So cool – it's for our band. Laura plays bass, y'know?'

Ravi glanced at me. 'Safe. How long you been into that?'

'Oh, jussa bit, no big deal.'

'Don't let her fool you, she's good. Anyway, gotta go . . . You on your bike, Laur?'

'Yeah.'

'What about you, Rav?'

'Uh, yeah.'

'Well then, neighbours, you'll be ridin' back to your yard together, huh?' Adi turned and strode off down the corridor. Me and Rav stood there for a moment in super-bad silence.

'OK, then,' he said. 'I've just got to get my jacket. Wait here 2 minutes?'

'Sure.' Heart pounding.

And then along came Thanzila Amar.

'Oh, hey, Ravi,' she pouted. 'How's my vid phone coming on?'

His eyes went a bit dazed. 'All fixed up.'

Thanzila gave a little squeal. 'Really? Can I pick it up, like, now?'

'Er, yeah, it's in my – uh . . . locker . . .' He turned to me. 'Um . . . this might take a while. So, catch you later?'

'Sure. No problem.'

I'd like to put Thanzila in my locker and leave her there over the Easter holiday. Wouldn't look so hot then, would you, girl?

The *hydro* tomorrow. Can't wait!

Fri, March 13th

Adi caught me in the Yard at break this morning.

'So?'

'What?'

He shot me a fierce look.

'All right . . . He was going to ride home with me then Thanzila rocked up so he didn't.'

'Gotta use your assets, Laura Brown.'

'What assets?'

He shook his head in disgust. 'See you tonight at 6. OK?'

I watched him walk away. Sometimes I'm so jealous of him – he always knows where he's at and what's going on. He's been with the same girl, Sarah, for 2 years. They're dead close, no big dramas, no big scenes.

1 a.m. Fired up like crazy. The *hydro* were so-oo cool. Once we got to Brixton, me, Claire and Adi followed the crowd to their warehouse just off Coldharbour Lane. The place was full of hardcore kids going mental, screaming *hydro, hydro* till the band came out. The set was awesome. It was like a 10-metre tower of recycled shit, wires and circuits poking out everywhere. Looked like it was gonna come crashing down on us. The best bit was the chorus of their last downloader *polootzute* when a whole bunch of kids took over the stage on hydro skates. They were flying thru the air, climbing the walls, looping above the crowd. A skater shot right over the top of us, liquid spraying off the back of his board.

'Urggh, what's that?' I shouted.

'S'hydrogen combustion! By-product is water,' screamed Adi. 'Here they come again, girl. Duck!'

When it was over hundreds of us stood out on the street. An old petrol Audi pulled up at the lights. It had those tinted windows so you couldn't see inside. Suddenly all the kids started chanting *Pig, pig, pig!* Then a girl broke out of the crowd, jumped on to the bonnet and sprayed a massive H symbol all over it. Whoever was inside must've been freaking out – this girl on the bonnet, thousands of crazy kids all around. As soon as she jumped off the Audi shot the lights.

'That was cool,' muttered Claire as we waited for the bus.

I shrugged. 'Maybe.'

'Oh come on, you've got to admit that took guts.'

'Surrounded by an army of her mates?'

Claire glanced across at me. 'Well at least she didn't just talk about it. She did it.'

'What are you saying?'

'Nothing.'

'Yeah you are. You're saying I haven't got the guts to do something like that.'

'Well, have you?'

Adi put his arms around both our shoulders. 'You two. Leave it out.'

I sat all the way home in silence. Adi walked me to my corner.

'Don't let her get to you, Laur. She loves winding you up.'

I sighed. 'Yeah, I know.'

When I got to my front door I turned. He was still there, watching. I waved goodnight.

Claire just messaged me. `Bet you wouldn't dare.`

I hit her back. `Watch me.`

Sat, March 14th

Saw Kieran in Alfredo's today, surrounded by paper. He was too busy even to look up.

Sun, March 15th

I went round to Arthur's and listened to horse racing from Kentucky on the net in front of his heater. He could see I was shivering so he turned on an extra bar just for me. I asked him again if he'd be my needy person for my Care Energy preservation and this time his NHS glasses went all misty.

I was climbing back over the garden fence when I saw Ravi locking up his shed. He looked up.

'Hey, Laura, sorry about the other day.'

'That's OK. Did you give Thanzila her stuff?'

He grinned.

'What's so funny?'

'That girl – she's pretty out there . . .'

A second's silence and then we both burst out laughing. Suddenly Mum's voice came shrilling out of the kitchen window. 'Darling! Laura! Could you come here a mo?' Pause. *'Now!'*

'Gotta go.'

'Yeah – see you in college . . . tomorrow?'

When I got to the kitchen, I nearly didn't go in. It was packed with strange, posh women. One woman even had an upturned shirt collar, like Lady Diana. And then it clicked. Had to be the Women's Skills Group. Mum was standing at the chopping board. Smiling bright.

'In my opinion, offal is the way forward. It's nutritious, extremely local, low on Carbon Points and, of course, ha ha ha, terribly trendy!'

She caught sight of me. 'Oh, hello, darling! Everybody, this is my youngest daughter, Laura – we often make this dish at home together! Sweetie, come on in.'

I took a step forward and then I saw what was on the chopping board. A pile of animal entrails, swimming in blood.

Kim walked in. 'Gross,' she snorted, before snatching up her house keys and striding out again.

Then Mum made the mistake of actually looking at the oozing organs. Her eyes rolled back and she staggered. What could I do? I went over and picked up a gizzard.

'Thank you, darling,' she gasped, nailing her smile back on.

So I stood there and demonstrated gizzards until Mum finally let me go.

When they'd all gone I crept back into the kitchen to get a Coke. Mum was wiping up blood spatters. And then I caught sight of my dad. He was on the sofa, pretending to read the paper, but really he was looking at Mum. His eyes weren't all kind, like normal.

Mon, March 16th

Ravi smiled at me in the Yard. Maybe he does like me. Like that. A little bit.

Tues, March 17th

Tonight we had band practice at Adi's for the first time in ages. Basically, his mum had banned us from the garage because she'd got a new freezer and had taken away Adi's band points to power it up. But there is some justice in the world cos the freezer broke down without anyone knowing. His mum only found out when the neighbour's dog started howling outside the side door cos of the stink. Plus Adi's brother, Shola, had done a home biology experiment with blowfly eggs in the garage 2 weeks before, and they hatched and multiplied big time. Adi said it was awesome – a total fest of rotting meat and swarming flies. So the *angels* are back and it's got a kind of gothic death vibe in there now. Cool.

Anyway the real news is that Stacey's-friend-Chris's-cousin-from-Vauxhall's-buddy-at-work said to Stace that he's gonna get us a gig at the Hope and Anchor in Greenwich in a couple of months. This is it, the beginning!

Claire caught up with me at the end. 'When?'

'Friday night. Come round to mine.'

She grinned. 'Can't wait.'

What am I doing? Now I've got to scratch up a Jeep to impress Claire bloody Connor.

Weds, March 18th

There's a fuel protest happening. Lorry drivers are blocking petrol stations all over West London. They're angry cos the Gov's piled this massive tax on fuel and they say they're already on the edge cos of rationing anyway.

Thurs, March 19th

The protest is getting bigger. It's spreading over London.

Ravi sneaked me a piece of Wrigley's Extra in Design Tech and whispered, 'What you up to this weekend?'

'Nothing.'

'D'you wanna hook up or something?'

'Sure.'

'I'll bell you.'

Oh yeah!

Fri, March 20th

Claire came over at 8. As soon as she stepped inside she grabbed my hand.

'There's only one way to go.'

'What d'you mean?'

She opened the front door a couple of centimetres and nodded towards Tracey Leader's Jeep.

'Oh, you've got to be kidding. That is death.'

Claire's massive eyes lit up. 'Cool.'

'For you, maybe; but I live here.'

'She ain't ever going to know.' She curled her lip. 'Well, if you won't, then I will. Thought you had more guts.'

'Claire, stop talking shit. I've got guts, it's just too close . . .'

'Yeah, right.'

I knew I was being manipulated, that she was messing with me, but I just had to face up to her.

'You got a key on you?'

She gasped. 'You gonna do it?'

I pushed past her. 'Never mind. I've got one.'

And before I could stop to think, I was crouched on the pavement by Tracey Leader's Jeep.

'Keep a lookout!' I hissed. Claire ran to the corner by the bins.

I took out my house key and scratched one deep H into the side door. Oh man, it felt so good! Flash! I looked up. Claire taking a photo on her mobile.

'Quit it!'

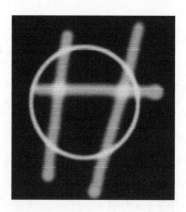

Suddenly there was the sound of footsteps. Claire whispered, 'Fat bird coming.'

'What's she like?'

'Blond hair; rough.'

I looked up. 'Shit – it's Tracey. We've got to hide. Now.'
I crawled over to the bins.

'Move up!'

'Where?'

'Behind you!'

We crawled into a disgusting, stinky pile of rubbish.
Footsteps up close now. Pause. Then a gasp.

'No. Way.'

I peered round the side of a bin. Tracey was punching
in a mobile number.

'Yeah, Karl. Some bastard's keyed up my car with a
shitty H thing. Find who it is and bring 'em to me.'

We stayed behind that bin for about a year till we got
up the guts to come out.

I'm lying on my bed now, thinking about it. What the
hell did I do that for?

Sat, Mar 21st

Stayed indoors all day. No call from Ravi. Now a bunch of
drivers are running their trucks off sunflower oil cos
there's no tax on it. They did a mass ram raid on about 50
Tescos around the M25 and ran off with thousands of
cans of oil. Weird.

The Mayor did a broadcast. He said: 'This behaviour is

unacceptable. We must pull together. Rationing will, by its very nature, involve some hardship until the transition to alternative fuels is in effect.'

Thanks for that, mate.

Sun, March 22nd

I've spent the day hiding from the Eye of the Leader and pretending to myself that I'm not waiting for R to call, like a stupid girl. But I am a stupid girl.

In the end I ran next door and buzzed Kieran. It took him ages to open the door and when I got in there I could see why. The entire flat, from wall to wall, was covered in scrawled-on, screwed-up bits of paper. Kieran was all pale, but when he saw me, he laughed and gave me a giant hug.

'Oh, Laura, Laura, I've had an epiphany!'

It was so nice to be with someone who was a) happy and b) pleased to see me. Even if the someone was clearly either a) insane or b) coming down off drugs.

'Let's celebrate!' He ran round his flat, flicking on lights and stereos and TVs and cranking the boiler up too. I threw myself on the sofa like a prisoner out on day-release.

'So, sweetie, you'll never guess what!' Kieran walked in with a bowl of microwave popcorn. 'I've been to the edge of the precipice; I've looked over and returned a changed man! Shall I tell you about it?'

'Mhh-hmm.' I crammed a fistful of popcorn into my mouth.

And so he did. It turns out that Kieran spent all of January going to bars, trying to pretend that everything was normal – but when he ordered a Smirnoff Ice and it came back warm for the 18th time, he realised he was living a lie. Over the month, every time he'd gone out to Soho something else had disappeared – the chill cabinets, the decks, the lighting, the late hours.

'It was awful, Laura, nobody knew what to do . . .' Kieran hugged his chest. 'And that's when I realised that nothing was ever going to be the same again, that the very act of dating was under threat . . . and that's when I started to think about the bigger picture – it's a new world out there and everybody's dating rituals are under threat.' He jerked his thumb at the balled-up paper lining the floor. 'So that's what all this is about.'

I picked up a piece at random.

```
Hetero/homo/inter/sexual = (orthodoxy)
          - CO₂ = fractalisation
```

Kieran sighed. 'Deep, huh?'

I nodded and re-crumpled the paper in silence.

'I haven't been able to sleep or eat. Been lost in a vortex . . . And then, suddenly, it *came* to me!' He flung his arms wide. My hand jerked, scattering a handful of popcorn across the room.

'Love, relationships, dating – they need a new form, a new language, a new set of rules – and I, Kieran, have the answer. *Carbon Dating!*'

We stared at each other in silence for a few moments. And then burst out laughing.

'Fabulous, isn't it?'

'Kier, that's so good!'

'I know, but I need to think more . . .' He started to scribble on a piece of paper. 'Think, think, think, think . . .'

I let myself out. It's not pretty watching a hairdresser think.

No RD. So much for hooking up over the weekend. I called Adi who said I have to go to college tomorrow and act like I don't know him cos being mean works with boys.

No traffic moving in London. No fuel. So quiet.

Mon, March 23rd

2 a.m. I've just been woken by a huge crash from downstairs. I jumped out of bed and peered down the stairs to see Dad slumped on the floor under a pile of coats and umbrellas. Mum shot past, wrapping her dressing gown around her.

'Honey, are you all right?' She bent over and lifted a fleece off his face. He just shook his head from side to side.

'What is it, Nicky? Tell me!'

He lifted his head. 'Been fired.' His face crumpled. ''Leven years and they jus' fired me, Ju.'

Mum straightened. 'Come on, there's no need to do this. You'll be fine.'

'How?'

'When one door closes, another one opens . . .'

'Oh, for cryinoutloud iss not time for pos'tive Prozac bollocks. Wha'bout mortgage? Can't get 'nother job. Evry'un outta work now an travel 'n' tourism's dead.' He finished with a slitting-throat gesture and flumped his head back down to the floor.

Mum tried to get him up, but he wouldn't move. He just lay there moaning, '*Lack of cuss'mers for the Trav'l 'n' Tus'm courss hav' render'd your p'sition redun'nt . . .*' over and over again.

But the thing is, he really hated that job anyway.

No Ravi in college today for me to ignore.

Tues, March 24th

When I got home Mum was wiping the hallway from where Dad's wet coat had marked the wax floor.

'You OK, Mum?'

She looked up with positive, laser eyes. 'Yes! Super! Why shouldn't I be?'

I went into the kitchen and turned on the TV. This time the Prime Minister was doing a speech saying no one had the right to take London hostage, blah, blah. Why are politicians so stuck up? He said unless the drivers back down he's going to send in the army.

Still no R.

A zillion lorry roadblocks have spread over the country. Manchester, Birmingham, Liverpool and Bristol totally surrounded. Tailbacks for a 100 kms. People are just leaving their cars on the motorways and walking. They interviewed one man. He went, 'That's it, I'm done with driving. That car can rot in hell before I get back in it.'

My dad hasn't got out of bed all day.

Still, still no Ravi. Maybe he's dead.

Weds, March 25th

A fuel battle's started on the M1. Right now tanks are rolling up the hard shoulder near Watford towards a line of lorries. There's panic buying going on everywhere. All the shops are jammed full of people clutching tins of pineapple chunks. I got home to find the kitchen loaded up with packets of food and Dad with a black eye.

I just stared at him. 'What happened?'

'Don't worry, love. I've got food for us, that's the main thing.'

'But Dad, you're just acting like everyone else now!'

'I don't care,' he muttered, slotting jars of jam into a cupboard. 'The way things are going we can't afford to be nice.'

Great. Now my dad's lost his job he's got to turn into some macho hunter-gatherer protector of the family. I preferred it when he was depressed in bed.

Thurs, March 26th

The army attacked at dawn today in Northampton. Soldiers, 500 riot police, tanks, armoured cars and choppers vs 1,000 fat pig lorry drivers.

Bob Jenkins got us all in the main hall at lunch time and smiled. 'And now I'd like to welcome a representative of the Carbon Department. He's here to give you an important talk.'

What is it with adults? They haven't got a clue what's going on, so they do this weird thing where they pretend they're in control, that they've got a plan. So we had to sit there while a grey little man got up on the stage and opened up a flash presentation. He cleared his skinny throat. 'Ah, hello young people, I'm here to give you some information on *What to Do in a Riot*.'

Adi scowled. 'Oh, man.'

'Firstly, stay indoors. Keep away from the windows. Listen for reports on the radio or television. If you think things are out of control or threatening your life . . .'

Stace nudged me. 'What? Hide under the duvet?'

'. . . find a way to leave that's secret. Exits could include windows, ductwork or the roof.'

Nathan put up his hand. 'What the f is ductwork, man?'

Everyone started laughing. Bob jumped to his feet and glared at us.

The skinny guy swallowed. 'Secondly, try and travel as a group, particularly if you have to run across an open area such as the front of a building, a wide street or a square. Gunmen will have several objects to focus on, not just one, and will not be as likely to target you.'

Adi put his head in his hands. 'S'too surreal, man.'

Fri, March 27th

It's over. The drivers have given in. This shit really scares me. Not the protest and stuff, but just the fact that the Government got so violent so quickly.

Finally saw Ravi. He caught up with me in the link and told me he'd had this evil flu and that's why he didn't get back to me last weekend. He was all pale and thin and I was totally believing him, but then Thanzila sneaked up behind him and whispered 'Thanks for the present!' before strutting off, shaking her arse.

So, is he on the level? I dunno. I hate liking people. It hurts too much.

Sun, March 29th

The sun came out this morning and it was *warm*, not just glaring winter sun. I cracked open a Coke and went and sat outside like a normal girl. And as I sat there, loads of neighbours started creeping out, like little animals coming out of hibernation. Arthur was digging his garden over, Loud Dad was playing with his kids, Mrs Datta was sweeping up her back yard. Mum came out and sat on the back step. And then someone in the row put on a real old skool Beatles track – it was *Blackbird*, I think – and everybody stopped what they were doing and turned their faces up to the sun, dazed with pleasure.

But then a really bad thing happened. Word got around that Brains Fitzsimmons had been found, beaten to a pulp, on our street. The gossip is that the Leaders did it, but no one knows why. Bet I do. They've done him for the H symbol on the Jeep.

April

Weds, April 1st

Woke up this morning and someone had polluted the world so much that the climate was messed up and the UK went on rations and nobody ever, ever had any fun again. Ha, ha, ha. Messaged Amy back.

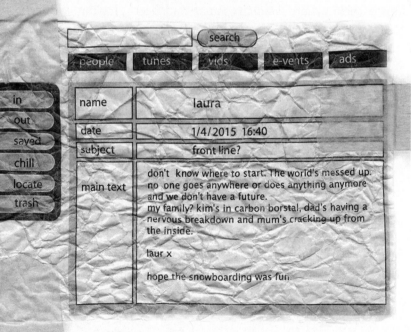

	search
people tunes vids e-vents ads	

in		
out	**name**	laura
saved	**date**	1/4/2015 16:40
chill	**subject**	front line?
locate	**main text**	don't know where to start. The world's messed up. no one goes anywhere or does anything anymore and we don't have a future.
trash		my family? kim's in carbon borstal, dad's having a nervous breakdown and mum's cracking up from the inside.
		laur x
		hope the snowboarding was fun.

Thurs, April 2nd

GPJ definitely needs more sex. She marched up and down the classroom, introducing this new enviro-presentation like she was having a really good time. She cracks me up – all the other teachers are on total death row, but the more depressed they get, the more she cranks up her Timberland boots and tool belt.

Anyway, at the end I was waiting for Adi to pack up his stuff and GPJ clocked me and asked me to help tidy up. So there I was, slaving around, straightening chairs and picking up bits of litter when I found this piece of paper near where Thanzila Amar had been giggling with her little girlfriends.

If she wants him, I ain't got the ghost of a chance. I guess the big question, though, is does he want her?

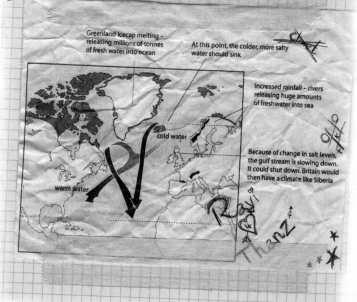

I got home and Kim called me from the end of the hallway.

'Laura. You seen this?' She jerked her head towards the laundry cupboard.

I went over and she lifted up a stack of towels with 3 bottles of Jack Daniel's hidden underneath.

'Dad's. He's turning into a total lush.'

'How d'you know they're his?'

'Oh, I know. Disgusting. He's not even *trying* to get another job.'

I don't know where she's got so moral from.

Fri, April 3rd

Brains Fitzsimmons is back in college with loads of teeth missing. Delaney Leader saw him in the link and spat in his face. 'Hydro scum. You can't prove nothing. Stay away from us.'

Claire caught up with me at lunch like nothing'd happened.

'Did you get that mail from the *hydro*? Y'know, the one about the demo at Heathrow on the 12th? They want to get on the tarmac and stop the A380 Airbus taking off.'

I frowned.

'Who's got the points to fly now?'

'Some still do – if they save, or get it on the black. But that flight's mostly passengers landing and refuelling here from the Middle East to LA.'

'I've got nothing against Middle Easterners.'

'Laur, we've got to stop people flying, and we've got to stop it now. All those fat pigs flying to California burns as much carbon dioxide as a car driver in a year, 2 drivers if they're using hybrids.'

'All right, Claire. Enough of the lecture. I'll think about it, OK?'

She crossed her arms. 'I know you're upset about Fitz . . . I mean, I am too. But what d'you wanna do about it? Are you up for telling the truth?'

I shook my head.

'Then stop being so moody around me like it's *my* fault.'

And then a bad thing happened. Louise Foster came out and sparked up next to us. 'Ooh, gossip!' She sucked a lungful of smoke down into her boots. 'Thanzila's dropped Samad for Ravi Datta.'

I went all cold.

Louise smirked. 'Yeah, Samad had to sell his Beemer – he walks to college now. Thanzila's not a girl who walks, you know.'

I shook my head. 'But Ravi hasn't got a ride either.'

'No, but the boy knows his shit – everyone knows if you need a download or a crack code or your batteries chargin', then Ravi's your boy. Mhh, hhm. Wouldn't mind him myself . . . Laur, you all right?'

'Yeah, sure.'

'Well, gotta go. History. Yawn.' Louise drew the last gasp of death out of her smoke and walked off. I turned to Claire.

'I don't believe it. He was laughing about Thanzila the other day.'

'When?'

'At home – we started talking.'

'You didn't tell *us* about any talking!'

I shrugged. 'Don't matter now.'

'Wait up, girl – let's find out if it's true or not. You know how rumours are.'

My mobile buzzed. Nathan Giles.

'Hey, you heard the news – Ravi and Thanzila?'

'I heard, Nate.' I locked off and turned back to Claire. 'Yeah, I know how rumours are.'

Sun, April 5th

Adi's ordered me to keep busy and calm while he investigates, so I went jogging with Kieran this evening; dead embarrassing cos he wears little jogging bottoms that are way too tight. Anyway it was good to get him out of his flat. His brain is in manic overdrive. It's like one of those toads that live buried under desert sand for thirty years – and then when the rain finally falls, tunnel out and go crazy for one night before dropping dead next day. For years, Kieran's brain has only been used for: *What would you like today?* and *Yes, I really think highlights would bring out your natural tones* and *God, he's got a nice arse.* He's gonna burn his cerebral cortex out if he carries on like this.

'Need, love, desire, craving . . .' he puffed as we turned on to Blackheath High Street. 'It's taken mankind millennia to develop sophisticated dating rituals . . . and now . . . do we have to go back . . . to the . . . bloody stone age . . . because . . . it's survival of the fit . . . test again?' He stopped and bent over, gasping. Talk about irony – he's going to have to give up the Marlborough Lights if he even wants to *be* in the survival race. Rationing's turned everyone into bloody smokers again. I mean, it's nearly illegal to smoke in any public place but everywhere I look people are dragging away, like it's a way to say piss off to all the control.

I leaned against a wall, waiting for Kier to get his breath back, and then Karl Leader bombed past in the fixed-up Jeep. It was like scoffing a bag of chips in a starving person's face. I don't understand it though, all the rest of us are obeying all the rules like stupid worker-ant drone things – and the Leaders have got a Jeep going. Bxstards. I'm kind of proud of that scratch now.

Mon, April 6th
No news on Ravi yet.

Tues, April 7th
Still nothing.

Weds, April 8th
It was better not knowing. Horrible day. To begin with, I got my Crit Thinking essay back – a D minus. Lisa Bell had written *Bizarre but very original. You have, however, not really addressed the idiomatic norms of mealtime conversation as required by the brief. Keep trying!* in her horrid handwriting across the top. She gave me this don't-blame-me-I-don't-make-the-rules smile as she handed me the essay back. Yeah, maybe she don't make 'em, but she sure follows 'em.

I was pretty down so I went out to the Yard with Claire. One minute we were alone and then a massive crowd came running round the side of the building, and we got caught in the middle of a battle between these 2 Asian kids, Naz and Faiz – although the word *battle* is kind of extra in this case, cos Naz is about 4 feet tall with arms like pipe-cleaners and a really girly voice, and Falz was reading his rhymes off the back of a KFC napkin. Still, it was a laugh, especially when Naz rhymed that Faiz wore a G-string and his momma wore the boxers. Faiz's mum runs the college canteen and carries industrial, mega-sized tins of baked beans around the building like they are feathers.

Anyway, me and Claire were right in there – and then I clocked Ravi in the crowd, almost directly opposite. Naz saw him at the same time and he spat on the ground. Naz's cousin is Samad, the boy Thanzila's just dropped. Naz pushed thru a bunch of people and pointed his finger in Ravi's face.

'Blood . . .
I see you done good
You stole my bro's gash
Showed her a piece o' flash
Blood, I don't mean to make you sore
But you ain't no place
That we all ain't been before
She talk pretty when she beg like a . . .
Blood . . .
She a 22-carat Gucci ho!'

There was a massive 'Ooooooh!' Ravi froze for a second – and then he stepped forward and knocked Naz flat to the ground.

'Don't start something you can't finish. Unless you want more of this.' He stood for a moment over Naz, before turning on his heel and storming off across the Yard.

So much for rumours. I walked out thru the gates with Claire, numb. Adi was leaning against the wire.

'I heard. I'm sorry, Laur.'

Claire snorted. 'She's best off without that loser.'

I looked at her, spiky blond hair and massive green eyes. She's never been dropped in her life.

'Shit . . . there they are.'

I followed her gaze. Ravi, standing at the bus stop with Thanzila wrapped around his ribs.

Claire grabbed my hand. 'Come on, he's just a stupid boy. Let's go on this Heathrow demo and kick some cop arse.'

I think it's the danger she's addicted to, not the carbon.

When I got home, Dad was sitting in the back garden with Arthur, my Care Energy *needy person*, drinking beer. There were loads of empty cans on the grass.

'Laura!' cried Dad. 'My luvv'ly, luvv'ly Laura . . .' and tried to hug me. Puke.

Watching Arthur finishing his beer can, I decided that I've got to do something to help him. He's about a trillion years old – why's he acting like this? His life must be so empty. I'm going to do my GPJ Care Energy presentation on the PROBLEMS OF THE ELDERLY, whether he wants me to or not.

I looked at myself in the mirror tonight for the longest time. I can't believe he's gone for her. I hate him.

Thurs, April 9th

Went to band practice. Broke my E-string. Don't care. Everyone was being really nice, which just made it worse. Dad is still drunk.

Sat, April 11th

I woke up to Dad shouting the words to some back-in-the-days Bob Dylan song. He's been drunk for 5 straight days. Basically he lies in his room till lunch time, drags himself to the kitchen, fries up a burning mess, wolfs it down straight out of the pan and then stumbles over to Arthur's to gamble and drink. He's never acted out like this before. I don't think Mum knows what to do either – at the moment she's going for the *ignore it and it'll go away* package.

The Women's Skills Group met at our house again. Mum locked the back door so Dad couldn't get in thru the garden (their relationship is so *healthy*). At one point I opened my curtains and looked down. Dad was roaming around the garden with a bottle of beer in his hand. He looked up and waved the bottle at me.

'Laura! You too young, get 'way from sad, bad, evil, no-sex wimmin!' And then he fell into the hedge.

What's next – carbon divorce?

Claire called. I let it go thru to answer. I can't face that Heathrow demo.

Sun, April 12th

House of badness. Dad's banned from the bedroom and is sleeping on the floor in his study. I took him in a cup of coffee and he whispered, 'Has it got any whisky in it?' I think I'm going to go into denial and pretend that everything's *super*. It's worked for Mum for the past 20 years. Oh God, does that mean she's been this depressed all that time?

Watched the news, but nothing on about Heathrow. I bet it was cancelled.

Mon, April 13th

It's all round college that Claire got arrested at the demo.

Tues, April 14th

Claire walked into the Yard like a superstar. A group of kids swarmed around her.

Adi stopped playing football, looked over at me and grinned. 'Why ain't you worshipping?'

I growled deep in my throat.

'C'mon.' He took my hand, dragging me forward. 'She's your mate, remember?'

When we got there, Claire was in full rant.

'So, by 8 we broke down the fence and got on to the runway . . .' She lifted her hand. 'Oh hey, Laur, Adi . . .'

Louise Foster tapped her on her shoulder. 'And . . . ?'

Claire spread her hands. 'When we bust through on to the tarmac, I realised how massive the Airbus really is. It's dead *menacing*. Just its wings are the length of a football field. Anyway, as soon as we got out there, we ran and got into position – we basically surrounded the whole plane and chained ourselves together.'

'How many of you?'

'At least a thousand people. It was dead weird cos you could see all the passengers inside, pressed up against the Airbus windows. Then Paul Rees, the bass player out of the *hydro*, climbed on to that ladder thing passengers use to board the plane, yeah? And he sprayed all down the side of the plane,

```
Climate Change = 250,000 deaths per year =
9/11 every week. Flying kills. Stop now.
```

'It was so cool. And then a load of protestors climbed up behind Paul on to the wings and sat there. The people inside were proper freaking out.'

'But where were the police?'

'Oh, they were there, but you know what they're like, they only get into it when they got the numbers to win, yeah? We held out till 12, but then a frigging *line* of armoured vehicles arrived – armed police, dog units, fire brigade. We didn't stand a chance. The pigs started throwing people to the ground. They had this whole system going – 2 of them grabbed a protestor and then a firemen came in and cut the chain. One by one, they dragged us into a hangar and took everything off us.'

'So you got arrested?'

Claire nodded. 'Held us in the hangar. No food, no water for 12 hours. Not even a phone call. Then they charged anyone over 18 with aggravated trespass and entering a restricted zone. The ones who climbed on the wings got charged with criminal damage.' She sighed. 'Then finally they began to let us go. Women first. This officer got up and told us the bail condition deal – no one was allowed within 500m of any UK airport – and if we talked to each other outside, they'd arrest us again for breaking bail. Then they released each of us, 5 minutes apart.'

Adi clicked his teeth. 'Who gave the police so much power?'

'Tell me about it. It's all those anti-terrorism laws. They can do what they want now.'

I frowned. 'But I watched the news last night. There wasn't anything on it.'

Claire turned to face me. 'I told you, they took everything off us. Vids, cameras, cells. There was even a BBC cameraman who got arrested. They took all his gear and footage off him. Destroy the evidence and it never happened. Right, Laura?'

I looked down. Man, that girl gets to me. I'm so jealous and so mad at her all at the same time.

Weds, April 15th

I bunked off college this morning and stared at the wall for hours. There's a big anti-capitalism demo on May Day. I know the others want to go, but I've got this sinking feeling inside. I don't want to be radical any more, I just want my old life back.

God, I sound like Kim.

2 a.m. Aargh! Just woken from wicked evil dream where Gwen Parry-Jones forced me to swim across a freezing lake in a fleece and I kept sinking under cos it was so heavy. I've got to face up to this Care Energy presentation.

Right then, problems of the elderly:

1) bad food
2) disease
3) dead friends
4) robbers
5) death

So depressing. No wonder Arthur don't care much about rationing; it's just another nail in the coffin.

Thurs, April 16th

The *angels* met at Claire's dad's vet's surgery tonight cos he was out on a call and Claire's been grounded after the airport demo. She was mad as hell when I got there.

'Look at this,' she hissed, throwing her carbon card on the pet examination table.

Stace let out a low whistle. 'Wow, you've used up three of your blocks already!'

'Oh, yeah, you reckon? Take a look at my Smart Meter reading. And there's more from last month.'

Connor, C	CO Acc No: 4347 6581 5569 7903	20/03/15 – 20/04/15	
Date	**Items**	**Payment**	**CO Points**
06/04/15	**Majestic Wine Warehouse:** Killawarra Pinot Grigio X 64 (origin: Australia) Zapata Merlot X 64 (origin: Chile)	Abbey Nat €364-56	40
14/04/15	**Esso Ltd, Lee Road:** 80 litres Premium Unleaded	Abbey Nat €130-00	20
15/04/15	**Wholefood Delights:** Basmati Rice 8KG x 10, dal, mung, channa, red split x 12, assorted pulses x 22	Abbey Nat €246-78	30

CO POINTS AVAILABLE: **200**
CO POINTS CONSUMED: **290**

Warning! You are in contravention of your allocated ration by 40 points. The extra 50 points have been charged at the Super50 rate. Contact the carbon department immediately

'But you don't drive . . .'

'Or drink red wine or shop at bloody Wholefood Delights. My card's been ripped off – and now I'm down to 4 blocks!'

'But you can get 'em back. I mean, this printout proves it wasn't you.'

'It don't prove anything. The Carbon Department don't know I don't drink Merlot. Don't worry, I'm going to fight it – but I dunno if they'll believe me.'

Adi frowned. 'These are such weird rip-offs. I mean, this ain't normal crime, is it? Rices and pulses. It's like you've been robbed by a vegetarian hippy.'

'Tell me about it. It's gotta be a black-market thing. All those middle-class pigs getting stuff on the black. Makes me sick.'

After she'd chilled out a bit we started to talk about Stacey's friend's cousin's mate's gig. It's gonna be in the first week in June and we're on with *Monday's child, dark force, fall of the rouble, potatoHead* and *SlashFist*. We're on second for 15 minutes and we've got to get 25 people thru the door.

'I don't know these bands – what kind of night is this?' asked Adi.

Stacey shrugged. 'It's run by this group called the New Punk Allegiance, at least that's what my cousin says.'

'Definitely punky, right? Not Straight X?' Adi once went on tour with a group of militant Straight X vegans who terrorised him for a whole week. They worked him like a slave – chopping carrots for 16 skinny bxstards every night. Plus no smoke break. Plus no phone calls to his girlfriend. They hurt him bad.

The flyer was totally lame. It had a blurry picture of a child with tears running down its face and *Monday's child* spread across it in gothic letters. All the other band names were tiny and stuck in the corner. Adi said that we should have an angel with a crucifix sticking out of its chest for our flyer, but Stace said that was disrespectful, cos her family was Catholic. Adisa went, wasn't that the whole point of the *angels*, to disrespect? Stace said, yeah, but couldn't the angel just *hold* the crucifix? Adisa sucked his teeth and went, 'Stace, you such a girl!' Then Stacey snatched up her jacket and walked out, shouting, 'Right, I quit – see how much of a man *you* are without a drummer!' Adi turned to us and said, 'She needs to chill way out!' and when we didn't straightaway go, 'Yeah, you're right,' he walked out too.

Then the phone rang. Claire picked up and I sat there under the strip lighting, full of dark, dark thoughts, while she was going, 'How long has Chu-Chu been vomiting for, Mrs Bradley?'

Everything is falling to pieces: my home, Ravi – and now the band. Rationing has really dicked all over my life. Claire finally slammed the phone down, stormed out and came back with her dad's brandy decanter.

We ended up having a real laugh in the end. There was this poster about overweight cats on the surgery wall and we changed it in Photoshop to being about my dad. She says hers is just the same.

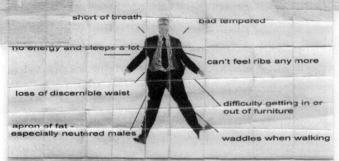

short of breath

bad tempered

no energy and sleeps a lot

can't feel ribs any more

loss of discernible waist

difficulty getting in or out of furniture

apron of fat – especially neutered males

waddles when walking

What about Treats?

Don't think FOOD/DRINK = LOVE. Play with your dad – cards, Monopoly etc. and even chat to him, but shut him out when you are eating or drinking.
If your dad is visiting the neighbours for food or drink tell them not to give in to him.

SOMETIMES you may have to put a collar around his neck with 'Don't offer me food, drink or sympathy until I've owned up that I've got a problem' written on it in LARGE LETTERS

Sun, April 19th

Why did I have to pick the boy next door to obsess over? Like I'm some dumb girl out of a dumb movie. Plus now I'm scared to go out in case I see him. I was supposed to go into town with the *angels* this afternoon, but the fight between Stacey and Adisa messed up that plan. I sulked around in my room until about 2 – and by then it was either go out or go crazy.

Pulling my hoody over my ears, I dodged out on to the street and smacked straight into Kieran.

'Whoah! What's up with you?'

I just stared at the ground.

'Your mum? Kim?'

I shook my head.

'Er, what else is there?' He scratched his chin. 'Teenage pregnancy, drugs . . . oh – *boys*?'

I nodded.

'C'mon.' He hooked his arm thru mine. 'Want to join me? I'm going to check out the Leaders' warehouse opening. Mmm, I'm such a sex god!'

'The Leaders' what?'

'Warehouse. They've set up a recycling business.'

'That explains it,' I muttered.

'What?'

'Brains and all that. Wondered why he was hanging round with them.'

'Who?'

I shook my head. 'Nothing.'

Kier hooked my arm thru his. 'Well come on then, mystery. You can tell me all about your love issues on the way.'

'Ooh,' he said, 15 minutes of heart-pouring later. 'Complex.'

'What's wrong with me?' I wailed.

Kieran stopped at the entrance to the warehouse. 'Stop right there, Laur. I spent ten years thinking there was something wrong with me . . . and then one day I just woke up and stopped feeling so damn sorry for myself. All those wasted years! I know it's a really cheesy thing to say, but life *is* what you make it. Now, are you a fighter or a quitter?'

I rolled my eyes.

'That's no answer.'

'Don't make me say it, Kier . . . s'embarrassing.'

'Go on.'

I looked up and down the street.

'Say it for me.'

'Imafighter.'

He punched me in the arm. 'Shitty delivery, but co-rrect! You gotta be so damn cool that Ravi Datta's gonna come crawling back on his hands and knees! Call those stupid people in your band now and get them all to join you in town. Things don't just happen on their own, y'know. You gotta work it, girl.'

I glanced across at him. He's started to talk in this weird, positive, American way.

Kieran was peering inside the warehouse. 'Blimey, is this it? It's like the Turner prize!'

I looked over his shoulder into a huge basement warehouse space. It was piled up high with toasters, stereos, TVs, washing machines, microwaves, fridges, kettles – all with their guts spilling out all over the place – and crowds of people crawling over the whole lot.

'It's recyclin', Leader style,' came a voice from behind us. Tracey Leader. 'Wot you reckon?'

Kieran nodded. 'Pretty impressive.'

Tracey threw back her head and gurgled like a troll. 'Yeah, weird, ain't it? Leaders doin' this stuff. But mate, there's money in this shit now – everyone's got to buy the new energy 'ficient stuff, but they can't do it all in one go, like – it's too 'spensive – so they fix up the old, while they're savin'.' She jerked her thumb towards a mound of white goods. 'That dishwasher there's only a year old, but nobody'd touch it now – it'd drain a month's worth of points in a week . . . All right boys, chill out! Plenty more where that came from!'

She stormed off to break up a fight. 2 men punching each other over an old Hotpoint.

Kieran nudged me. 'Isn't that Kim over there?'

I looked over and there she was, over in a far corner, sitting at a stall with a *Carbon Advice* banner draped over it. There was a crowd of people around her.

'Yep. Must be something to do with her Offenders Programme.'

'I tell you what though, for Lee Road, that's a bit of a strange crowd she's got round her.'

I looked again. It was true, they were all really middle-class looking, almost posh. And then I saw Tracey Leader look over at Kim and give her a sly nod. Strange.

We stepped back outside.

'So, what now?' asked Kieran.

I stood in the sunshine and looked about me. The cherry blossom was all out on the street, and I suddenly got this huge hit of *Spring*. I took a deep breath and called Claire. After a few rings she picked up.

'Right. Let's get the band sorted. You call Stace and I'll call Adi – and I'll see you in town in 30?'

'Good girl!' said Kieran. I kissed him before legging it across the road to catch the 53. Sometimes I think I'd sink right under without him.

When Adi and Stace first saw each other it was like a nature programme where the animals do the pecking order thing and kind of circle each other warily, then bit by bit they calmed down and pretty soon they were sharing a burger.

It was mad getting into town, though. There was just

no traffic on the roads, and my bus zoomed along at about 2000 miles an hour. Those drivers need to go into retraining to deal with their new freedom. And another thing, when I got off the bus at Westminster, I heard a bird singing in a tree.

Mon, April 20th

It's hot. I know this is really bad, but I kind of love this side of Warming. I lay in the garden and finished the elderly persons' checklist for my presentation. Later I took it round to Arthur's. God, his lifestyle is so far off from what's normal it's a miracle he's still alive. His house is full of cigarettes, even though it's been illegal to smoke in the home for the past 6 years. Why didn't I pick an easier *needy person*?

CHECKLIST	NO	YES	CARER COMMENTS
Are there smoke alarms fitted and working?	X		Arthur took out all the batteries because a) the damn winking and blinking got on his nerves and b) a fire truck came out every time he did his bacon *crispy* how he likes it.
Check that ashtrays do not contain smouldering cigarettes.	X		The house is a smouldering *volcano* of half-lit cigarettes. Arthur says it comforts him in his old age to have one lit in whatever room he's in.
Check that smouldering cigarettes have not fallen on or underneath the furniture.	X		Even when I was there a cigarette fell down the back of the sofa. There was a horrid whiff of burning plastic, which Arthur killed by flicking a used tea bag on to it.
Are deep flat-bottomed ashtrays available?	X		Mr Kipling individual apple-tart foil cups more like.
Are house keys in a safe place? Don't hide keys in the porch, or under plant pots or doormats - it's the first place a burglar will look. Leave a spare set with a trusted neighbour or relative.	X		Keys are under a plant pot on the doormat in the porch. Arthur won't give out a set to anyone, especially his only relative, a nephew in Penge, 'Harry's boy', who he describes as a 'thieving dog'.
Are there non-skid strips on backs of rugs?	X		Not sure if possible to apply non-skid strips to skinned Arctic-fox-with-head-still-attached rugs in sitting room.
Do shoes have Velcro straps, which are easier to put on/take off?	X		Arthur refuses to wear 'children's shoes'. He owns one brown and one black pair of Church's, which he says will see him out *and* do for his funeral.
Is there a walker/cane for unsteady gait if needed?	X		Arthur says he once nearly beat a man to death in India with his cane and has refused to carry one ever since.
Check eyesight regularly. Use sunglasses or cap to help prevent glare.	X		Arthur says at his time of life you don't want to see too clearly. He also refuses to wear anything that will make him look like a 'slipshod Yankee'.

Not a single YES!

Tues, April 21st

Mum came into my room and asked me to 'retrieve your father' like he is a bad dog. I was just about to say no, but then I took a look at her ageing face. She is like the bad example woman in a make-up advert, the one who hasn't moisturised daily.

I went out the back to look for him, then I heard Arthur's and Shiva Datta's voices coming from Arthur's porch. I peered over the hedge, and Dad was there too, slumped in a deckchair holding a can of beer. I was just about to call out to him when Arthur went, 'Yes, but what's wrong with the modern marriage is a woman doesn't know who's in control. It's all muddled up nowadays.' Arthur patted Shiva on the arm. 'Look at old Shiva here. No doubt who wears the pants in his house.'

Shiva nodded. 'Yes, we each have our designated path in life. My wife's path is to serve me.'

Dad slapped the arms of his deckchair. 'Huh, fat chance. It's all right for you . . .'

Shiva shook his head. 'No, Nick, every life is looking greener. Me, I come from Hyderabad – you know it? Famous for cow project, turning manure into gas for the people's homes. So, my family, three generations of cow shit and finally, finally, I get the chance to escape, come to England, God Save the Queen, long-distance lorry firm with my wife's brother. Then working, working like the dog – getting TV, stereo, good German car, kids going

McDonald's and drinking Coca-Cola – all one hundred per cent Western style – and then they do this to me. Rationing! Business gone! Hyderabad number two.'

Dad slumped again. 'Yeah, but at least you wear the pants.'

'Pants are not everything, Nick . . .'

'I told you, old boy, rein her in. Women are like hosses, need to know who's the boss. Makes 'em happy – trit, trot.'

I couldn't take hearing this crap any more. I stood up sharply. Dad's arm jerked as he turned towards me, spilling beer down his shirt.

'Mum wants you.'

'Well . . . I'm busy.'

I looked from his stubble to the tin of beer in his shaky paw. I was trying to be angry with him inside, but really I quite like this new dad. Not the stone-age woman crap, but just that he's stopped being such a walkover.

'OK, but don't say I didn't tell you.'

He gave me a shy smile. 'I won't.'

I can't work Arthur out. He's totally corrupting my father but he is also very kind and posh.

Elise Penatata came this evening for our final *Procedure Review Check-up*. Talk about role reversal from her last visit. Dad stank of booze, so just before she arrived Kim poured a mug of black coffee down his throat and put a fresh fleece on him to hide the scum that lay beneath. Then we propped him up on the sofa and sort of balanced him with cushions.

'We'll pretend he's got flu,' said Kim, re-bending his left leg to make it look more normal. Dad's head lolled over to one side, like a stroke victim's head.

'Flu? Ebola more like,' my mother snarled from her chair.

Elise took one look at Dad then totally blanked him and went and sat at the kitchen table, flicking thru our Government file. We are *so* the property of the state.

'Hmm, hmm – yes, definite improvement. The family has met its March and April targets . . . and *exceptional* improvement from you, Kimberley.' She held up some papers and flashed her pointy teeth. 'I have received excellent reviews regarding your participation on the Youth Carbon Offenders Rehabilitation Programme.'

Kim sat there with this mock humble smug face.

'It's so wonderful to see young people taking on such responsibility.' Elise held out some papers for Mum to look at, but Dad suddenly sat up in his chair, reached out and closed his fist around the papers; the forward movement releasing a thin drizzle of drool from his lips.

We all watched in fascination as it spiralled downward before coming to land on Kim's report.

'My dad's been pretty stressed out lately,' said Kim.

Elise turned away, disgusted.

Weds, April 22nd

Things have gone bad. My dad's 15 years of silence have shattered. CRACK! That's the trouble when you keep things locked up inside – when it finally breaks, oh boy. He stood out on the street in his Marks and Sparks' boxers and matching socks, waving a bottle of JD at the sky like a madman. The whole street turned out to watch. Mum screamed, 'Give me a break, Nick!' and my dad screamed back, 'Why? Why? Why? When did you once, ever, ever give me a break?' and then he hurled his whisky bottle and it smashed into a thousand pieces.

My head went all numb and I walked out into the back garden. I stood there, cold and trembly, and then I heard the most disgusting sound. Thanzila Amar's giggle.

'Oh, Ravi,' she drawled, 'you're so cute.'

Death take us all.

Thurs, April 23rd

We are officially the bad family on the street now, the family that other families call the cops on. Basically, the new Leaders. Dad didn't come home last night. Mum went around to Arthur's and said, 'I hope you're satisfied now,' and then came home and called the police. I made her up a cup of tea. When I took it to her she was staring out at the garden, looking all little. I put the cup down and just stood there for a minute. Very strange: my mother and silence. I turned to go.

'Laura?'

'Yes?'

'It wasn't always like this, you know.'

When the policeman arrived he was dead kind, with gloomy eyes. He cleared his throat. 'Is there any possibility that Mr Brown might have caused harm to himself?'

Mum clutched his hand. 'Oh, I knew it! You've got him, haven't you? Take me to the body, officer!'

I had to take her upstairs. Then I came down and sat in the kitchen and described my own father as *Caucasian, above medium height, hazel eyes, greying at the temples, possibly suicidal.*

The policeman told me not to worry too much. 'I reckon your dad'll be fine. Give it a day or two. In my experience, everyone needs time-out sometimes, y'know?' he added, casting a quick glance upstairs.

3 a.m. I've got my Care Energy presentation tomorrow. I'm so going to mess it up.

Fri, April 24th

Oh, God.

Key Questions	Please check box	Tutor feedback Gwen Parry-Jones	Candidate feedback Laura Brown
Did the candidate... Speak clearly in a way that suited the subject, purpose and situation?	YES ☐ NO ☒	*You spoke for **approximately 2** minutes on recent research that you have undertaken into food safety and principles of health and safety in Mr Stoat-Wilson's home. You **followed** this with a **further 15 minutes** on various thoughts concerning alcoholism, dead animal rugs, principles of making moonshine, marriage as a defunct institution, gizzards and evil in the home.* *The **positives** are that you spoke clearly and maintained good (if slightly glazed) eye contact with the class. **Unfortunately,** however, by the end no one **understood** what had taken place, whether Arthur was real, why your father was having a breakdown, why leopards are beautiful, what is the point of being radical, where your mother found gizzards, why your sister is fundamentally evil. **Disappointing, Laura!***	Pippa James went up just before me and did her presentation on, like, how she is single-handedly saving the planet when everyone knows she is a **brown-nosing**, goody two-shoed **hypocrite** who two-timed her boyfriend with Stace's ex-boyfriend, Ash. When it was my turn a red ball of **flame** blew up in my chest and I just wanted to tell people what it's really like. So I did. I didn't expect **anyone** to **understand.**
Did the candidate... Listen and respond appropriately to what others said?	YES ☐ NO ☒	*In your **defence, initially** you did listen closely to other members of the group. Your interest was obvious through your body language and the way you calmly waited for others to finish before responding. Unfortunately, you did not maintain this maturity.* ***I have no choice but to suspend you from college and shall discuss what happened next with you and a parent/guardian at the earliest opportunity***	I listened to Pippa James **taking the piss out of** me for a full **2** minutes before I threw a plastic cup of **water** over her. It's not my fault that it was **coffee.** Anyway I don't **care.**

There's no way any parent/guardian of mine is gonna find out about this. College always sends suspension letters straight out. I'm gonna have to get up early and cut the post.

Mon, April 27th

First day of Easter holiday and the suspension letter came right on time. I snatched it out of the postman's hand and marched round to the recycling bins. I was just about to throw it in when Delaney Leader appeared from the back of the white goods recycling crate with an old PC in his hot hands. I quickly closed the bin lid, but not before he clocked the college crest on the envelope.

'Nice one, Laur, best place for them tossers.'

Dad's just called Mum. I don't know what he said, but the conversation lasted for about 10 seconds before she hung up. At least he's alive.

Thurs, April 30th

I've been in bed for 3 straight days. It's too complicated getting up.

May

Fri, May 1st

This morning I made my mind up. I'll have to pray I can cover up the suspension – but after that I'm not bunking off or messing up any more. I've got to get an education, it's my only way out of here. And then I got up and went to the May Day march.

I met up with the others in Soho and we joined the crowds of people going up to Trafalgar Square in the dazzling sunshine.

'Urgghh, crusties! Away! Away!' Adi flapped his hands as a dirty girl on rollerblades zigzagged across the pavement towards us. 'Ra, why do radical people have to be so ugly? It's the same with Straight X. Is there a law that if you care about shit you've got to get dreads and a dog on a piece of string and never wash?'

'C'mon.' Claire grabbed his arm. 'If we're going to be revolutionary we've got to get hard to this.'

We caught up with the march by the church of St Martin-in-the-Fields. Stace nudged me. 'God, remember when we came to that classical concert here with school? S'like another life.'

I scanned the scene in front of me. All of Trafalgar Square and the surrounding streets choked up with a heaving mass of people.

At first it was rubbish. We got stuck with a bunch of protestors moving away towards the river. They were pushing a huge globe, with people popping out of holes in the top and sort of trying to dance. So lame. And even when we got past them we got caught up with thousands of uni students chanting 'One Solution, Green Revolution!' like a bunch of wimps. Claire and Adi dodged to one side.

'Let's get to the action. These ones look like they know what's going on.' Adi pointed at a bunch of about 3,000 trade union guys. They had a line of drummers and were really moving. We crossed the road and joined them. As soon as we slipped in behind the drums, I felt the adrenalin start to pound thru my body.

The police were trying to get everyone to move down Whitehall, but our group kept turning right, away from the main march and back towards Trafalgar. The pigs were trying to block us, but there wasn't enough of them. But when we got up to Charing X Station another massive group of marchers suddenly appeared from the opposite direction. Lines of riot police came out of nowhere to stop us all coming together. They came right up alongside and started to push us with their riot shields. A couple of fights broke out, but nobody wanted any trouble so we got pushed back down Whitehall towards Parliament Square. After 15 minutes it started to get scary. It was so packed, we couldn't move any further.

Adi tripped up in front of me and went down. He yelled out and then it seemed like everyone around us was shouting, getting angry. There was the sound of smashing glass – I looked up to see the entire plate-glass window of a McDonald's shatter into a million pieces. A moment's silence – then a voice shouting orders. I whirled round. Mounted police charging us from a side street. People started to lose it, screaming, shoving, shouting.

'Shit.' I grabbed Claire's hand. Adi and Stace just behind. It was like being caught in a massive wave. Pushed forward, dragged back. After what seemed like hours, we finally made it to Parliament Square.

Once we got there, police wouldn't let anyone leave, just kept us blocked in the square for hours. No one in or out. Officers went round, blatantly photographing everyone, taking names and addresses. After a while I kind of went outside of myself and watched the scene. The police confuse me. They're supposed to protect us, but then they do this. Who do they really work for? And another thing, when I finally got home I watched the news. They said we hurled stones and sticks and blocked the streets with trash, but they never said anything about police on horses charging a group of teenagers.

Sat, May 2nd
Finally. Arthur's brought my dad back.

Mum ran across the room. 'You're alive!' she sobbed. 'Oh, Nicky, don't you ever leave us like that again.'

'I won't,' he mumbled, tears spilling down his cheeks. And then something weird happened. One minute they were really close and then Mum just pulled away. It was like watching a door close.

'Well, that's good.' She brushed at his coat. 'Where've you been to get so filthy? Honestly.'

'Julia, I want you to know . . .'

But Mum was already halfway to the door. 'I'm going to run you a bath!'

Dad stood there for a moment, looking so lost I couldn't stand to see him. Arthur cleared his throat sharply. 'Well, Nicholas – I'll be off.' He patted me on the head, turned on his heel and marched out the back door.

I woke up in the middle of the night to a flood of

moonlight pouring thru my bedroom window; it was all shivery and magical. I went to the kitchen to get a glass of water and found Dad curled up on the sofa. I just stood there for a moment, looking down at him.

'Laura?' he said, softly.

'Yes, Dad?'

'Are you OK?'

'Yes, Dad.'

'I'm so sorry.'

'I know.'

'My lovely girl.' He took my hand – and we just stayed like that for a bit.

Sun, May 3rd

Totally annoying *thunk! thunk!* noise coming from the garden this morning. I opened the window to see Dad attacking the nettle patch at the far end of the garden with a pickaxe. Kim stepped out across the grass towards him, balancing a cup of tea and plate of biscuits on a tray. Evil witch.

I was so mad with her perfect little daughter act I ran into her bedroom and punched her old teddy bear in the guts. It fell off the bed on to the carpet – and guess what was underneath? A mini mobile, one of those new kinetic ones that go on your wrist. How's she affording that? It lit up. I so wanted to answer it, but then the back door slammed so I ran out sharp. She is *so* up to something.

The sunshine's changed everything. Our street's come out of its winter slugdom big time. All day there's been cleaning, planting, fixing, painting. I kept hearing laughter coming from the garden – and when I looked out there was Mum and Mrs Datta cackling together over the fence. I don't know when they got so friendly.

Mon, May 4th

Back to college. Grr. But we had ourselves a totally hardcore band practice at Adi's. We've got a date for the gig now, it's June 7th. His mum's given us extra practice time cos she's saving carbon on heating during the warm weather. We've picked *so funny, messed-up world* and *death to capitalist scum*. 15 minutes of pure *venom*.

```
death to capitalism
a new world waiting to be born
murder is capitalism
cast off the cloak of scorn

you selling us mercedes, nike, mp3
gucci, rolex, toys R us –
```

```
trying to sedate us - but the tragedy
is that in reality you are killing us
```

It's sounding so hectic right now – especially as Stacey's finally nailed her chorus harmonies on *mp3* and *tragedy*.

In the break, Claire came and sat next to me. 'How's it going?'

'How d'you mean?'

'Just in general.'

'Yeah, good. Busy.'

Claire raised an eyebrow. 'Well I hope you ain't got too much on, cos I know someone who's well into you.'

'Yeah, but I got so much on with the band and . . .' I paused. 'Who, though?'

'John Clarke. You know, the drummer for Dogshit.'

My heart sank. 'Claire, he paints his fingernails black.'

'Keeps good time, though. Steady.' Stacey nodded approvingly.

I shook my head. Is this the best they think I can do? 'No.'

'Just think about it, is all.'

'Would *you* go out with him?'

'Sure! It's not all about fingernails, Laur. Thought you'd be more open-minded.'

It's all right for her to say that, she goes out with

gorgeous Sean with his gorgeous body and unpainted cuticles. I looked over at Adi, but he was deep into restringing his guitar.

Claire showed us the flyer design she's done for the gig. It rocks. We all looked round at each other with shining eyes – we are the *dirty angels* . . . oh yeah!

Tues, May 5th

Dad's out in the garden 24/7 with Arthur and Shiva. I got home to find they'd pulled down the dividing fence and dug up loads of grass. Arthur called me over and put one end of a ball of string in my hand before setting off across the soil in a series of lines, unravelling the string and winding it around cane sticks.

'What's going on?' I asked.

'Seeds, drills, new life . . . But no time for gabbling, Laura . . . Late start – all hands to the pump. Marvellous, isn't it!' he cried, crisscrossing the garden like a giant spider. 'Reminds me of my halcyon youth on the estate, don't you know!'

Somehow I don't think he means *council* estate. I must ask Arthur how come he's living in Charlton – talk about riches to rags!

Ravi came out and sparked up.

tHE dIRTy anGels

8 pm

june 7th

Hope & Anchor

Blackheath

we're gonna puke all over your pretty lives!

'Hey, Laura.'

'Oh, hi!'

Cool as a cu-cum-ber.

I think I'm getting kind of obsessed with him. The more he ignores me, the more I like him.

Anyway, had the best night. Didn't think once, just watched trashy TV with Stace and Claire in her dad's surgery. He gets a special carbon allowance for screening this vet channel called Pet Aware! But Claire's sorted out a crack code for tuning it to US MTV. It was really mad, cos loads of it was teenage boy-bands singing about girls and jetting round the US all blinged up in a Ferrari. Things have changed so much for us in 5 months, it's like watching sci-fi.

Oh yeah, last thing. I reckon I've got away with it. Tutorial was cancelled cos GPJ's at a conference, but anyway I reckon she's forgotten about the suspension thing. Once you get over 40 you can't remember stuff any more. Whatever, I don't care, I've been charged by police horses. What's she gonna do . . . make me write an essay? *Huh.*

Weds, May 6th

Mum called me down from my room this evening. When I got downstairs, my jaw nearly hit the floor. Gwen Parry-

Jones was sitting at the kitchen table. Kim smirked as I walked in.

'Laura, is this true?' Mum asked.

'What?'

'Don't *what* me, young lady – the presentation, the . . .' her eyes began to fill up, '. . . the coffee?'

I swallowed hard, I could feel the tears starting. Why do I let them do this to me?

Mum crossed her arms. 'I simply can't believe—'

But GPJ cut in. 'If I may, Mrs Brown . . . I don't think that anger is always the appropriate response.'

Mum snapped her jaws shut, like a terrapin. GPJ turned on me with her nailed-on teacher smile. *Do you want to disappoint your parents? Do you understand the gravity of the situation? Do you wish to continue your studies or do you want to throw your life away because that's where you're headed, young lady . . . blah, blah, blah.*

Dad tried to lighten her up a bit. 'Well, if Laura doesn't want to go to college, there's plenty of work to be done around here.' He smiled. 'I mean education isn't every—'

'Mr Brown.' She uncrossed her legs, planting her boots down hard on the rug. 'I presume you are trying to be amusing, but it has taken womankind several millennia to escape the constraints of a patriarchal society operated

135

by men, dominating women and oppressing them. Education is freedom.'

Dad looked down at his slippers. They looked dead small and girlish compared to hers.

GPJ cleared her throat. 'However, the college *is* prepared to let your daughter continue with us, on the condition that she performs some, uh, community service in order to show how sorry she is.'

Kim's smug grin widened. Gwen Parry-Jones turned to me. 'Laura, the only way we can let you back to college is if you attend the Carbon Young Offenders meetings at the local Blackheath branch. We feel this is an appropriate space for you to put your, uh, *creative* talents to better use . . .'

I couldn't believe what I was hearing. 'But this isn't fair—'

'It is more than fair in the circumstances,' GPJ interrupted. She looked around the table. 'Are we all in agreement?'

Mum shook her head and sighed. 'Oh, Laura. Why can't you be more like your sister . . . ?'

I glanced up at Kim. Her smile had gone.

'I think this is very harsh, I mean . . .' Kim started.

'It is the only way she can come back. Don't you care about your younger sister's education?'

Kim looked at the floor.

'Well, that's settled then.' She stood up and suddenly there was a weird groaning noise and the table tipped over, like it was exhausted with all the bullshit.

Mum jumped forward. 'Oh, I'm so sorry. Nick's been promising to fix that for months now.' GPJ ducked under the table. 'I see the problem – leg's warped. Just need a . . . little bit . . . shaving off with a chisel.' She reached for her rucksack. 2 minutes later, the table was back up.

She smiled into Mum's face. 'There, that's fixed. No need to ever wait for a man, Julia.'

'Well, thank you . . . I'll . . . er . . . see you to the door then.' Mum walked her out of the room with little panicky steps.

'Dad!' I began as soon as they'd gone. 'You know this isn't fair!'

'It's all for the best, Laura. It'll do you good. Look at Kim now. Much better.' He reached for a seed catalogue. I stared at him for a moment – it's like he's totally buried himself in this new garden project. And then I had this dazzling insight. He's just like Mum. Keep busy and don't think!

Thurs, May 7th

Mum's grounded me. Revision and 4 walls and watching

Dad planting beans. There is no justice.

Fri, May 8th
In this world.

Sat, May 9th
Or the next.

Sun, May 10th
Unbelievable. No rain since the beginning of April and they're saying there's going to be a water shortage. Turns out London's had less rain this year than Ethiopia. Who makes this stuff up? All I can remember is rain and snow.

Mum is dressing like a teenager. She's been all over Dad since he's got all revved up in the garden. Today she was wearing low-slung hipsters, a baby doll T-shirt, platforms and a silvery belt and spent the morning chasing him all over the garden with the hosepipe. Puke.

Mon, May 11th
Finally got out of the house. I went to college and welded a water-pump tube for Dad. He begged me to do it, cos the garden's getting dry. Basically he wants to set up a system to pipe bathwater outside in case there's a hosepipe ban. And another thing – he's not going to try

and find another job, he told us at breakfast he's
6 months off and living on his redundancy pay. H
his arms. 'It just feels great to be doing something I really
believe in. Thanks for being understanding. And it's not
just me – I want everyone in the family to be happy.'

He caught my eye. 'Laur, I don't want you to be
miserable at college. If you don't want to be there, then
I understand.'

'Excuse me. Once of us taking time off is all we need
in one house.' Mum smiled, but her face looked like
an old lemon.

I glanced at Dad. I know he's trying to be nice, but
what am I going to do without an education – stay at
home like a weird spinster daughter with bottle-end
glasses and thick ankles?

Weds, May 13th

I can't believe what's happening. When I got home Kieran
and Kim were deep in talk on the sofa. I stopped dead
when I saw them.

Kieran looked up. 'Ooh, good! We need you to look
at something.'

'We?'

Kim rolled her eyes. 'Yes. We. Kier's asked me to help
set up Carbon Dating. Got a problem with that?'

'C'mon and sit down, Laura.' Kieran patted the sofa.

I crossed my arms.

'*Please?* This is really important to me. I've traded in my Alfa and everything.'

'You sold your car?'

'Yep, for a G7, five thousand flyers and six months' rental at the Leopard in Soho.'

He dug into his pocket and brought out a business card. 'Like it? Kim did it.'

love in the new age

carbon
d8

kieran@co2d8.com

Thurs, May 14th

It's happened. Thames Water's putting London on a hosepipe ban from next week. No watering the garden, no washing the car. Dad was dead upset. 'It's not like I'm growing roses out there now. It's real food, things we need to live on.'

'You could always get another job, darling,' said Mum.

He stuck his hands in his pockets. 'Where? You know there's a recession on.'

'Well, you could get yourself on one of those Gov retraining courses – y'know, for renewables engineers, turbine fitters . . . there's a massive skills shortage . . .'

'Hmm. Well, maybe. But first I want to get the house self-sufficient.'

Mum glanced at the shrivelled-up lettuces, but said nothing.

Sat, May 16th

Kim has just been in my room. She came in, shut the door and leaned up against the wall. 'Listen, don't rock the boat.'

'What boat?'

'Just don't rock it, little sis, or it'll be bad for you.'

'Why don't you just piss off?' I hissed.

'With pleasure,' she hissed back and left.

Weds, May 20th

So bored. Mum still won't let me go out with my mates, cept to college, till I start *Offenders*. Did stupid revision for the environment exam. Later I went round to Arthur's for him to test me.

'Hmm,' he said at the end. 'The general environmental

141

impact stuff is OK, but let's just pray you don't get any questions on air travel. Very weak. Why's that?'

I shrugged. 'Dunno. It's just stupid. I mean, all this stuff's going on around us for real – and it feels weird doing an exam on it. Like if you were married and someone made you sit down and write an essay on love.'

Arthur glanced at me, sharply.

Thurs, May 21st

Flopped it. Opened up the exam paper and went all cold inside. The whole exam was about air travel. When is my luck gonna change? Ravi was in the hall at the same time doing some triple maths paper. When my row got up to leave, he glanced up for .46 of a second, grinned, then put his head down again.

Came home and found this on the kitchen table. Huh.

Name .... Age ....
Height .... Eye colour ....
Occupation .... Hair colour ....

Dear Applicant,

Findin' love ain't easy at the best of times and in these days of carbon rationing, the rules are changin' before our eyes. You used to be a hero and now you're a zero. The lasers are gone, the music's low and suddenly everyone can hear every word you're saying, which ain't always good. A pumped-up gym body is burnin' too much carbon and you had to trade in your wheels for an energy efficient boiler. It just ain't sexy!
You bankers, IT boys, designers, agents, media types, paper-chasers - you're so out o' style. It's all about fixers and menders...
Boys and girls who are good with their hands...

But don't despair - Carbon Dating is here to get you on your way!

Personal Spot Check!

First of all, you've gotta find out where you're at, carbon-wise. We've split this *personal spot check* section into **Caring, Fixing, Socialising** and **Moving.** It ain't **SEXY** as we used to know it, but unless you're down with the basics, you ain't never gettin' to first base with the love o' your life!

Just circle the number that best describes you and when you've done, add up your score and then check out our guide below!

Fri, May 22nd

I'm not going to panic, I'm gonna write out key revision points for the Crit Thinking exam on individual memory cards. Like that will turn me into a normal teenager who can pass exams.

Sat, May 23rd

Interactionalism – dramaturgical model.
The society is constructed like a play or drama. The society operates through the dramaturgical scene. You learn the part you play. Socialisation.

Mon, May 25th

Feminism.
The society is constructed by men dominating women, with a hierarchy with men at top and women at bottom. Social change happens due to the uprising of feminism. There are no apparent conflicts because men deny it.

Tues, May 26th

Globalisation – has world become smaller?

Nothing will stay in my head. I read it and 2 minutes later it's gone.

Weds, May 27th

On top of everything else I've got this stupid bloody Offenders meeting tomorrow.

Thurs, May 28th

10 p.m. Oh Jesus, I just got back from Offenders. Too exhausted to write more now. Exam tomorrow morning, which I am going to 100% fail.

Fri, May 29th
Advanced Subsidiary GCE

Critical Thinking	**2450/1**
Paper 1	
Friday, May 29th 2015	**Morning**

Time 1 hour 30 minutes

Instructions to Candidates

- **Write your name and candidate number in the spaces provided on the answer booklet. Do not write on both sides of the paper.** *(Mr Harris, the fat PE teacher, cracked a joke about us being sure to write* *on at least ONE side of the paper. Like he's ever had to take an exam in his life.)*

- **There are three questions – you must answer either A OR B AND C.** *(What?)*
- **Read each question carefully and make sure you know what you have to do before starting your answer.** *(Yeah, right)*

A) Critically evaluate the argument below.

Having a 'gap' year between A-levels and university is now very popular. However, a number of questions need to be raised about the practice in the rationing era.

The year-long luxury of a gap year is so radically different from the way life is organised in our current society that it might prove difficult for students to readjust to normality. 50% of lbiza carbon exiles are individuals who have never managed to readjust after taking a gap year. As a result they have attempted to permanently drop out. Such a dose of freedom is a poor preparation for the disciplined routines that the modern world demands – and, indeed, may be a direct cause of socially unacceptable behaviour.

1) Identify the overall conclusion of the argument. (2)

The person who wrote this exam paper is probably a middle-aged parent who has reached the overall conclusion that they want their teenage snot-bag to grow up and stop sponging off them.

2) Construct an argument that either **challenges** or **supports** the conclusion. Your answers should include a developed discussion. (8)

I am going to *challenge* the conclusion with reference to a real-life example – that of my sister, Kim Brown.
Challenge:

If my sister Kim *had* been allowed to go on her gap year to New York to work in a designer clothes store, like she was meant to, then she would NOT have gone off the rails and dragged my family into carbon bankruptcy. Following this, she would NOT have been sent for reprogramming at Carbon Offenders, where she would NOT have become involved in Tracey Leader's carbon crime ring.

Although I have no definite proof as yet, my suspicions were aroused last night on my first visit to Carbon Offenders. I was forced to sit in a circle of offenders and throw a ball to the other members and say my name and my offence each time I caught the ball. And then a girl next to me leant over and whispered, 'Laura Brown, you're not Kim's sister are you?'

When I nodded, she looked at me with great respect and asked me if I could 'introduce her'. When I expressed surprise at this request, she gave me a hurt look, and said, 'Oh right, I'm not good enough for you' and turned away.

When the meeting was over, I was about to leave when I saw a small group of people huddled around a familiar-looking 4x4 in the dark outside. I sneaked over. They were all nice, educated people, their whispered conversation was all about how they *really needed* this holiday, how they simply *couldn't survive* without the car, etc.

Suddenly I heard the slam of a door. I looked to see a woman of my mother's age emerging from the 4x4. She came over to a friend in the group and whispered, 'Tuscany, what luxury!'

I remained in my concealed location for over an hour, hoping to catch sight of my evil sibling, but she did not appear. After a while, I began to believe that I had made a mistake and I set off for home, but as I tramped the lonely streets, the 4x4 appeared at the lights alongside me. I ducked behind a bin and peered inside to see my sister and a laughing Tracey Leader. Then they disappeared into the night. Coincidence?

All I have to say in conclusion is that it is clear from this example that in my sister's case a gap year would have been a VERY GOOD THING. She would have gone to New York, clubbed, snorted ching, gone anorexic, dated a record producer, etc., like a normal, fricked-up, spoilt, 20-year-old from the West.

Instead of this, she is at home and somehow involved in peddling black-market carbon to the corrupt middle classes in alliance with Tracey Leader, new friend to the bourgeoisie. The same Tracey Leader who will ditch her like a piece of dogshit on her shoe if the pigs come knocking on the door.

I realise this is maybe not the answer you are looking for, but the fact is if you were living my life right now, you'd fail this exam too. Sorry.

Sat, May 30th

Urggh, I woke up with my head full of trouble. I haven't got any real proof, so there's no point telling anyone. I don't even wanna tell Adi – I mean, what if it's true?

I saw Arthur outside weeding, so I went and sat on the grass.

'Arthur . . . was there a black market in the war?'

He tugged at a dandelion. 'Course. Couldn't have survived without it.'

'Didn't you feel guilty?'

'No time for guilt. You were hungry and if you could

get something to fill your belly you did it. Within reason, of course.'

'But . . . what about now? Carbon fraud. Isn't it kind of different . . . ? I mean, it's not about starvation, it's just about wanting it easy.'

Arthur looked at me. 'Hmm. Well, I wouldn't be too hard on people. It's such a difficult thing we're doing, there's always going to be some rule bending.'

'I bet it wasn't like this in the war. People had more style back then.'

'Well, I don't know. In some ways it was easier – we had a clear enemy – but this time it's almost like we're fighting ourselves. It was difficult in other ways then; the whole country was turned upside down. Poor people and rich were forced together, y'know, eating the same food, wearing the same clothes. City children were evacuated to much richer families and all the old rules were broken.'

'But at least everyone worked together. They weren't rioting and looting just cos they couldn't get what they wanted.'

Arthur shook his head. 'Don't believe all that Government whitewash "Spirit of the Blitz" stuff, Laura. I remember one time when there was a direct bomb hit on the Café de Paris in Piccadilly – it had a famous underground ballroom, as I recall, so couples would go there for a night on the town because it was supposed to be safe. Anyway, it turned out it wasn't so secure, and when the military police got to the scene it was like a tomb – all the elegantly dressed people still sitting at tables without a mark on them, but *stone dead* – I suppose from the shock of the blast. But the really awful thing was the looting. Gangs had sneaked in there before the rescue crews and cut the fingers from the dead to steal their rings.'

'What, they stole *whole fingers*?'

'Yes. Gruesome, isn't it? But Laura, what we're going through now is very extreme. It wasn't supposed to be like this, was meant to be a more gradual reduction to sixty per cent. But the Great Storm changed all that for ever and now we've got to do the best we can.'

Arthur sighed. 'At least we're not at war. War is awful. I hope we never have to go through anything like that again.'

Summer. June

Mon, June 1st

No rain for weeks and weeks. Dad tried to hand out a load of new house rules at dinner today. He wants us to shower in a bucket for 1 minute max and then throw the water on the garden. No more dishwasher, no more washing machine, one clothes wash per person per week, by hand. The toilet rule's the most disgusting part: basically – if it's yellow let it mellow, if it's brown flush it down. Dad tried to make a joke out of it. I saw Mum give him this look like she wondered how she'd ever fancied him. She went over to the cooker.

'So what are you learning at Offenders, Laura?'

I could feel Kim's eyes burning into me. 'Umm, dunno. Stuff.'

'Honestly, darling, do try to articulate better . . . Well, what about you, Kim? Are you doing anything exciting?'

Kim blinked. 'Umm, yeah – we like went into a prison and gave a lecture on staying clean in the new world.'

'Oh, marvellous! And aren't you doing something with

Kieran now, too? You see, your gap year worked out in the end!' Mum began to offload huge mounds of lumpy mashed potato on to our plates. She glanced at Dad. 'Did you hear that, darling? She's doing so well!'

He grunted.

'Laura, surely you've got something to tell?'

She fixed me with her biggest positive smile; it was like being under a massive sunlamp.

My forehead began to prickle with sweat.

'Lumps.'

Her smile slipped. 'Excuse me?'

'This mash is full of lumps,' muttered Dad, poking at it with a fork.

'Well, I'm sorry, Nick, there wasn't time to finish it properly, what with everything else . . .'

He pushed it to one side.

'Don't like lumps.'

Are they starting to fall apart again already?

2 a.m. Wide awake, drenched in sweat from yet *another* mare – this time I was being chased all over the Leaders' estate by a pig-dog beast with slavering jaws. It was wearing a little dog jacket with KIM embroidered on it. Huh. Interpret that, Mr Freud.

I couldn't get back to sleep, so I went into the kitchen, opened the fridge door and just sort of gazed inside for a few minutes. Even the fridge has had a revolution; it used to be stacked up with Waitrose ready meals and plastic packaging – and now it's like looking into my granny's fridge in Devon. There was left-over stew, 5 spuds, a bottle of milk of magnesia (??), a beetroot, some wizened apples and a bag of old carrots. All very British – the exotic stuff just costs too many points. I could have murdered a slice of really tacky Domino's pizza – salami with extra jalapeno.

Suddenly the front door slammed. I froze. It could only be Kim. I stood there, willing her to go straight to her room – but when did she ever do anything I wanted?

'Oh God, you gave me a shock,' she gasped, standing in the doorway.

I just stood there.

She fixed me with a level stare. 'So, how was Offenders the other night?'

'Whatever.'

'What does that mean?'

'Well, it was kind of weird, cos as soon as they knew I was your sister, everyone wanted to know me. Why's that, Kim?'

There was a pause. I stood there, waiting for the explosion, but instead Kim just sighed. 'Yeah, OK. It's true. I fix people up with a bit of extra carbon.'

'It's more than a bit, Kim – there were women getting fixed up with enough black market stuff to fly to Italy.'

Kim scowled. 'No way! I deal in gas bills and bus passes, just a few chillers. Nothing more.'

'And what about Tracey – you reckon *she* stops there?'

'That's her business. Don't get involved.'

'Oh right, too late. I *am* involved, cos I'm your sister

and if you mess up then I'll end up paying for it cos that's how it works round here.'

'Listen, you have to believe me, I am not involved with what she does.'

'Then why were you in the Jeep with her later?'

'Jesus. You're quite the little spy aren't you? She gave me a lift, that's all. It's all right for you, little miss radical, all that anti-capitalism bullshit – but what about me? My whole life's been taken off me . . . It's not like I ever wanted anything bad – just to work in fashion, travel, you know, the usual shit . . . and now it's over.'

'You're breaking my heart.'

'You don't know anything about it, you don't know anything about me. At least I live in the real world, instead of some little moral fantasy . . .'

'Why shouldn't I tell Mum and Dad?'

Kim laid a hand on my arm. 'Don't be stupid, Laura. Look, you're really overreacting here. I *am* going to stop soon, anyway.'

'When?'

'Soon. That's why I'm doing this thing with Kier.' She looked at me hard. 'Trust me.'

I stared back at her.

'Just this once?'

I sighed.

She smiled. 'C'mon, little sis! It's not so bad – it's kind of underground, y'know, like 2 fingers up at the state.'

I went back to bed and thought about it. The trouble is, right now I *am* the state. I don't want spoilt pigs to go to Tuscany, I want them to clean up and sort their shit out once and for all. Can I trust Kim? Almost definitely not. But I *want* to.

Weds, June 3rd

Me and Adi gave out flyers for the *angels* gig around college. Loads of kids say they're coming . . . We were standing in the link, talking to a bunch of people, when Thanzila cruised by with Ravi.

Adi held out a flyer. 'Hey, you wanna come?'

I hissed, 'Adi!'

Thanzila stopped and looked at him like he was a bug crawled out from under a log. 'Oh, right, your band. That's sooo cool.'

'So see you there?'

'Ohh, right . . . The thing is it's not really my scene. I'm more of an R&B girl, I mean, isn't this kinda like white people's shit?'

'Take a look at my skin,' replied Adisa, coolly. 'It's not about colour, it's about *giving* a shit, Thanzila.'

'Well, yeah, course! Umm, what's the date?'

'The 7th, this Sunday.'

'Oh, no!' A look of pure fake distress crossed her perfect face. She turned to Ravi. 'We're going to that party in Hackney that night, isn't it?'

He shrugged. 'Dunno. This looks safe.'

Thanzila gave him the evil eye, but Ravi smiled shyly at Adisa. 'I'll take a flyer, if that's cool?'

'Sure, it'd be good to see you there, Rav.'

Thanzila turned on her heel. 'Yeah, well,' she smiled sweetly, 'as I say, I *think* we may be busy.'

After they'd gone, I gave Adi a shove. 'What did you go and do that for? I don't want her there. Or him, for that matter.'

'Just testing it out is all.' He watched them walk down the link. 'It's not over till it's over, Than-zi-la.'

I've just tried some new bass moves in the mirror. What if he does come? He won't, though. Anyway, I don't like him any more.

Fri, June 5th

I went to Offenders and did a workshop on pollution. Bizarre.

Sun, June 7th

Day of The Gig!

Close one. Mum found the *angels* flyer in my jeans pocket this morning when she was loading the washing machine.

'What's this, honey?'

'Oh, s'nothing.'

'But it says you're playing a gig tonight . . .'

'Oh, yeah – it's kind of a joke. The girls just made it up in Photoshop.'

'Really? I'd love to see you play sometime, you must be really good now.'

'Course, I'll let you know . . .'

She sighed and folded the flyer. 'My little girl! You're getting all big now.'

'Yeah!' I picked up my college bag. 'Gotta go, Mum!'

There's no way *ever ever* that my mother is coming to the gig. And Mum, if you're reading this right now, I mean it.

5 a.m. Can't sleep, just too fired up!

We got to the gig in a total sweat, cos our ride – Stacey's friend's cousin's mate, Dodgy Gary from Wicklow – had a blow-out on the North Circular in his untaxed, carbon-illegal wreck of a white van – and he had to push it half

159

a mile off to the next slip road so the pigs wouldn't bust him. By the time he fixed it and got to us, it was almost time for the sound-check. Claire banged on the van door in rage when he pulled up.

'All roight, darlin', keep yer knickers on!' he grinned.

'Keep your own bloody knickers on!' screamed Claire, throwing a snare drum into the back. 'And don't just sit there like a stuffed pig – help us get the kit in.'

Gary's face went all white; I don't think girls talk like that in Ireland.

It was the Van of Tension. The traffic was all snarled up because of some road works so Gary was forced to go down the back streets, even though the pub was only a couple of Ks away. We were making him so nervous that he took about 500 wrong turns. I thought Claire was going to strangle him. Even Adi, who is normally one very chilled human being, went into some kind of stress trance. He wedged himself tight against the passenger door, going 'juss-gotta-get-there-juss-gotta-get-there' like a zombie until we finally screeched up outside the pub.

'Sweet Jaysus.' Gary wiped his damp face. 'Oi been on some dirty rides before but youse lot is lethal.'

'Better believe it, buddy. We're the *dirty angels*,' snarled Claire.

You'd never believe she lives in a 5-bedroom house in

Blackheath. We piled out of the van and I picked up my amp and set off around the corner behind Stace. Suddenly she stopped.

'Oh my God!'

I stopped too. The outside of the Hope and Anchor was swarming with kids – hundreds of 12-year-old, Straight X kids in chains and tats. Stace tapped a skater-boy on the shoulder.

'Er, are you here for the gig?'

'Yuh. *SlashFist* are playing. Vegan death. Bare cool.' He flipped his board up on his toes.

'What's Adi gonna say?' I whispered.

There was a groan from behind me.

'Oh, you got to be kidding!'

Then Claire appeared. 'Wow, there's like 400 people here!'

Adi stuck his hands on his hips. '400 *edgers*. They'll kill us if they catch us with as much as a Coke Lite in our hands.'

'C'mon, Adi,' said Claire, 'it's time we broke down those old barriers. That's what we're about – we aren't punks, we aren't Straight X, we're *us*. We're here to rock out.'

He shook his head. 'Whatever.'

As soon as we walked inside a girl with about 50 thousand face piercings and blue hair skated over to us.

'Yo! Mia Metziger,' she drawled in a US accent. 'You the *angels*?'

'Yeah,' Claire drawled back.

'Cool. We gotta problem, though. Running order's changed – the *Mondays* have pulled out, so you're on third now. Just before us, *SlashFist*. Cool?'

'Yeah,' said Claire.

'Cool.' Mia skated off.

Claire turned to us, eyes shining. 'Our first gig, 400 crowd and we're nearly headlining! Come on, Ad, it's awesome.'

He grinned. 'OK, but just keep your smokes hidden, girl. Or they'll kill ya.'

I felt my stomach twist.

After we'd done a fast sound-check I wandered around backstage. There was a reporter in there with Mia Metziger. I turned to go, but she waved me to stay. 'Cool if you wanna chill . . . Er, yeah,' she turned back to the journo, 'I came to London cos of the whole new rad rationing scene here. The States suck right now – they been talking for 10 years 'bout a hydrogen revolution, but like *everyone* knows the oil people still call the shots in Washington. Anyhowz, I play drums for a political/personal/anti-thug sXe hardcore band from Little Rock called *SlashFist*. We're like total hardcore enviro punk but I'm also deeply into political/social justice issues, art, baking, skating, tattoos and booking shows.'

The reporter nodded. 'So, how did you get into the scene?'

Mia fiddled with her eyebrow bolt. 'Well, I was always into music a whole lot. It sounds kinda sad, but I din't really have many friends of my own, I just kind of hung out with my brother's crew. I wanted to play keyboard in a band so bad in elementary school but this music teacher told me my hands were all wrong to play. I was really down, but then one day I picked up my bro's buddy's stix and it all started from there.'

The reporter smiled. 'OK, so just one final question. What was it about hardcore/punk that appealed to you in the first place?'

'I think what got me into it was the aggression.' Mia frowned. 'Not aggression in a macho sense – because I was never really that big into bleeding at shows. It was just the fury, the anger, the whole attitude of "Yes, I'm mad, I'm not happy like YOU think I should be, everything isn't OK, and I'm gonna do something about my life!" I liked that a lot, that I could be in a band, go on tour, be part of something – instead of just living through bands on MTV and youtube and facebook and whatever.'

'Awesome!' The reporter switched off her recorder. 'Have a great show. I'll be out front.'

Once she'd left Mia blew out a deep breath and smiled. 'Journos. Gotta love 'em . . . Anywayz, what's your name?'

'Laura.'

'From the *angels*, right?'

I nodded. I kind of felt shy, but I really liked what she said about the anger thing. She twisted her smartphone round. 'Wanna touch? Us radicals gotta stay in touch.'

The gig was mind-blowing. The club was just one big sweaty mosh pit by the time we got on. I nearly threw up, but once we were onstage and Stace clicked her sticks, I just stepped into my bass stance and rocked out. All our college crew were there, right at the front. I saw Louise Foster go down in a pool of blood, laughing her head off. We wound up for the final track, *death to capitalist scum*, when suddenly I saw him. Ravi. He was standing on his own, right on the edge of the crowd. Our eyes locked and my whole world went cold, my fingers froze to the fretboard. Adi turned to me, frowning.

'Laur?' His voice coming from a thousand miles away.

'Ravi's here.'

He threw his head back and laughed. 'Then let's mess this place up good!'

Stacey screamed, '1 2 3 4!' And the place just EXPLODED!

After the gig finished we hung out with the others outside. Ravi came over to me. 'I'm going home soon, if you wanna walk. I reckon it's as fast as the bus . . .'

'Oh, I've got to pack the van up—'

Adi cut in. 'I got it covered – we're all done here, girl.'

Ravi shrugged. 'I'm ready if you are.'

We set off and walked for the longest time in deep, deep silence, Ravi viciously chain-smoking.

'So, thanks for coming,' I finally blurted out.

He nodded.

'No Thanzila then?'

He turned to me, with a half-smile.

'Nah.'

'Oh.'

Another deep pool of stressy silence. I've never felt so good as when we turned the corner into our street. I pulled my keys out too fast and dropped them. Ravi bent down and held them out to me. 'I'm not with her, you know.'

I didn't know what to say, just stared at him like an idiot.

'Laura . . . you were, uh . . . really cool . . . tonight.'

He leaned in towards me, the world went so quiet and still – and then his cell buzzed. He flipped it open. 'What?' And then he suddenly moved away. 'Look, Thanz,

I told you I don't want . . .'

I turned, sharply. 'Got to go.'

'No, wait . . .' Ravi smooshed the phone up against the palm of his hand. 'I got family shit tomorrow, but see you Monday? College?'

Once I got inside I leaned up against the door, heart pounding. Basically it was the best night of my whole life.

Mon, June 8th

I feel like I've been floating around on a cloud – everything's kind of unreal. I drifted into the kitchen this evening.

'What's up with you?' Kim growled.

Mum looked up from her knitting. 'Yes, darling, you do seem kind of . . . different.'

I was feeling so happy, I almost thought about telling them.

'Maybe she's in *lurve*,' said Kim.

I yanked the fridge door open and pulled out a juice. There's no way I'm telling anyone in this family what's really going on with me.

'Girls, girls . . .' Mum sighed and put her knitting needles down. 'Well, there, that's done! My first sweater, for your dad. D'you think he'll like it?'

'S'great,' I said. Kim said nothing.

Mum tutted. 'Don't sound too enthusiastic.' She went over to the kitchen door. 'Nicky!' After a few moments he appeared at the door. Mum made him close his eyes and then she held up the sweater.

'You can open them now. *Voilà!*'

He took the sweater in his hands, turning it over, trying to find the neck. And then he did the worst thing – he started to laugh.

'It's . . . *terrible* . . . it's the . . . crappest thing I've ever seen.'

Mum just gave a little shocked gasp. I wanted her to shout at him, like usual.

'Oh, c'mon, Ju, it's funny. I mean . . . the arms don't even match.'

She sighed. 'Nothing I ever do is going to be good enough, is it?'

He tried to put his arm round her. 'Let's face facts, you're never going to be very good at practical stuff – it's just not . . . you.'

Mum pulled back. 'But that's just not all right for you any more, is it? Looks like you married the wrong woman, Nick.'

It's like a loop. One of them gets happy and the other gets sad. Again and again and again.

Tues, June 9th

College was awesome. Loads of people came up and asked us when the next gig was. For the first time in my life I am popular. Except with you-know-who. She must have an evil 6th sense – cos when she swanned past us in the link with a bunch of pretty girls she gave me the filthiest look.

'Scratch your eyes out!' hissed Adi. 'So, anyway, how was the walk home?'

'Fine.'

'Fine? You're not getting away with that.'

'He said he wasn't going out with her.'

'And?'

'Nothing . . . I think he was going to kiss me, but then he got a call. Thanzila.'

Stace gasped. 'No! Why's that if they're over? So what did you do?'

'I just went indoors, left them to it.'

'Hmm. Playing it cool. Like your style, Laur – as long as he's not stringing you along.'

I shook my head. 'I don't think he's the type.'

Adi frowned. 'Well, just remember you're better than him.'

'Yeah, right – I mean, he's gorgeous.'

He turned away, sharp.

I grabbed his arm. 'What?'

'Nothing,' he muttered. 'I didn't say nothing.'

I wandered along the corridor towards the Design Tech lab and when I got there Ravi was inside, bent over a piece of steel tubing.

'Hi.'

He barely looked up, just held out a piece of wire. 'Here, can you hold this please?'

I took it silently, all my cool melting away like a snowflake on skin.

'Wrap the end around that screw – there . . .' He flicked the hair out of his eyes, irritably. 'No, not like that – *anticlockwise*.'

I unwound it. 'All right! Only trying to help.' I jerked my hand away too quickly and pulled the wire out of Ravi's hand. Blood welled up across his thumb.

'Oh God, I'm sorry.' I stared at the wires. 'What is it, anyway?'

He sucked his thumb. 'A crossbow.'

'A *what*?'

'You know, for shooting with. S'for my mum . . . to keep my dad in his place. He's such a jerk.'

We looked at each other for a moment and then we both cracked up, big time. So much for the perfect Dattas.

'Can you do one for me too?'

'You got the same shit?' he asked softly.

I nodded. 'My sister.'

He gave me his shy smile. 'D'you want to come to the park this Sunday? There's a softball game . . . could be cool . . .'

'Sure.'

Boom, Boom, Boom went my heart.

Fri, June 12th

A category-5 hurricane has hit the east coast of the States. That's the fiercest type, even stronger than the one that wiped out New Orleans back in 2005. It struck this place called Wilmington in Carolina in the middle of the night. Everyone was asleep because the local news media had told people not to evacuate. It's not even hurricane season yet and the weather bureau said the winds would only be 50 mph. So wrong. The outer wall of the hurricane slammed in with 150+ mph winds that went up to 250+ mph. They don't know what the full damage is yet, but by this morning 9,000 mobile homes and 10,000 apartments have vanished off the face of the earth. They don't know how many people are dead. The really chilling thing was this local broadcast that they kept repeating. It was like something out of a movie.

We interrupt this programme to bring you an emergency alert from the National Broadcast Emergency Center. This is an emergency alert! We repeat, this is an emergency alert! The outer winds of Hurricane Vanessa have just reached the North Carolina coast. Hurricane Vanessa has unexpectedly shifted twelve degrees north. We repeat, Hurricane Vanessa has shifted twelve degrees north. Vanessa is expected to strike Wilmington within minutes. We repeat, Vanessa is expected to strike Wilmington within minutes. All Wilmington residents should take immediate cover! We repeat, all Wilmington residents should take immediate cover! This is an emergency alert!

Watched the news at college. Vanessa isn't stopping, she's swept up north along the coast and formed hundreds of mini-tornadoes thru Baltimore, Maryland and Washington. All my mum's family lives there. We don't know if they're alive or dead. The death total is up to 2,400 with nearly a million people homeless. All the reporters look sick and shocked.

Adi shook his head. 'This ain't no New Orleans, this is rich white people getting killed. Everybody bothered now.'

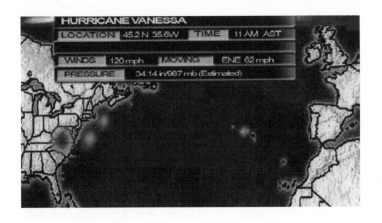

HURRICANE VANESSA
LOCATION 45.2 N 35.6 W TIME 11 AM AST
WINDS 120 mph MOVING ENE 62 mph
PRESSURE 34.14 in/987 mb (Estimated)

Sat, June 13th

Still waiting to hear from our family. Dad's cousin died in the Great Storm, but we didn't know for weeks. Mum's really upset. She keeps calling and emailing the States, but all the lines are down. When I got back tonight, she was sitting at the kitchen table looking thru some old photos. I leaned over her shoulder.

'Look, there's your grandparents with that stupid speedboat. Their pride and joy. Wouldn't be allowed now – it only did about two miles to the gallon.' She stroked the surface of the photo and sighed. 'I just want to go back and be with them. Stupid really, I couldn't wait to get away, couldn't stand my crazy mother – but now it's so hard to go back . . . A return to the East Coast would use up nearly two months' points.'

Sun, June 14th

We finally heard from Mum's sister in Washington. She could only talk for a couple of minutes before cutting out. They're all safe, though they've been in shelters for a week. Vanessa is now down to a category 1, but thousands of miles of coastline are still flooded. Endless shots on the TV of stranded people paddling across flooded towns.

This leading hurricane expert, Dr Lewis, did an interview from his Colorado State University office. He was all normal, then suddenly in the middle of the interview he just lost it. He banged his fist on the desk: 'The Gulf Stream is desalinating and shutting down right now and it's not going to stop. Storms on this scale are going to happen again and again – and we're going to see damage like we've never seen before. We have to act now, before it's too late.'

I was really looking forward to this afternoon with Ravi, but then I kept remembering about America and my family and feeling dead guilty. Anyway, it turned out there was no need, it's not like anything good happened to feel guilty about. Basically he called round for me at 1 – we walked along the hot dry back roads to the park, he smoked, played softball, he smoked some more, had a burger, had a beer, he smoked even more – and then we came home.

At the end Ravi turned to me. 'Look I've gotta totally focus on my exams for the next 2 weeks, but I'd really like to hook up with you after then.'

Was that a date? No idea.

I talked it over at band practice.

Stace said, 'Well, I always said he's a techno nerd. I reckon he's using you as cover to mask his geekiness.'

'Thanks.'

She shrugged. 'Just a theory. S'better than him not fancying you.'

'Yeah, look,' added Claire, 'can we get our priorities straight, Laura? We're here for practice, not emotional counselling.'

'Fine,' I said. I really, really, really hate her sometimes.

Adi mouthed *ignore her* from behind Claire's shoulder.

When we were packing up at the end I asked him what he thought.

'About whether he fancies you or not?'

I nodded.

'Hmm . . .' He coiled up his guitar lead. 'Honestly? I got no idea, but I do know it's always like this with you – I guess you like it that way. I mean, who else would pick the emotionally-unavailable boy next door to fall in love with? It's not like he's the only one—'

'Only one what?'

'Ah, nothing.' He grinned. 'Face it. You got issues, Laura Brown.'

I forced myself to smile, but only cos there was something wrong with his smile. It was only in his mouth.

Weds, June 17th

No rain for 9 weeks and counting. Thames Water has applied to City Hall to bring in a 2nd level drought order. That means no watering of parks and sports grounds, plus they want to put all of London on a water Smart Meter system, like the electricity one. The Mayor refused them. He said it was their fault there's a water shortage in the first place – that over the past 2 months they'd lost 50bn litres of water in London thru leaky pipes – enough to fill a thousand of those stupid Olympic swimming pools every day. Makes me crazy. What's the point in us dicking around with showers and not flushing shit down when that kind of stuff's going on?

Gwen Parry-Jones called me into her room today.

'Ah, Laura! Just a quick check to see how the Offenders meetings are going.'

I stared at a poster on the wall behind her.

'Well?'

'Fine.'

She smiled. 'Miss Brown, you remind me of myself at the same age. You don't have to keep everything so . . . bottled up, y'know? I'm not your enemy.'

'Can I go now?'

'Of course. But I'd like to see one of your parents, just for an update. Could you ask your mother to come in?'

'My mother?' I stammered.

'Yes. She is a family member, *n'est-ce pas*?'

Fri, June 19th

I spent tonight packing up medicine for America in Offenders. My packing group started singing some disgusting girl-guide song. They all knew the words. How? I always feel like there's a bit of normality training that I missed or slept thru or something. Anyway it made me feel kind of sick. People really love a crisis that's happening somewhere else to someone else.

Sun, June 21st

Got this from Amy.

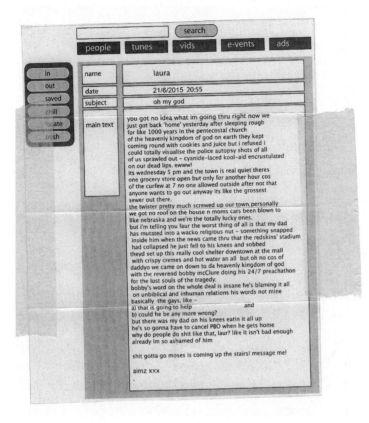

search

people   tunes   vids   e-vents   ads

in
out
saved
chill
date
trash

name	laura
date	21/6/2015 20:55
subject	oh my god

main text

you got no idea what im going thru right now we just got back 'home' yesterday after sleeping rough for like 1000 years in the pentecostal church of the heavenly kingdom of god on earth they kept coming round with cookies and juice but i refused i could totally visualise the police autopsy shots of all of us sprawled out - cyanide-laced kool-aid encrustulated on our dead lips. ewww!

its wednesday 5 pm and the town is real quiet theres one grocery store open but only for another hour cos of the curfew at 7 no one allowed outside after not that anyone wants to go out anyway its like the grossest sewer out there.

the twister pretty much screwed up our town. personally we got no roof on the house n moms cars been blown to like nebraska and we're the totally lucky ones.

but i'm telling you laur the worst thing of all is that my dad has mutated into a wacko religious nut - something snapped inside him when the news came thru that the redskins' stadium had collapsed he just fell to his knees and sobbed theyd set up this really cool shelter downtown at the mall with crispy cremes and hot water an all but oh no cos of daddyo we came on down to da heavenly kingdom of god with the reverend bobby mcClure doing his 24/7 preachathon for the lost souls of the tragedy.

bobby's word on the whole deal is insane he's blaming it all on unbiblical and inhuman relations his words not mine basically the gays, like –
a) that is going to help   and
b) could he be any more wrong?
but there was my dad on his knees eatin it all up he's so gonna have to cancel PBO when he gets home why do people do shit like that, laur? like it isn't bad enough already im so ashamed of him

shit gotta go moses is coming up the stairs! message me!

aimz xxx

Mum came into Dad's study, just as I was reading it. She peered over my shoulder. 'Jesus, I always knew Eric was a jerk, deep down, but this is beyond . . .'

Dad walked in.

'Nick, have you seen this?'

'What?'

'My sister Carol's Eric has gone Pentecostal. Joined the

church and is blaming the hurricane on homosexuals and liberal society.' She began to laugh.

'Well, maybe he's got a point. I mean, if we'd stuck more to the basics then . . .'

'Then *what*?'

'I don't know, things might not have got so out of hand, people would have had their own roles and been satisfied with less.'

Mum stared at him, open-mouthed. 'I'm going to pretend you didn't just say that.'

Dad shook his head. 'Ah, you're a true liberal. Free speech for everyone, unless they disagree with you.'

Mum headed out the door. 'I'm not sure I know who you are any more.'

She's got a point about Dad. He's gone self-sufficiency crazy. Yesterday he gave me a whole speech about this new waste bucket system he's set up. Apparently now I'm not to chuck orange peel in the same bin as cabbage leaves – it messes up the pH balance(??). I just zoned out and watched his lips move.

Weds, June 24th

It's getting dead hot. When I got home I stripped down to my T-shirt and knickers and threw the bedroom window open just to cool down. I timed how much electricity my fan uses on the Smart Meter. It's not good. I guess I'm gonna have to save it for when I really need it. Or get one of those tacky Spanish fans. The last one I saw was on my nan in Devon's fireplace. With a dancing bull on it.

Fri, June 26th

The Mayor's given in to Thames Water and approved the 2nd drought order. Guess who's got the power there? He's forcing a compulsory water-rationing system on us. Effective immediately. Basically everyone's got to get a water meter fitted in the next 3 weeks. Government vans will deliver them street by street across the city and then we've got to put them in ourselves. The limit's going to be 90 litres per person per day. That's a cut of 60 litres. Go over and the taps run dry. The Mayor said our current levels are unbelievable. He looked up from his notes and spoke directly into camera: 'If you had to fetch all that water from a well, each person would have to carry over eighteen buckets of water home every day. Think about it.'

Patronising pig. Why don't *you* think about the thousands of litres pouring away every minute cos you're too weak to stand up to Thames Water?

Sat June 27th

I stepped into my house and heard *howling* coming from upstairs. I ran up there like a mad animal and yanked open the bathroom door. At first all I could see was Dad's legs. The rest of him was hidden under a weird blue plastic bag.

'Dad! What's going on?' I screamed.

He writhed about like a monster.

'Goddamn bloody, bloody thing! Get it off me.'

I bent down and ripped the wet plastic off his head.

'Ewww. What is it?'

'*Infernal* devil . . . toilet hippo,' he spat, struggling to his knees. 'It reduces the volume of flush inside the lavatory system from nine to seven litres. And now I've got to put in the water meter. I . . . can't cope.'

Watching him panting on the bathroom floor, I suddenly really felt his pain. It's living death being a dad.

I've got my final Energy Saver exam this Friday. I'm supposed to be revising, but I can't face it after the mess I made of the last one so I sat out on the decking in my shorts instead.

'Laura! Hi, hi. Got a favour to ask you.'

I looked up. Kieran leaning over the edge of his balcony.

'I'm doing a focus group for Carbon Dating. Will you come and be my teenage spokesgirl?'

'Er.'

'*Pleeeease.*'

I sighed.

'That's a yes then? Fantastic! Ooh, take a look at this. I just finished it!' He tossed a piece of paper down. 'I'm going back to basics even on what a relationship is. We can take nothing for granted in the new world order.'

How hot's your relationship?

relationship

seeing each other

affair

one night stand

sofa petting

quick snog

Somehow, I don't think Kieran's basics and my dad's are the same thing.

Sun, June 28th

Exams are over. I'm free!

July

Weds, July 1st

I don't believe it. Without asking Mum, Dad has traded in her car for a wheelbarrow full of tools, 5 hens, a cockerel, a scooter, a *pig* and a sty! He's like a village idiot.

Mum came back from work and stared, dumb, at the empty spot where the Saab used to be parked. Then she went upstairs and started to throw clothes into a suitcase. I followed her and leaned against the doorway. 'Where are you going?'

'Away from that man,' she ground out between clenched teeth.

'Are you coming back?'

She hurled a Prada loafer into the bag.

'I'm your goddamn mother, Laura, but if I don't take a break from . . .' she waved an arm towards the back garden, echoing with pig squeals, '. . . I'll go mad, plain mad.' She zipped up the case and dragged it on to the carpet.

'But at least he's happy. You're always saying that's all you want.'

She took my hands in hers. 'Honey, I know what I am. I'm a difficult, neurotic, *silly* woman who bangs on about the past and pokes her nose into where it's not wanted. I drive my husband and my daughters crazy and I can't make a soufflé or sew a button to save my life. But I do love you and I am trying. But right now, it's not good enough, for any of you, or for me either. I've got to get away. Now. D'you understand?'

I had never heard Mum make sense like this. I just nodded.

'Good girl,' she whispered.

I sat on the bed, staring at the pattern on the carpet for ages after she'd slammed the front door shut behind her.

'Laura!' Dad's voice, panicky. 'Where are you?'

I dragged myself off the bed, opened the bedroom window and looked down into the back garden. He was covered in dirt, battling the pig in a headlock. I bit back a laugh.

'Well, don't just stand there, come and help me! Wo-ah. Good pig . . . no!'

The beast threw up his pink head and strained towards a row of baby carrots. I went down very slowly to find Dad locking the sty gate on the pig. 'Blimey! It's got some balls that one.'

'Dad, what's going on?'

'Ah! It's the next logical step. This pig is no ordinary pig. It's going to be the neighbourhood pig, we're all going to feed it our scraps and then it's going to feed us. It's not just me – Shiva's got some rabbits.'

'But what about Mum's car?'

'Oh, I know I should have asked her, but I was in the pub and there was this guy and it was too good an offer to pass up on . . .' He blew out his cheeks. 'Look, she never drove it anywhere, it's just been sitting there for months, losing money. She'll calm down . . .'

'She's gone, Dad.'

He turned, sharply. 'What d'you mean, gone?'

'She packed a bag and walked out the door.'

Dad ran his finger along the wooden gate. 'Your mum and I . . .'

My heart began to thud, waiting for the *sometimes people just don't love each other in the same way any more* speech.

'A pig! Marvellous! What breed is he, Nicholas?'

I looked up to see Arthur leaning over the fence.

'Oh – er . . . a Gloucester Old Spot.'

'Well, let me at him! *Go-oo-ood* piggy,' he crooned, holding out a custard cream. The pig let out a small grunt of pleasure.

Dad leaned over the gate to watch, face bursting with

pride. 'He's a beauty, ain't he?'

I went indoors. What is happening to fathers? The way mine's heading he's gonna turn into one of those crazy American backwoods survivalists – you know, the ones they have to send the US Marines in to hunt down and kill. His brain's gone doollally. No way do pigs and shit add up to a Saab hybrid Convertible. It's just really bad maths. I'll come home one day and he'll be chewing tobacco, dressed in old Vietnam vet uniform, timing himself as he strips down an AK47 and makes plans to sell me to his friend's cousin.

I messaged Aimz back. Told her my dad's lost the plot too. Just cos he can't get a job don't mean he's allowed to lose all self-respect.

Thurs, July 2nd

Last few days of college. Oh yeah! We had our final Energy Saver session with Gwen Parry-Jones today. Nathan came in dead late. He was totally wiped out after trying to fit his family's water meter. Basically, he drilled into a pipe and totally flooded the kitchen.

'Man, it was hectic. My mum was bare angry, there was plates and carrots floatin' around the room. She kep' screaming *where the stopcock, where the stopcock, you fool!*

Like I know! I ain't no plumber.'

GPJ spread her hands. 'Yes, but soon you're going to have to know. We can't take water for granted any more.'

Nate sucked his teeth. 'What's wid that? All it do is rain, rain, all winter long – and then as soon as the sun come out I get me mum screamin' at me.'

'Well, the water industry got privatised in 1989 and since then Thames Water's been taken over again and again. Right now it's owned by a bunch of Germans—'

'Yeah, man, they don't care about us, it's just business.'

'But soon it's going to be political. Water's rapidly becoming the most serious social issue of this generation. You can see it starting already in Spain. There's been no rain in North Africa for two years and thousands of immigrants are flooding across to Europe through the Spanish borders.'

'Yeah, yeah, world comin' to an end. I know, miss,' Nathan growled. 'But look at my trainers – all messed up.'

So much for chilling out after the exams. Dad's cockerel is one manic bird. It kicked off at 4 a.m. and crowed for 3 hours straight. At 6 I gave up, went into the lounge and buried my head under the sofa cushions, only to have them ripped away moments later. I squinted up into Kim's face.

'What's going on? What are all these wild animals doing here?'

'They're Dad's,' I moaned. 'He traded the Saab in for them.'

'Oh, you got to be kidding! What's Mum say?'

'Packed a bag and walked out.'

Kim sat down heavily on the sofa. 'Well, that's it. They've finally lost it.'

'She said she was coming back. It's just a break.'

'Yeah, right. But where would she go, anyway? The Hamiltons?'

I shook my head. 'Didn't say.'

'Does Dad know?'

'Yes, but he's too into that pig to care. I think this might be it, Kim.'

'I'll give him pig. He's not treating her right!'

I stared up at her in surprise, realising that we were actually talking and not fighting – maybe for the first time in 2 years. She looked dead tired, dark circles around her eyes.

I struggled to sit up. 'Are you just home now?'

'Yeah, yeah. Right, we've got to find out what's happening.'

'Since when did you care?'

'Look,' she snapped, 'if they wanna get divorced that's

fine, but it's not going to be over a pig. It's too *humiliating*. And besides . . . there's something dodgy about this. Mum wouldn't leave unless she had somewhere to go to. Oh, hi Dad!'

I glanced up. He was gazing at us from the doorway. His daughters awake at dawn, plotting.

Kim smiled. 'Want some coffee?'

'Er, sure.'

She went over and filled the kettle. 'So, we starting up a farm?'

'A pig, some chickens . . .'

'A pig! That's so cool!'

'Really?' Dad looked hopeful.

'What's he called?'

'No name yet. Any suggestions?'

'Hmm. What about Larkin? Y'know, like the poet. Philip Larkin.'

'Oh, right. A poetic pig.' Dad smiled. 'Why's that then?'

'You know how he wrote about your parents messing you up.' She fixed him with her blue eyes. 'Forever.'

Damn she's good.

Dad slammed his hand down on the kitchen counter. 'Look, young lady, I've had just about enough—'

'Where's Mum?'

His voice went quiet. 'I don't know.'

'Haven't you called her?'

'Look, she's probably with Marcia Hamilton.'

'Probably? Way to go, Dad. Care factor zero.'

'Right, that'll do. I don't need to be lectured by someone who's been acting like a killer zombie for the last year. Have you ever thought about that? She might be sick of you, too.'

'I didn't trade her car in for a lousy pig!'

'No you didn't,' muttered Dad, 'I did. And I'm not going to apologise. I'm a forty-six-year-old terminally unemployed man. I hated teaching anyway, I don't want to go back to it, and I don't want to go back to being bossed around and treated like a pet dog in my own home – and if you or your mother have a problem with that, then . . .' He kicked at a bucket of vegetable scraps. 'And you know what else? I'm really enjoying myself out there. I could be good at this, buy some land and get some bloody peace and quiet!'

'And what are you gonna buy it with, bacon rashers? You aren't exactly bringing in the mega bucks.'

Dad rapped the kitchen wall with his knuckles. 'Oh, there are ways and means.'

Kim gasped. 'You wouldn't sell this place . . .'

He picked up the bucket. 'It's a new world out there. London isn't everything, you know. You've had it easy for way too long, young lady!'

He strode out thru the back door. 'Here, piggy, piggy! Here, Larkin boy!'

Kim gazed at me across the room. 'That's it. He's lost it big time.'

Fri, July 3rd

Last day of college!

Mum called this morning.

'Hello, darling, it's me.'

'Where are you?'

There was a scuffling sound followed by that old-fashioned phone-box pips noise.

'Mum?'

'Got to go, no more money, all's well, back Sunday—'

Where still has those old red phone boxes? Outer Space?

Just downloaded the new *hydro* release, *deathscum*. It rocks.

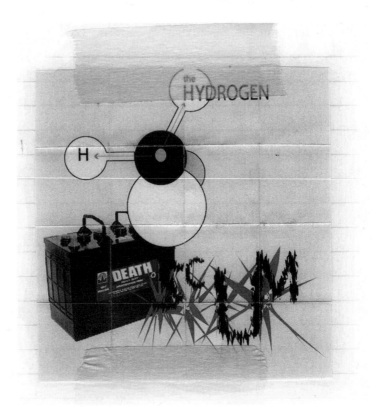

Sat, July 4th

Living chicken torture. Plus it's so hot. I got so angry trying to find a cool place on the bed that in the end I dragged my duvet over to the open window and lay there looking at the night sky. It's full of stars now that they've cut the streetlights after midnight.

I walked all the way to Offenders tonight only to find it cancelled. I nosed around for a bit, but there was no sign of Kim or Tracey. Maybe I did overreact that time. So

I stomped all the way home. Chickens running around the kitchen and my dad disappearing thru the back door with a bucket of pig food. Animal Farm, basically.

'Could you carry that water out to Larkin?' Dad cried over his shoulder.

I can't believe I'm saying this but Larkin is one cool little pig. When I poured the water into his trough, he flipped his head back and grinned before pushing his hairy snout thru the bars of the sty towards me. What could I do? It's not his fault. I bent down and rubbed behind his ears and he scrunched his tiny eyes up into creases of joy.

'Hello, Laura.'

My hand jerked back.

'Oh hi, Ravi.' I tried to keep my voice as normal as a girl-scratching-a-family-pig-talking-to-a-boy-who-she-is-maybe-or-maybe-not-dating can manage. 'How'd your exams go?'

'Yeah, good. Finished yesterday . . . So – what's with the porker?'

I shook my head. 'He's Dad's – it's a long story.' This huge longing to be normal swept over me. Behind me Larkin suddenly did a kind of pig back-flip, squealing at maximum volume.

'So, what – your dad's setting up a farm?'

'Traded in the Saab for all this.'

Ravi let out a low whistle. 'Mental.'

'And it's not only him – haven't you seen your rabbits?' I jerked my thumb towards his shed.

His face darkened. 'Where? No!' He stomped up to the shed and flung the door open. 8 pairs of ears twitched from within.

'Where's my stuff?'

'Ah, Ravi.' Shiva stood on the doorstep. 'I did not wish to disturb your exams . . . As you can see, we—'

'What've you done? Where's all my kit?'

'—are now having some new friends, the rabbits.' Shiva smiled. 'Very nutritious, very productive.'

'Screw nutritious, this is my place.'

Shiva frowned. 'Do not speak with such language to your father. Your equipment has merely been relocated for this exciting family project . . . Ah, sorry, darling.' He moved to one side as Mrs Datta appeared with a sack of vegetable choppings.

'Oh right, a *family* project. Then why's Mum doing all the work again? You make me sick.'

'I don't mind,' said Mrs Datta with a tired smile.

'You see, she is not minding. Men do not peel vegetables, but when killing time comes, that is the man's time. And you, boy, should watch your words. I am the father in this house, the man.'

Ravi just shook his head. 'Whatever.'

Sun, July 5th

Mum came home for about 10 minutes this morning.

'Where is he?' she hissed.

I nodded towards the garden.

'Good!'

She started throwing clean underwear into her bag. 'Have you had a good week, sweetie? I missed you.'

'Then why are you packing your bag again?'

'Special Sunday, darling. Must dash, can't explain now.'

'Mum, you haven't quit work or anything, have you?'

She glanced scornfully out the window. 'Course not. Somebody needs to work in this family.' And then she kissed the top of my head, zipped up the bag – and disappeared again. Is she having an affair?

Another mail from Amy.

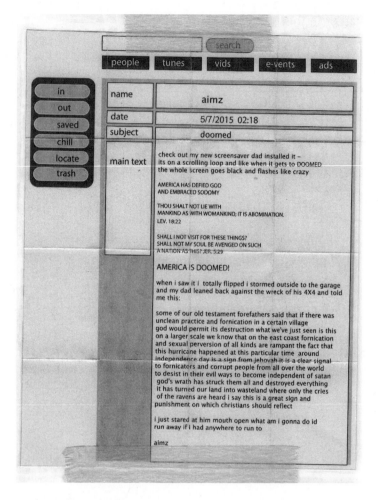

name	aimz
date	5/7/2015 02:18
subject	doomed

main text

check out my new screensaver dad installed it –
its on a scrolling loop and like when it gets to DOOMED
the whole screen goes black and flashes like crazy

AMERICA HAS DEFIED GOD
AND EMBRACED SODOMY

THOU SHALT NOT LIE WITH
MANKIND AS WITH WOMANKIND; IT IS ABOMINATION.
LEV. 18:22

SHALL I NOT VISIT FOR THESE THINGS?
SHALL NOT MY SOUL BE AVENGED ON SUCH
A NATION AS THIS? JER. 5:29

AMERICA IS DOOMED!

when i saw it i totally flipped i stormed outside to the garage
and my dad leaned back against the wreck of his 4X4 and told
me this:

some of our old testament forefathers said that if there was
unclean practice and fornication in a certain village
god would permit its destruction what we've just seen is this
on a larger scale we know that on the east coast fornication
and sexual perversion of all kinds are rampant the fact that
this hurricane happened at this particular time around
independence day is a sign from jehovah it is a clear signal
to fornicators and corrupt people from all over the world
to desist in their evil ways to become independent of satan
god's wrath has struck them all and destroyed everything
it has turned our land into wasteland where only the cries
of the ravens are heard i say this is a great sign and
punishment on which christians should reflect

i just stared at him mouth open what am i gonna do id
run away if i had anywhere to run to

aimz

I don't know what to say to her. I've got nothing. I feel
like I'm drifting down a river towards that . . .
whatsitcalled? Oh yeah, Heart of Darkness.

Mon, July 6th

So good not getting up. I love holidays.

Mum is back and my parents are being weirdly polite to each other. I overheard them in the hallway this morning.

Dad: 'I'm installing solar panels on the roof. It might be a bit messy in the house for a few days. Terribly sorry.'

Mum: 'Don't worry, darling. What's a bit of mess? Ha, ha!'

When people go polite you know it's really bad. She's got a new haircut; it's dead short with loads of gel. I said it was nice.

She did a little twirl. 'Thanks, honey. I felt I needed a change.'

Personally I am relieved. She's definitely not having an affair with that mop.

Tues, July 7th

I was sunbathing in the garden this afternoon when Ravi came out. I pretended not to see him, but all the time I could *feel* him checking me out, and then finally I couldn't stand the tension any more and I looked over – only to see he was reading *Carbon Times*, this pukey-green manufacturing magazine Dave Beard gets for Design Tech.

I lay back down, dead disgusted. Suddenly Arthur turned up his solar radio and shouted, 'Weather forecast!' and loads of neighbours came swarming round him, like a tribe of Aztecs praying for rain. There's no grass any more, loads of leaves have dropped from the trees and the Heath looks like the moon.

Weds, July 8th

Europe is starting to cook. Old people dying, *again*. It's hot and dry here, but it's basically OK – seems like whatever we get they get twice as bad. They've got to go on rations soon. I mean, they've just got to.

Thurs, July 9th

I went to Kim and Kier's bloody focus group this evening. Talk about a bunch of randoms.

Kieran – former hairdresser.

Kim – evil witch.

Donna – gorgeous, works in advertising.

Miles – media boy about town.

Jules – used to work in IT-support. Retraining to be a plumber.

Tabitha – florist.

Phil – Aussie surfer dude.

Laura – teenage mutant girl.

Kieran cleared his throat. 'So, welcome to the focus group session! Thank you all so much for being here. The purpose of this thing is for everyone to give their angle on dating – y'know, how it's changed, what are the issues, what you want from the new scene, basically. So who wants to start?'

Everyone went dead quiet.

Kier took a big gulp of wine. 'All right then, I will. The reason we're setting up Carbon Dating is that we don't think anybody knows the rules of dating any more. I'm hearing the same thing from everyone – a general loss of *confidence*—'

'Tell me about it,' interrupted Surfer Phil, running a hand thru his golden mane. 'Useta be, I'd step into a bar, flex me arms, and the chix'd be clambering all over me. Well . . .' he smirked, 'that bit still happens, but now . . . they wanna know what I do before they'll take it any further. Like, they wanna know what I *do for a living!* What am I supposed to say, I bum around the world and catch big waves? I'm a surfer, for chrissake. Useta be enough.'

'And even if you've got a job, the question is, are you making any money out of it?' Tabitha added. 'I've run my shop in Blackheath for fifteen years. At the classy end. I sell exotics, you know – bamboos, callas, orchids – but now I simply can't afford them – the carbon rating is sky high. So I'm down to roses, daffodils, pansies!' She shuddered. 'Who's going to buy pansies in Blackheath?'

'And your point?' asked Kieran.

'My point is, there are a lot of people like me now, y'know. Struggling. I used to love eating out. Well, even that's gone. There's no flying in fresh lobster from Norway or organic pomodorinos from Italy. Today's menus are a travesty – a sort of dreadful new carbon fusion, sourced from inside the M25.' She sighed. 'It's like all the glamour's gone out of my life, poof, in a cloud of smoke.'

Everyone nodded in agreement.

Miles loosened his tie. 'Well, my problem's kind of different. Y'see, I work in film, so there's loads of freebie parties happening, but the problem is my old lines don't work any more. Before, I was always travelling. I could take a girl away for the weekend, spin her around in the company Merc, whatever. Now it's like I've got nothing to offer. I'm bankrupt. All I can say is *Hi, I'm Miles.*' He put his head in his hands. 'Do you know how lame that sounds? I'm really starting to lose it – not gone out for a month. I've even . . . been reading nineteenth-century novels, looking for old-fashioned pick-up lines, pre-electricity! How tragic is that?'

'I'll give you tragic,' the gorgeous Donna snorted. 'The other night I got off with this guy. He's been chasing me for a while and, well, you know, the time had come . . .' She crossed her 200-mile-long Armani legs. 'Anyway, the point is, the next morning, right, he said *what about a cooked breakfast, beautiful?*' She rolled her eyes. 'Like I know how to cook breakfast! So I just laughed and the next thing I knew, he just upped and left. I mean, we had it all going on and then he never called me again. Over *breakfast*. Have I got to turn into a bloody housewife now if I want to keep a boyfriend?'

There was a pause. Everyone lost in a world of pain.

'What about you, Jules?' asked Kim.

She shrugged in her baggy T-shirt. 'I'm doing OK – retraining to be a plumber.'

'So rationing has turned out a good thing for you?'

'Yeah. Everybody loves a plumber.'

The group looked at her with hatred in its eyes x 6.

'Laura?'

All eyes turned to me. 'Oh, well, it's like . . . dead confusing . . . all this stuff—'

Donna cut in. 'Oh, God, yeah. Teenage love. Tough.'

'Can you be more specific, Laur?'

I felt myself blushing. 'Uh, well, like there's this boy at

college, right? He's kind of gorgeous but no one used to really notice him cos he was a bit quiet, a bit techie – but now that girls know he can fix things up for them, they're all over him.'

Kim smirked. 'Is this a personal example?'

'No! Well – yeah, but that's not the point . . . I mean, *everything's* changed now. People are more political. You know, maybe dating isn't the most important thing any more – survival's got to come first.'

Donna clutched my arm. 'But what about the pretty girls? They're still getting the boys; right?'

'Well, yeah, but they gotta have something else beside. It's not good enough to just strut any more.'

'So . . . ' Kieran glanced at Kim. 'What we're getting is that Carbon Dating's got to offer something different – people need a space where dating can be exciting . . . it needs to be stylish, but not expensive, it needs to offer people a place where they can learn new skills without feeling like they've had a personality transplant, it needs to—'

'. . . Find a way to make rationing sexy,' cried Donna. 'Cos right now dating's finished.'

There was a loud cheer.

'All right!' said Kieran, laughing. 'Meeting over. We've got our orders!'

Fri, July 10th

A group of housewives have rioted all over a golf course in Essex and chained themselves to the sprinklers cos the club keeps on watering the grass.

Sat, July 11th

I just got a message from Mia Metziger.

```
u guys rock, wanna hook?
```

I said yes. We're going to meet up at the Ollie, which is some back-street, vegan skater café just off Covent Garden. Stace and Claire are away, and I'm not sure about Adisa. He might freak out and throw scalding herb-tea drink in Mia Metziger's face.

Sun, July 12th

About 6 clouds came into the sky and drizzled on London this afternoon. Rain stopped play at the Oval – England vs Australia – for 10 whole minutes. The entire crowd stood up and cheered.

Tues, July 14th

I took Adi to the Ollie for a laugh. We got there before Mia, so got a juice and hung around in front of the noticeboard.

Adi frowned. 'These people are strange.'

'Shh, they're not deaf.'

'Like I care.' He nodded at a row of notices. 'I mean, what is this? Some kind of lonely hearts? Check this one out.'

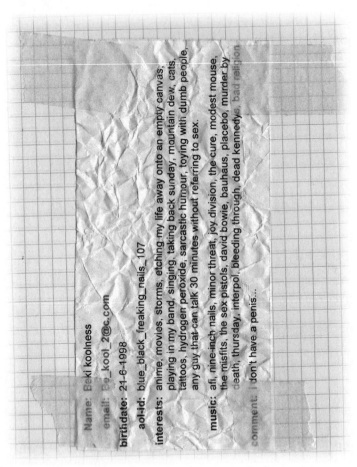

Name: Beki koolness
email: Be_kool_2@c.com
birthdate: 21-6-1998

aol-id: blue_black_freaking_nails_107

interests: anime, movies, storms, etching my life away onto an empty canvas, playing in my band, singing, taking back sunday, mountain dew, cats, tattoos, hydrogen peroxide, sarcastic humour, toying with dumb people, any guy that can talk 30 minutes without referring to sex.

music: afi, nine-inch nails, minor threat, joy division, the cure, modest mouse, the misfits, the sex pistols, david bowie, bauhaus, placebo, murder by death, thursday, interpol, bleeding through, dead kennedys, bad religion.

comment: i don't have a penis...

We started to giggle. 'What does that mean, at the end?'

Adi shrugged. 'Who knows? But if you're gonna be a radical you gotta stop etching your life away.'

'Yeah, but all edgers aren't like that. I mean, Mia said some cool stuff at that interview, like how we've got to stop being so pathetic and passive.'

'I know – I wanna bring the system down too. It's just I wanna do it in style, not with mountain dew or pissy cats.'

The door banged back on its hinges and Mia skated in. 'Yo, Laura! Howz it hangin'?' She unzipped a bulging backpack and pulled out a wad of flyers before turning to a skinny geek standing by the juicer. 'Baggy, is it OK to *distribute*?' She handed me a flyer. 'Totally cool – dayfest in Camden. July 22nd – you should come down. So?'

'So – what?'

Mia is so speedy, she makes me feel like I've had a stroke and can only form words really slow.

'So, howz it all goin'?'

'Oh, pre-tt-y go-od.'

She grinned. 'Hey, Baggy, what about a Mia special, to go? I gotta be south of the river by 3.'

He smiled and reached for an avocado.

'He don't say much, but he's the king of the smoothie.

Wait till you see this puppy, it's got organic soya pulp an' all.'

Adisa smiled dangerously.

'Anyhowz, Laur, the point is I got something you guys might wanna get hooked up on. It's a 7-day tour/showcase of politico bands in like, the west country . . . whatever . . . Anywayz I'm hooked up with these booking people and this one band's just dropped out and these friends of mine were like, hey Mia, d'you know any cooooool bands and I said, well, yeah, I totally do – thinking of you guys – and so I told 'em I'd get on to it . . . so waddya think? It's in September.'

My heart began to thud with excitement. 'A tour? For the *angels*?'

'Ab-*so*-lute-ly. 2 other bands, you drive around in this big old bus, pull up and do your thing. Takin' the message out to the country. It needs it, man.'

I turned to Adi. 'What d'you think?'

He gave his coolest shrug, like he was sick of people offering him tour dates.

I smiled at Mia. 'Er, OK . . . I guess I'll have to ask the others – could take a few days . . . Claire's on holiday . . .'

Mia shook her head. 'No can do, gotta tell me by tomorrow . . . Hey, Bags, is that smoothie done? I gotta head.'

'OK then, tomorrow. D'you really mean it, though – a whole tour?'

Mia grinned. 'For real.' She skated over to the counter, picked up her drink and then she was gone.

Me and Adi stepped out on to Neal Street. 'Shit, Adi, what's up with you? You could've been more positive.'

He scowled. 'Do we got to chop vegetables for them?'

'Who?'

'The other bands.'

'I dunno. Why?'

'Cos I ain't doing it, is why.'

I put my hands on my hips. 'C'mon, this is the chance we've been waiting for. D'you want to stay in your mum's garage for ever?'

'No-o.'

'What about Stace and Claire, though? Can we say yes without asking them? I tried calling Claire last week but there was zero connection, not even voicemail.'

'Stace'll definitely be up for it – anything to get out of the house. So Claire's in, whether she likes it or not.'

'Can we do that?'

'You give that girl way too much power, Laur.' He burst out laughing. 'And you're right. Shit, if I got to chop, then I got to chop!'

Weds, July 15th

I called Mia this morning and said yes, so she's going to get back to me with the full details. Now all I've got to do is sell it to my parents. I talked it over with Larkin, who is definitely my closest family member right now. We reckon it'll be cool – like he says, I'm not exactly the centre of their world. He was just crunching down the last bits of some toast crusts, when suddenly there were voices from the Datta garden.

'So, what? You ditched me? *You?*'

I crouched down.

'Thanzila, we were never . . .'

'Oh, right. That's not what you said in the café . . .'

'Look.' Ravi's voice went a bit desperate. 'I don't want to disrespect you, but this was never gonna work.'

'Yeah. You wanna know why? Cuz you're a total loser, a real embarrassment.'

'You only hung with me cos I gave you cool shit.'

'Yeah, well I'm all done now, buddy. Why don't you go crawling to that girl next door? She's pretty much on your level.'

'I ain't gonna go crawling to anyone. She's cool and I like her.'

'Huh, I soo-oo knew there was something going on between you two.'

'Thanz, please, just leave it now . . . And there's nothing going on. Why would she even—'

Thanzila squealed. 'What's that *disgusting* smell?'

'It's a pig.'

'*Laura's* pig?'

'Well – it's her dad's . . .'

'Oh *gross*! Yeah, well that *so-oo* sums it up. Goodbye, loser.'

Why can't people finish sentences? Why would she even *what*?

Fri, July 17th

A local water battle broke out on a river in Andalusia in southern Spain. It started with local Spanish people driving back Moroccan immigrants with sticks and stones. The Moroccans fought back by fencing off a mile of river – and now it's totally kicked off. Bombs and rifles all along the banks and locals dressed like soldiers patrolling the area.

Sat, July 18th

Totally normal breakfast scene this morning. I was staring at a map of Devon, Dad was staring at the garden, Kim was staring at the back of a Frosties pack, plugged into her e-pod. Suddenly Mum slammed the milk down on the table. 'Why don't we ever talk to each other any more?'

Kim pulled a headphone out of her ear. 'Cos we don't like each other. And now there's no escape except silence.'

I hate to admit it, but I really admire my sister sometimes.

Sun, July 19th

I've started to sneak into the kitchen in the night and open the fridge door so I can cool down. Man, I'd kill to sleep in there, next to the cottage cheese.

Thurs, July 23rd

There's colossal forest fires all over France, but they're down to 50% of their water and so they can't put them out. Meanwhile our garden's turning into a desert. I can hear the baby carrots' little gasps of thirst. The shower water's nothing like enough.

I've got to do a final Offenders presentation in 2 weeks, then I'm officially a good person again.

Fri, July 24th

I saw Ravi in the garden and a big ball of fire flamed up inside me. I'm sick of being this stupid little girl who doesn't know things. Before I knew what I was doing I was standing in front of him.

'Ravi, d'you like me?'

His eyes widened in shock.

'Sorry?'

'Don't make me repeat myself.'

'What, *like* like?'

I nodded.

'Like on a date?'

I nodded again, all my courage burning off like petrol fumes. Horrible pause, broken only by the sound of grinding rabbit molars.

Ravi smiled.

'What's so funny?'

'You are. Laura Brown, you're really quite something.' And then he leaned over the fence and kissed me.

I'm in shock.

Sat, July 25th

I cycled with Ravi in the blazing heat all the way to Oxleas Woods and we lay side by side on the withered, dead grass and stared up into the blue. The thing is, at first I didn't want him to be all over me, but when he didn't even try and kiss me, I really wanted him to so I leaned over and kind of caught him off-guard and our teeth clashed. Maybe it was better in my head.

Mon, July 27th

Feel so good! Hung out with R all afternoon and finally, finally did some dead good kissing, but then I came home and watched the news and now I feel so bad. The Prime Minister's called an emergency debate in Parliament about whether to bring in a 3rd Level Emergency Drought Order. If it gets passed the Government will cut off private water and put us all on standpipes in the street.

Tues, July 28th

The House of Commons emergency debate started at 8 a.m.

Weds, July 29th

10 p.m. After more than 24 hours of solid talk they've passed the emergency law. Big sections of the country are going to be cut off. We are first on the list. Thames Water's cutting all London houses, borough by borough. There'll be a standpipe for every 20 homes. The weird thing is when they announced it I didn't feel anything. That's starting to happen loads. Even with Ravi. I know I really like him, but I can't always seem to connect.

Dad stood in the garden with Shiva, looking at the dried-up beds.

'All that work for nothing. I can barely keep it all going

with our shower water. Once they switch us off, I don't know what's going to happen.' He shook his head. 'I'm going to join the march on Thames Water's headquarters in Reading tomorrow. We've got to force them to do *something*, at least start building a bloody desalination plant. Y'know, for making clean water out of the sea.'

Shiva frowned. 'How does it work?'

'Not sure – something to do with osmosis and the Thames.'

'But Nicholas, the Thames is a freshwater river. Where's the salt?'

'Well, a lot of it's tidal, so I guess they do it closer to the sea.'

'But . . .'

'What?'

'It sounds like a big process. Isn't it going to burn a lot of fuel?'

'Yeah well, I guess that's the choice now – pollute or burn.' Dad stamped his foot. 'There's got to be another way to get water in this town.'

Thurs, July 30th

Portugal's gone up in smoke. Mum handed me the paper. 'God, Laura, we only went there two years ago!'

Fri, July 31st

Fire Consumes Algarv

THE FIRES GROW - SATELLITE IMAGES OF PORTUGAL

0600 29/7/15
Fire and smoke clearly visible

0600 30/7/15
Smoke pollution spreads rapidly

0600 31/7/15
Smoke entirely obscures re

Abrupt change in wind direction set to destroy millions of hectares across the Algarve.

Today has seen a terrible worsening of conditions in the Algarve in Southern Portugal. An abrupt overnight change in wind direction has set the stage for the worst outbreak of forest fire in modern European history.

For the past three days entire villages and towns across the region have been evacuated as fire-fighters attempt to contain the situation in controlled areas. The hardest hit civilian areas have been the towns of Alcoutim, Lagos, Albufeira and Castro Marim, with around 625000 hectares of surrounding forest and agricultural land lost.

The UN has convened an emergency session and a major aid initiative is underway.

'We're fighting for our lives, please help us,' pleaded the Portuguese interior minister yesterday in an emotional appeal. Neighbours Spain, Italy and Greece today sent the limited aid they can spare from their already stretched resources. All three countries have sent man-power, with Greece also contributing 2 water distributor Canadair planes.

But it may be too little too late. The situation has deteriorated rapidly with fires breaking through the containment areas. A further 1 million hectares are now at risk with the major conurbations of Faro, Albufeira, Lagos and Portimao under serious and immediate threat.

The authorities are facin potential evacuation of milli To compound matters, all n roads in the region are bloc

This new disaster is the la in a series of severe fires to hit beleaguered Portugal in past ten years, but too tragedy is set to dwarf previous outbreaks.

In 2003 eighteen people in forest fires in the sum heatwave and a record 424, hectares were lost. In 200 huge fire at the Arrabida Nat Park, 50 km from Lisbon, judged to have caused 'irreparable loss for diversity nature'.

In the period 2008 -14 it been estimated that fire claimed the lives of 260 pe including 40 fire-fighters work in the region.

Evacuation alert! Thousands on the move

Aljezur

Silves · Castro Marim

Portimao · Sao Bras de Alportel · Tavira

Lagos · Albufeira · Loule

Almancil

Faro

214

August

Sat, Aug 1st

I spent all morning doing research for my stupid Offenders presentation on effects of heat on the human body. Some bits are dead cool, though. Arthur's letting me use his net for research cos he's powered it by solar panels hooked up all over the roof. I'm down to only 3 blocks on my card. Everything I like burns so much carbon.

The human body is always fighting to keep its core temperature at 37C. This is the heat at which the organs function normally. To stop overheating, the body pumps blood to the skin's surface. This makes extra work for the heart. Added to this, as water from the blood evaporates, it thickens the blood, which can increase chances of strokes or heart attacks.

If the core temperature gets hotter, muscles stop working properly because of all the water and salts being sweated out. When the brain reaches 38.5C, the body suffers a heatstroke. When the body gets to 42C, it starts cooking. And it's irreversible. The proteins in each cell change, like an egg white when it boils. Even before that, the brain shuts down because the heart can't pump enough blood. Muscles stop working, the stomach cramps up, you go crazy. Death is inevitable.'

The problems of heat stress on the body get worse with age. The older a person is, the less efficient their body's temperature regulation. 'They are not as sensitive,' says Dr Peter Arnton, senior lecturer in Geriatric Social Policy at UCL. 'An older person doesn't feel the cold or the heat as soon as a younger person does and that's a problem because they don't respond to it quite so quickly.'

I started to read it out to Arthur, but when I got to the egg whites he bounced up out of his chair. 'That's quite enough, young lady!' he barked. I think he's in denial about being old.

There was a knock on the door and Dad stepped in with a dirty old map in his hand. He flattened it out on the kitchen table.

'Look at this . . . I've been looking for alternative water sources. D'you know there are loads of underground rivers in London? The closest to us are the Ravensbourne and the Quaggy. See?' He traced the rivers with his finger. 'The Ravensbourne rises in Keston then flows through Bromley, Lewisham and lastly Greenwich, to the Thames. So does the Quaggy – and then it joins the Ravensbourne next to Lewisham Station. That's only a mile down the road from here – we just need a way to access it.'

Arthur frowned. 'What, by digging a well d'you mean? In the main road by the station?'

'Well, no-o. But there's other places, parkland like Hayes and Bromley Common.'

'But are the rivers still there? I thought they were all covered over or turned into sewer tunnels now. And how on earth do you think you're going to get away with digging down ten, twenty metres? The police are all over us if we as much as turn a hosepipe on.'

Dad threw his hands up. 'I don't know. I'm just trying to find a way . . . All right. If we can't dig a well, what about opening up an existing one? The River Fleet was full of springs and wells, right across the city, until they covered it over. Look at this one, St Chad's Well. It was open till the nineteenth century, just behind Kings Cross Station, in an area called Battle Bridge.'

'Never heard of it.'

'They say it's right where the final battle between Boudicca and the Romans took place and eighty thousand British were slaughtered. Anyway, hundreds of people used to go to the well every day and drink the waters.'

Arthur sucked his teeth. 'Well, we could try, I suppose. What about dowsing? I was a dab hand at finding water that way as a lad.'

'With a hazel twig? There's got to be more scientific ways of doing it.'

'What's dowsing?' I asked.

'It's the art of finding water. Some people have got a gift. Traditionally you use a fork-shaped hazel branch and you walk across an area. When you're over water, the branch bends towards the source. It's a bit unclear how it works, but it's something to do with changes in magnetic fields. Basically, water conducts electricity and the human body is mostly made up of water, and so it is a sort of natural conductor. And that's how you "feel" the water. A lot of people swear by it.'

'What, so you're going to wander around Kings Cross with a twig?'

Dad glared at me. 'It's just an idea. Have you got a better one?' He grinned suddenly. 'Anyway, we might find a buddy for Larkin. When they covered the Fleet River over there was this eighteenth-century London myth about underground pigs.' He pulled out a sheet of paper. 'This is from a newspaper from the twenty-fourth August, 1736: *A fatter boar was hardly ever seen than one taken up this day, coming out of the Fleet ditch into the Thames. It proved to be a butcher's near Smithfield Bars, who had missed him five months, all of which time he had been in the common sewer . . .*'

Ravi walked me up to Offenders this evening and then we kissed outside for ages. I don't even know if I want to kiss him now, but I so want to feel *normal* that I'm doing it anyway. Why is everything so complicated?

I went inside and saw Tracey Leader standing by the entrance. She was leaning up against a table, staring at me. I smiled. She didn't. As I went past her she pulled me close with one of her meaty crab claws. 'Tell your girl to keep going. No time for gettin' cute.'

I just had to stand there with Tracey's Big Mac breath all over me till she released her grip. And then I went inside and talked about egg whites.

Sun, Aug 2nd

I walked into Kim's bedroom this morning.

She turned. 'What the—?'

'Yeah, exactly. Just passing on a message from Trace. She wants you to keep going, sis.'

Kim sat down heavily on the bed. 'Shit, she's a psycho.'

'Is that supposed to be news?'

'I don't need another lecture from you, all right? I'm trying to get out, build something with Carbon Dating now. It's serious.'

'Kim, look at what's going on around us. How can you do the black mar—?'

'It's just . . . she . . . won't let me stop. It's all messed up.'

'Maybe you should tell Mum and Dad.'

She snorted. 'Those two? What a joke!'

She's right about my parents, though. I wish they'd stop being so polite to each other. I think they're doing it for the sake of the children, but I, the children, would like them to please start shouting at each other again. At least it's real.

Tues, Aug 4th

I passed my Offenders presentation. I am now officially an ex-offender, but it don't mean anything with what's going on. The country's starting to lose it. In Axminster, where my nan lives, they're only giving people water every other day. It's the same all over the South West. My dad is dead worried about her. He wants her to come to us, but she won't. It's bad in Yorkshire, too. The council's been supplying half of the county's villages thru tankers, but they don't know how long they can keep it up, cos the groundwater tables are sinking so fast.

Our water gets cut off on Thursday.

Weds, Aug 5th

An underground waterpipe burst last night all over the street and whole families ran out with buckets to collect the water. Mousy Woman from no 6 leaned on her front gate and sobbed over the waste. Today all our water is dark brown. The forest fires are out of control in France, Spain and Portugal. It feels like it's never gonna cool down again. Why is it always old people who die? They found 20 dead in an old folks' home in Paris. All of them with 41°C body temperature.

I went round to check on Arthur. He's made a kind of tent in his kitchen out of layers and layers of sheets. When I walked in he was lining up a load of empty water bottles on the table.

'Ah, Laura! Come in.'

'Are you all right?'

'Perfectly cool. Secret is keep still, lots of fluid, lots of layers – lets the air flow. Learnt it from the Bedouin. Glad you're here actually . . .' He nodded towards a steaming pan on the cooker. 'Can you check if that water's boiling yet? I'm making safe water.'

I went over and lifted the pan lid. 'Er, what's this tin cup on the side for?'

'Catching the evaporation. Anything in it?'

I peered inside. 'Yeah, nearly full.'

'Ah, marvellous . . . bring it over. We need to evaporate and distil the water to get rid of all the impurities.' He took the cup from me and poured the water into the nearest bottle. 'And now we do it all over again. Hmm, how much do we need? A three-day supply at one gallon per person per day – a lot, basically.'

I looked around the kitchen. 'You're joking, aren't you? It's going to take for ever. And anyway, things aren't so

221

bad – the standpipe'll have clean water again.'

He glanced at me sideways. 'Of course, of course. I'm just being cautious.'

I put the cup down. 'They can't cut *all* our water off. I mean, how will we . . . *live*?'

'By being prepared. And if you don't want to do this, apparently you can drink toilet water.' He smiled. 'Unless it's blue. Then don't.'

'How can you joke about it?'

'Because that's the way you get through things. Unless you want to go under. Now if you wouldn't mind filling up that pan with fresh water?'

Arthur should be the Mayor of London instead of the idiot we've got.

Thurs, Aug 6th

It reached 43°C in Birmingham today. The hottest ever recorded temperature in the UK. Our water goes tomorrow. Only hospitals and vital industry's going to stay connected. Not that you'd want to go to hospital, they're all packed out. Queen Elizabeth Hospital's got a tent set up in the car park to deal with all the people collapsing in the heat.

Fri, Aug 7th

Totally forgot. Went to the bathroom this morning and no water in the taps. Had to spit out my toothpaste and clean my teeth off with a towel.

Later, me and Ravi stood at my bedroom window and watched all our neighbours crowding around a standpipe outside Arthur's house. 2 buckets a day per person.

Ravi ran his hand over his forehead. 'When's this gonna end?'

I glanced up at him. 'D'you get . . . scared, sometimes? I mean, what if we're too late—'

He cut me off. 'Nah, we can fix up. That's what I want to do, invent stuff. Make things cleaner, better.'

I didn't say anything. The way he'd said it, so positive. It sounded kind of fake. I looked down at Loud Dad standing in line with his kids. I wanted him to shout at them like normal, but he just stood there, looking dead knackered.

'You know what this reminds me of? Those old black and white photos of early settlers. Y'know, in America or Australia. I can't believe we used to fly abroad to get hot weather. It's only good when you've got showers and air con, otherwise, it's like . . . hell on earth.'

Sat, Aug 8th

I went down to see Kier at the Leopard. The streets are all empty cos no one's going out in the day now. All the shops are opening up at 6 in the evening, like in Italy. Kier met me outside this grand old Victorian pub just off Brewer Street. He's dead mad cos they've just had to cancel their Carbon Dating summer festival. Kier shook his fist at the sun.

'Thirty years of rain, rain, rain – and now I've finally got something good happening I've got to cancel cos it's too frickin' hot. Unbelievable. Anyway, can you help me with these? We've got to get all our stuff out of the festival tents.' He loaded me up with candlesticks. 'Just go round the back and up the fire-exit steps, you can't miss our floor – it's the one with the *Welcome to the New Era of Style* banner draped across the doors.'

I crossed the cobbled stones and was halfway up the steps when I heard this huge, terrifying human growl 'Rrrraaagghhh!' coming from the next door building. It was followed by total silence, then a single female voice.

'Feel – The – Power – Within!'

I stopped and peered across into a large, lit-up room. It was full of sweaty women standing in a circle, and in the centre, standing tall and proud – Gwen Parry-Jones!

'Come on, slowcoach, no time to waste,' puffed Kieran, trotting up behind me.

I jerked my thumb towards the building. 'What the hell?'

He dropped his voice to a whisper. 'Women Moving Forward! They're *wimmin* – you know, like in the seventies. Hairy armpits, no bras, hard-liners.' He grinned. 'Super scary, huh?'

I nodded.

When I got home I found Mum on the stairs, crying. 'God, I need to get out of this city. It's driving me crazy.'

Sun, Aug 9th

Thames Water has cut off the standpipes where Adi lives in Lewisham. They've said it's for emergency repairs, but everybody thinks the water's run out. Shops everywhere are packed out with people buying water, milk, any drinks they can get their hands on.

Mia Metziger called with the dates for the *angels* tour. It's the first week of September.

'But we can't go anywhere in this, Mia.'

'You're cancelling? The country needs this message.'

'Mia, the country don't need a message, it needs rain.'

I went to my room and felt so bad. But the *angels* don't mean shit when people are dying. Adi texted me to say he was OK. Is he telling the truth?

I've got a blister low down on my back. It really hurts.

Mon, Aug 10th

I went round to Adi's and rang on his bell for ages, but no answer. Man, it's like a police state. There's a 24-hour patrol all over the city – and a hotline for grassing up your neighbours. It's prison for stealing water – what happened to drugs and mugging? My blister's getting worse, spreading, but I don't want to tell anyone cos there's no way I'm going to hospital.

Tues, Aug 11th

38°C. And after 3 days of no water Lewisham exploded. Huge crowds marched on City Hall on foot to demand drinking water. The Mayor responded by bringing in the riot police, who sprayed them with tear gas and fired shots into the air, but for the first time this year, people didn't back down. The news spread across London and thousands went down to the Hall to back them up. It started to kick off; and then a really bad thing happened – the police shot directly into the crowd with live bullets. They killed 5 people. I'm so scared about Adi. I've been calling him all day, but no answer.

Later, when it was all over, the Mayor did a broadcast, explaining why he gave the order to open fire. Protection of democracy, blah, blah. It's a load of bullshit. People are literally starting to die from the heat. I'm starting to get scared in a way I never have before. We're in crisis and nobody knows what to do. Adi finally called me at 3 a.m.

'Are you OK? D'you want to come here?' I asked.

'We'll be all right. They've promised us water by tonight.' His voice sounded weird. Like something's changed inside him.

Weds, Aug 12th

I woke up with a really bad pain low down in my back. Mum's scared it's my kidneys and wants to take me straight to hospital, but I've refused. She says she'll give me one more day at home. She's given me her water ration. I feel so bad. Her lips are all cracked.

Mrs Brown the hen staggered into the house and collapsed.

Thurs, Aug 13th

Feel dead light-headed, but no worse. Mum's given me *another* day. But the real news is that thunderstorms are sweeping across Europe. They came in from the Atlantic overnight. Spain, Portugal and western France have got torrential rain. Please, please let it come here too.

Fri, Aug 14th

Storms have spread across France, Italy and southern Germany. Come on! The swelling's starting to go down in my back, but I can't remember when I last slept. We can't spare the water even to wet a towel to wrap around my head.

Sat, Aug 15th

No rain. France had 8 centimetres just last night. The Met Office don't know if the storms are going to make it here. I don't know how much longer we can hold on. I lay in my room all day, listening to the radio.

There are demonstrations in the US cos of a big climate bill that got voted down in the Senate last night. It was about cutting emissions by 60%. All the senators who voted against it were from the industrial, oil states, and everyone's saying they've been bribed or bought off.

They had to call out the National Guard in Times Square and shoot water cannons at people to get them to break up. There were tens of thousands of protestors, going crazy, fighting, petrol bombing, charging the barriers. By midnight the military had a curfew over all of central Manhattan, all the way down to 8th Avenue.

The best thing is happening in California. 4 million

people have lined up all the way from Santa Barbara to LA and at midnight they're gonna link hands and jump in the air. It's called the Big Jump. They want to crack the San Andreas fault for good. They say it's the only way they can get California away from the filthy States.

A boy from college died. Claire's just called and told me.

'Happened last night.'

'But how?'

'Dunno. Wasn't a disease or infection or anything. Just heat collapse.'

Sun, Aug 16th
Still. No. Rain.

Mon, Aug 17th
The US demos have spread to Europe. Protests started today outside churches in nearly every major city in Italy, France, Germany, Belgium, Spain, Portugal, Poland . . . They're planning to walk to Brussels to do a massive demo in front of the Parliament. There's an emergency EU leaders' summit there next week. All the presidents and prime ministers have come back off holiday cos of the crisis. Gee, thanks, guys.

Tues, Aug 18th

I woke up in the night. Someone was shaking me. Mum.

'Can you hear it?' she cried.

I ran to the window and flung it open. We stuck our heads out as far as we could and screamed.

RAIN!

Weds, Aug 19th

Torrential rain all day. Everyone is crazy happy. We've got every single bucket and bowl out in the garden to catch the water.

People are actually doing it. All across Europe, from villages, towns, cities, walking across fields, down lanes, roads, motorways, to Brussels, to demand action on rationing. The whole continent just looks burnt out.

Thurs, Aug 20th

More beautiful rain. Hundreds of thousands are on the move now. They've created like a new city just outside Brussels. Tents and fires stretching out for miles. The army is there, but they don't know how to act cos the protestors are doing nothing wrong. It's so exciting.

The Euro leaders are *flying* in for the meeting tomorrow. Talk about stupid. They put out a joint statement saying they wouldn't be held hostage by the 'common crowd'.

Fri, Aug 21st

Big mistake, calling them the 'common crowd'. It really did something to people's heads. By the time the march began in the morning there were about 3 million people. The trouble wasn't anything big to begin with. It all kicked off in this suburb called La Marolles – a few car windows smashed, shops and bus stops spray-painted, a few Molotovs. But the police went in hard, opened fire with rubber bullets and tear gas – and that's when it got out of control.

By 2, the European Parliament was in a huge face-off with protestors trying to storm the building. The outside of the Parliament was bristling with 4,000 troops, armoured cars, tanks and machine-guns, but the crowd wasn't backing down. It was hard to see what was going on cos all the early footage was live feed – coming from one little guy sticking his camera out of a 12th-floor toilet window. But basically it was one massive battle.

There was one bit where a man leaped on to the steps and tried to take a rifle from a cop. The other cops around jumped on him and smashed their rifle butts into his face and the crowd roared like a huge monster. The army opened fire, the police charged on horses, but the mob carried on forward, till finally it was pushed back with water cannons.

But they didn't give in and within an hour, protestors got control of 2 tanks and drove them at army lines. It was so cool. I reckon that's when they started to believe they could win. Finally they fought their way thru the lines and got inside. I couldn't believe what I was seeing. Nothing happened for ages, all you could hear was gunshots and shouting. The mass outside chanted and screamed for the leaders to come out and show themselves.

And then suddenly there they were, a bunch of grey-faced, shaking men and women. The protestors forced them down on their knees and the crowd went silent. Dead silent. A man stepped forward and cocked his gun into the European President's face and shouted:

'We need action! You're elected by us to act. Not to do nothing while we die like animals around you.'

The crowd roared again. The man turned to face the line of leaders. 'On behalf of the people we demand immediate—' And then there was the sound of a single gunshot and he fell to the ground, blood pumping out of his neck. Suddenly 6 military choppers appeared overhead, firing directly on the crowd. The square dissolved into chaos. The front of the Parliament building swarmed with soldiers – and everywhere you looked there was screaming, running, falling, blood and beatings.

Sat, Aug 22nd

Running battles all day in Brussels. The army are beating the shit out of people. It's guns, tanks and water cannons vs stones, Molotovs and pure, pure rage.

Huge thunderstorm in London tonight. Lightning gashed the sky over Oxleas Woods.

Sun, Aug 23rd

It's over. Guess who won? They've arrested thousands and thousands, got them all lined up in the square like criminals. I am so angry, I can hardly breathe.

Mon, Aug 24th

Exhausted, can't watch the news any more.

Tues, Aug 25th

Mia's just called.

'So, hey. Want the good news? Tour's green to go.'

'Huh? I didn't know it was cancelled.'

'Yeah, well, the promoters kinda agreed with you before, but now they're good. Tour. Back on. In or out?'

'You know what? I don't care.'

'Laura, you *gotta* care. This Brussels thing makes me sick too, but this is the only solution – to fight back. Right?'

I sighed. 'Right.'

God, that's dead soon – next week. I'll have to call the band and work out how to sell it to my parents in like, 5 days. I'm so tired I can hardly think.

Weds, Aug 26th

Talk about totally surreal. Mum got us all round the kitchen table tonight.

'Right, your dad and I have decided we need to get out of the city as a *family*. The weather forecast says it's going to be wet and cool for weeks so it's the perfect opportunity. I know it's a bit sudden. But these people are very welcoming – and they have their own well.'

'Which people?'

Mum slid a leaflet over the table. 'I know it's kind of unconventional, but I've met some of these guys, and it's what *we* feel we need . . .' She gave Dad a sharp glance on the *we*.

'Oh, you *got* to be joking,' said Kim.

Mum turned to me.

'Laura?'

'Mum, people are dying. I don't want to go on holiday.'

'Spare me the lecture. We're *all* exhausted, but while you both live under our roof . . .'

'I don't know, Julia,' said Dad. 'I mean, if the girls really hate the idea and what with this weather and the garden, the animals . . . maybe we should rethink . . .'

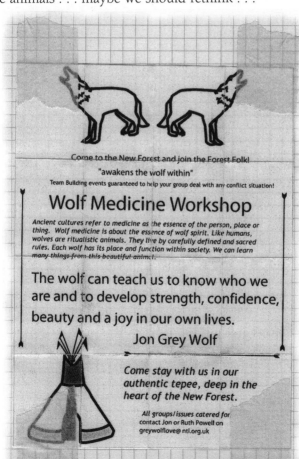

Come to the New Forest and join the Forest Folk!

"awakens the wolf within"

Team Building events guaranteed to help your group deal with any conflict situation!

Wolf Medicine Workshop

Ancient cultures refer to medicine as the essence of the person, place or thing. Wolf medicine is about the essence of wolf spirit. Like humans, wolves are ritualistic animals. They live by carefully defined and sacred rules. Each wolf has its place and function within society. We can learn many things from this beautiful animal.

The wolf can teach us to know who we are and to develop strength, confidence, beauty and a joy in our own lives.

Jon Grey Wolf

Come stay with us in our authentic tepee, deep in the heart of the New Forest.

All groups/issues catered for
contact Jon or Ruth Powell on
greywolflove@ntl.org.uk

Mum zapped him with an evil stare. 'You're not backing out of this, Nick. They've had this sudden cancellation and I've booked it now.' She turned to face me and Kim. 'Right, you two – come on. If we're going to work as a family, we've got to get away from this house and *redefine our dynamic* – otherwise, I, for one, am finished. I'm sick to death of being the stupid woman around here . . .'

'You said it,' muttered Kim.

Mum whirled around to face her. 'Oh, you're so funny.'

Dad spread his hands on the table. 'All right, all right, no more fighting. After what we've just been through we do need a break, but I don't know why you couldn't pick something more normal.'

'There isn't anywhere normal now. Europe's burnt to a crisp and full of revolutionaries and most places in the UK are shut for tourists. These guys have got water and shelter and a – a friend recommended them.'

'Some friend.'

I got this sudden stab of fear. 'Wait. When is this?'

'This weekend. I know it's a bit sudden, but—'

'But I can't.'

'What d'you mean, can't?'

'The *angels* have got a tour . . . it's all set up—'

'Set up by who?'

'Mia!'

Mum thinned her lips. 'Excuse me, but who's Mia? And when were you going to ask *us* about this?'

'I only found out it was back on yesterday!'

'Well, I'm sorry, darling – you can go with the band another time.'

I stood up. 'So unfair!'

Silence.

'Please? Mum?' I could feel my voice breaking.

She shook her head. 'Sorry. No. This time the family comes first.'

'What family?' I shouted. 'Take a look at yourselves!'

So instead of touring with the *angels* I'm going to the New Forest with my messed-up family for a week in a tent. Messaged the band, I can't face telling them in person.

Thurs, Aug 27th

Soft summer rain all day so Ravi came to mine and I spent the afternoon in deep depression lying on my bed, watching him sand down, varnish, sand down, varnish, sand down, varnish his mum's crossbow.

'And so now Mum's trying to make us *communicate as a family*. Puke. Does your mum do that?'

Sand, sand.

'Ravi!'

'Umm?'

'Do your parents make you sit down and discuss things as a family?'

'Nah.'

I poked him with my toes. 'Never?'

He glanced up. 'Laura, I'm making my mum a crossbow so she can shoot an arrow thru my dad's head.'

'You're not serious, though?'

He narrowed his black eyes. 'My dad's a loser – India-shmindia, vark, vark, 22 years, Jai Rama, cowshit. He wants my sister to get married to some nice Indian boy from home and he wants me to go into the business. He lives in some back-in-the-days fantasy, but the trouble is he's messing up my present.' Ravi sighed. 'But the worst of all is he treats my mother like dirt, never lifts a finger . . . and she never, never says anything back. You take the piss out of *your* mum, but I think she's got balls. She's a real woman.'

I sank back into the pillows and looked at him with a sudden bad feeling. Maybe I'm not the main attraction, maybe he's one of those boys who fancies girls' mums . . .

'No, I fancy you,' he grinned, snaking his hand inside my T-shirt. And then the door flew open. Mum.

'Oh, Laura . . . oops!'

I caught the smile on her face before she closed the door. Oh God, now she's going to sit me down and talk about contraception. Why can't she be all repressed like other mums? I bounced up off the bed.

'Wassamatter? Get back here.'

'No,' I said, crossing my arms. 'Ravi Datta, I hope you're not going to turn out to be a jerk. I ain't no Thanzila.'

'Thank God,' he said quietly, focusing along the barrel of the crossbow. 'C'mon, let's go outside and check this puppy out.'

It's a beauty. Ravi totally pinned a rat that was footling about in the pig-nuts. Footle no more my friend.

I can't believe what's just happened. I finally got up the courage to go to band practice and see them all face to face and I get there and . . . they're going to do the tour without me!

Claire spread her hands. 'Well, the thing is, if you can't make it, we have to get someone else for the tour. Short notice, though.'

I gasped. 'What, you're gonna find someone else?' Looking round at the others. Adisa staring really hard at his fretboard.

'Adi?'

'It'd only be for the week – we'll get Rrriot Mary to do it.'

'You're joking, right?'

'Oh, look Laur, cut the dramatics,' snapped Claire. 'This tour is for the good of the *angels*. Just let Mary fill your boots for a week.'

I stared at her, didn't dare say what was really on my mind – what if Mary is for ever? Mary laughs at Claire's jokes.

I went home and just felt sick.

```
a rush of silence sweeps
thru the heart of the crowd.


a kick of adrenaline
jolts thru my body.
```

```
The strokes of music
vibrate my soul
and I feel every beat
like my own heartbeat.


I live for this feeling
```

Fri, Aug 28th

Adisa called round.

'Hey,' he said.

I jammed my fists in my jeans.

'Can I at least come in?'

'What for?'

'Don't go all moody on me, girl. Mary's in for one week only. No one's ever gonna replace you.'

'Whatever.'

'C'mon. After everything we've just been thru, we need this.' He took my hand. 'It's one week and then you're back. Trust me.'

Adi left me the tour dates. The last one's at the Purple Turtle in Poole. That's like 20 miles from where I'm staying in the New Forest. So unfair.

Sat, Aug 29th

I said goodbye to Ravi tonight. We had a dead passionate kiss and I promised to message every day.

Sun, Aug 30th

7.30 a.m. Left home with family.

1 a.m. Just crawled inside my tent. Too tired to write.

3 a.m. Can't sleep. Surrounded by death screams of hunted woodland creatures.

5 a.m. Woken by the Forest Folk didgeridoo warble.

I've left my family behind, gone deep into the woods and I'm writing this on the bank of a stream, watching the rain fall into the water.

Mum had already found out by dawn that the Forest Folk group leader, Jon Grey Wolf, had a solar-powered shower, and she's been flirting with him like mad all morning. Meanwhile, Dad was trying to drive extra tent pegs into the mud and bending them all like a classic weakling loser dad. Then Kim slid out of her tent like a viper and got straight into a scrap with Mum. A little kid with white-blond hair and weird blue eyes suddenly appeared between them.

'Are you havin' conflic?'

Kim took a step back. 'Urggh. What is it?'

'Sh-sh.' Mum held out a hand. 'No, honey, we're . . .
just expressing a difference of opinion.'

'Soun' like conflic,' said the child, wiping its nose.
'Yes'day we did conflic. I gotta star. I'm a woodchip. My
name is Lucius. Wuju like to see my drawin'?'

'Er, sure,' replied Mum.

Lucius pointed at Kim. 'No, I want show the *cross* lady.
She's bad, smokeded puff back in the bushis las' night.
'Gainst camps rules.' He grinned, showing a perfect set of
tiny milk-teeth.

Kim rolled her eyes. 'OK, woodchip. Show me the
drawing.'

conflic tree

responses 2 conflc

avoydance   diffus hum   konfrontashun

mask ignore   postpone   wait

vyolently   nonvyolently

yuse physical vylence   yuse sycological vylence   threaten yuse verbal vylence

talk diskus feelings   heer uther persons poynt of vew   agree to disagree   no attak   problem solving   decyd together   jenerate lots of solushuns

He pointed at a bit of tree with a grubby finger. 'I fink you was doin' non-vilent cong-frun-tashun with your mummy.'

'Maybe, buddy.' Kim tapped a different branch. 'But I could go up to *vyolent* congfruntation. Easy.'

'Kim!'

Lucius started to snivel. 'You mussen' talk to me like that. I'm a woodchip.'

Suddenly, across the campsite came a cry: 'Lucius, darling, come to Mummy!' A woman in a poncho with American Indian braids waved. Lucius wiped his nose again. 'I'll be back!' he trilled.

Who are these people? Messaged Ravi but nothing back.

Autumn. September

Tues, Sept 1st

Got a message from R in the night.

> messed up rabb

What does that mean?

I couldn't get back to sleep, so I wandered thru the woods for a bit. Super bored. When I got back, Dad was already up, drawing weird shapes in the dirt around the campfire.

'Hey, Dad.'

'Oh, morning.' He frowned and scratched out a line. 'I'm working on this swill-feeding mechanism. Can't decide if it should be on a timer or if I should let Larkin's body clock dictate the pace. What d'you think?'

The sound of a didgeridoo floated over the air. I felt a sudden wave of panic – like I needed something, just one thing, to be normal.

'Dad?'

'Hmm?'

'Don't you ever want a job again?'

'Aha – a *weighted* pulley lid system! If he's hungry enough to pull the lid up, he's hungry enough to eat!'

'Dad!'

Pause.

'Yeah, yeah.' Drawing sulky circles. 'Would it be so terrible if I didn't?'

'But how will we—'

'We'll find a way.'

'But don't you ever want to do some of the stuff we used to do? Y'know – fly abroad, eat KFC, just normal shit?'

He looked around the campsite. 'No, not really . . . I know this holiday is stupid, but everything's different now. We can't go back. Rationing is going to happen in Europe too, soon. You *do* know that, don't you?'

'Of course,' I replied. Automatically.

'Hey Nick, you jamming?'

'Oh Christ! It's the men's dawn music group. You haven't seen me, OK?' He legged it down a forest trail. An incredible feeling of loneliness swept over me. In a way, he was right. In my head, maybe I did just think rationing was temporary. But standing there, in a campsite in the New Forest, I finally got it. This is my life now. How did people let things get so bad? Selfish bastards.

I've just got another weird message from Rav.

> got no mob - grounded - gotta go - sorr

I logged on to message back and then my cell made this weird death bleep noise and totally died in front of me. I think it got wet in the bloody tepee. In the end I had to go to the shop (about 5 Ks away) and write Rav a postcard with a New Forest pony on it. It's like modern life never happened. I can't remember the last time I put a stamp on anything.

Huh, got totally bullied by a gang of ponies on the way

back from the shop. I was innocently crossing a field when a squinty, black pony shot out from under some trees and went for my pack of Monster Munch. And then a load of others came up behind him. It was dead scary. I had to surrender the Monsters and make a run for it. When I looked back they were all tearing at the plastic like piranhas. The countryside is so brutal.

Weds, Sept 2nd

I'm trying not to think about the band. They play Poole tomorrow night and I'm so jealous. Plus I don't know what's happened to our family communication plan. Mum's spending her whole time with Jon Grey Wolf doing 1-2-1 intensive therapy. Yesterday she burst into tears, and he put his arms round her in the most puke-making new age style rocking cradle hug. Puke, puke, puke. His 'partner', Poncho Woman, looked pretty sick, too.

Dad's pretending not to notice, but Kim and me saw him kick ash on da Grey Wolf's towel this morning when he thought no one was looking.

'Go, Dad,' growled Kim. 'That's what this place needs, a big fight. Poncho Woman's mine . . . she's a bad mother.'

'Thought you hated Lucius?'

'Nah, he's cool. Taught him how to swear yesterday.

That woman's not bringing him up right – a kid's gotta know how to swear.'

'He's what, 5?'

'Never too young – I started you at 4. You were *so* cute when you first swore . . . Uh-oh – group work!' Kim jumped up, snuffling the air like a wild animal. I looked over. Mum was waving from the centre of a group of Forest Folk. 'Girls! It's family workshop time. Come!'

I glanced back, but Kim'd vanished. Mum patted a space on the ground between her and a miserable-looking Dad. No escape.

'Sit, darling. Where's your sister?'

I muttered something about her being lucky.

'But this is important! If Kim wants to be part of this family, she'd—'

'Oh, leave her alone,' groaned Dad.

'Well, isn't that just your solution to everything. So goddamn passive.'

8 pairs of woodland eyes gleamed at my parents. My ears started to burn.

'If I may stop you a second, Julia.' Poncho Woman held up a calming hand. 'Before you proceed with this conflict, you must ask yourself – *am I UNFAIRLY taking my anger out on the other?'*

Mum looked up, startled. 'Well, I don't believe—'

'Oh, you've got no idea. You wouldn't know unfair if it slapped you round the face!' interrupted Dad.

'And you, Nick, must ask yourself – *are my actions or words HURTING the other's feelings?*'

Dad shut his mouth with a snap.

Poncho threw her braids back, opened her throat and *howled*.

'*G-r-ou-ou-ou-p j-oi-oi-oi-oi-n!*'

The group linked hands. I, of course, got Mum and Dad. They began to chant, '*Mother Wolf, we, the group, feel their pain. We pray You take their anger, release their inner wolf. Snatch their conflict in jaws of steel and run it through the woods, over the prairie, into the foothills!*'

Prairie. What bloody prairie? I tried to pull my hands free, but my parents' inner wolves had me in their slavering jaws.

'*Julia, you know what you need to ask yourself,*' chanted the group.

'Yes, yes!'

'*Say it! Release the words!*'

Mum threw her head back. 'Am I – trying to – control him – against his – will?'

The group threw back their skinny heads. '*G-o-o-o-d! Feel your pain, take your anger, release your inner wolf.*

251

Snatch your conflict in jaws of steel and run it through the woods, over the prairie, into the foothills!'

'And now, Nick – *what do you need to say?*' squealed Poncho Woman.

Dad sat with bowed shoulders. 'I can't.'

'*Nick!*'

'No-o!'

'*Yes! Yes! Release!*'

Suddenly he leapt to his feet. '*All right*, I need to say *this!*' He stared down at Mum, wild.

'Julia, I don't know if I love you any more. Everything's changed. I keep trying to get it back, but don't know if I can!' And then he burst into tears.

Dead silence fell. Mum gave a little shocked gasp and I grabbed my chance, snatching my hands free and running down a track. And then I wandered for ages, just couldn't get her face out of my head. I made for the river and suddenly heard an angry voice up ahead. Kim.

'No! I don't want to, any more! You can't make me!'

I peered round a tree to see her throwing her mobile on the ground.

I ran up. 'Kim. You OK?'

She whirled round. 'Go away!'

'Who were you talking to?'

'Look, Laura, just piss off.'

I turned to go, but then a hot flash of anger surged thru me. 'Why are you so angry with me? What did I ever do to you?'

She closed her eyes. 'It's not you . . . I'm . . .'

Suddenly there was a massive yell and a scream of '*Nick!*'

'What the—?'

'It's Dad!'

We turned and ran back to the campsite to find Dad rolling on the ground with Jon Grey Wolf, both pounding the shit out of each other.

Kim seized Mum's arm. 'Jesus, why don't you do something? It's all your fault!'

Mum stared at Kim for a second and then she slapped her, hard, right across the face.

'I hate you!' Mum screamed. 'And you all hate me. I don't want to be in this family any more!'

And then *she* ran blindly into the woods, leaving us all staring at each other in shock.

I've had enough. I'm going to find the *angels* tomorrow.

Thurs, Sept 3rd

2 a.m. Mental day. I'm on the way

back to London, surrounded by sweaty bodies in the back of the tour van. I started out at dawn, walked 15 Ks to Brockenhurst before I even saw another human being. I went into a Spar and picked up a Snickers – and then had to put it back cos I'd forgotten all my money. The man in the shop looked at me like I was a gippo. There was no way I was giving up, though. I set off down the A337 in the drizzle, with smug families gliding past in their family cars. When my blisters got too bad I hitched a lift. The woman driver looked dead sorry for me. I stared out the window the whole time I was in the car so I wouldn't cry.

I got to Poole at about 4, and then walked all over town looking for the Purple Turtle. God, I know what homeless people feel like now. My T-shirt and jeans were all messed up from when I'd fallen down a bank in the woods. After asking a zillion people, I finally found the place down a back street, but it was all shut up. I didn't know what to do, so I slumped down on some dirty steps and waited and waited.

'Laur, what the . . . ?'

I looked up. Adisa.

'Hey,' I smiled, 'just come to check out this hot new band, the *angels*. You heard of them?' And then I burst into tears.

Sometimes I don't know what I'd do without him. He just squeezed my hand until the tears stopped.

'I hate – my family – I hate them all.'

He nodded.

'I can't take the pressure any more. I can't, Adi. I'm gonna do something bad . . .'

'Nah,' he said, looking into my eyes. 'I don't see that. Not my buddy Laura Brown.'

'Why are they doing this?'

'Cuz.'

'Cuz what?'

'People mess up. They don't mean to, but they do. But that's their shit.'

'But what if it is me, too? Maybe I'm all messed up like them.'

'You'll be OK, I promise.'

'Promise?'

'Yeah.'

'Laura, thank God you're here!' Claire stood at the bottom of the steps. 'I've had it with that bitch, Mary. She's so out.'

'What this time?' asked Adi.

'Says she won't play. Again.'

He rolled his eyes.

'What's been going on?' I asked.

'Don't even ask.'

'But it's cool, cos Laura'll do it,' said Claire.

I looked down at her, felt my heart thud in my chest.

'Claire. First. You need to apologise for ditching me in the first place. Second. You need to *ask* me. Nicely. Third. When we get back, I'm going to write some lyrics and you're gonna at least look at them.'

Claire stared up at me in shock. 'What's up with you?'

'Nothing. It's just how it is.'

She paused a moment, hands on hips. 'OK. One, I apologise. Two – please will you play tonight?'

'And number three?'

She flicked her fringe back. 'Jeez. You been on assertiveness training in that forest?'

I wiped the snot off my nose with the back of my hand. 'I am at one with my inner wolf.'

At 10 I was pacing up and down the back of the stage with Mary's bass slung around my neck, trying to keep the panic down. And then suddenly the band was all gathered around me. Claire punched me in the shoulder. 'All right crew, we're back up to full strength!' She scrambled on to the stage and flashed her tits at the crowd.

'We're the *dirty angels*!' she screamed. 'And we're gonna crucify this place!'

We piled onstage behind her, Stace clicked her

sticks, we launched into *messed up* and the room went crazy. The adrenaline rush when I'm up onstage is like nothing else, I *love* it. It's like for one tiny moment I'm doing something real.

When it was all over I helped the others carry gear out to the van. Somebody shouted my name. I turned. Mum was standing by the back doors. I coiled my bass lead tight around my hand. She threw the *angels* tour flyer at me and grabbed my shoulders.

'Never, ever do that again. I've been out of my goddamn mind. If I hadn't found this flyer . . . Your dad's still out there in the woods now, looking for you.'

I shook free of her grip. 'Who are you to act so caring all of a sudden? After what you said? You don't care about me.'

Her voice cracked. 'Is that what you really feel?'

I shrugged and then she just stared at me for the longest time.

'Laura, I'm sorry.'

I couldn't help it, a great big tear rolled down my cheek.

'And,' she said, 'nobody in this family is going to pretend any more. You, me, your father, Kim. I'm moving out when we get back, I'm sick of trying to make us all something we're not.'

'But—'

'No buts. I don't have any answers. We'll have to work it out as we go along.' Mum sighed. 'I don't know if we were a mess before and rationing's just made it all come to the surface, but I know it's time to face up to it now.'

Fri, Sept 4th

As soon as we got home Mum packed a bag. Dad's offered to go, but she said no.

'You've got to look after all this . . . I'm a big girl now, Nick.' She held her hands out to me and Kim. 'I'll call you as soon as I'm settled.'

And then she was gone.

Found my exam results under a pile of junk mail. Pretty much sums it up. About 50,000 people died all around me this summer and I flopped my exams. I don't know what I'm supposed to feel.

I knocked on Ravi's door and Mr Datta answered.

'I have sent the bloody boy away. He will be back in a few days. Worst luck!'

What's going on?

Sat, Sept 5th

Kim's just been in my room.

'Look, I'm gonna keep a low profile while things die

259

down, so I'm going to be around the house a lot, working on Carbon Dating.'

'Uh, OK.'

'I . . . just want you to know I'm handling things.'

'Kim, maybe it's time to go to the pol—'

She cut in. 'Please, Laur. For me?'

Sun, Sept 6th

Got woken up in the middle of the night by a mad squawking and snarling. Dad ran downstairs, shouting, 'Fox! Fox!' I ran after him. There was a huge pile of feathers in the chicken coop. Mrs Black and Mrs White are gone and poor Mrs Pink was huddled in the corner, all covered in blood. Talk about shell-shock.

Mon, Sept 7th

People are going mad about the fox. It's taken loads of people's chickens since we've been gone. A bunch of neighbours gathered on the street this evening and got more and more angry – until finally one of the Leaders went, 'Let's hunt it down!' and everyone cheered.

'Scratch a liberal . . .' muttered Kieran.

'And what?' I asked.

'Reveal a fascist. Look at the bloodlust on those *Guardian*-readers' faces.'

In half an hour there was a big mob on bikes and scooters, all gathered round Arthur, who was outlining tactics. '. . . So is that clear? The beaters will flush the fox out of the gardens and along the train tracks and the outriders will chase him down on the roads once he's out in the open. When I blow this horn, we'll begin! Ready?'

The hunters revved up their mopeds. Pathetic. And then I saw Ravi, crossbow slung across his shoulder. I turned away. The bastard. I mean, I feel dead sorry for Mrs White and Mrs Black, but the fox don't know any better.

For the next hour all you could hear was tiny scooter engines and people screaming and shouting at each other. First they went around the back of the Chinese restaurant and then they started to spread out across the streets. I suddenly saw Dad zooming round the corner and jumping off his bike into the bins at the back of our road.

'He's over here!'

I glimpsed a streaking red body. The fox, weaving desperately between mountain bikes – and then it was all over. Delaney Leader revved up and down the street with a bloody foxtail stuck on to his scooter helmet, followed by the mob.

'Let's celebrate!' Shiva Datta punched the air with his dirty fist.

Dad called from downstairs. 'Laura! Come on, we're having a barbecue in the back.'

I slammed my door shut and went back to my desk.

```
red blood thin man dead now
you kill to eat but
we kill for fun
```

There was a knock at the door.

'I don't want to celebrate the death of an innocent fox,' I shouted.

'Laura?'

Oh, God. Ravi.

'What?'

'Can I come in?'

I opened the door a chink. 'Well?'

'Hey. Missed you.'

I stared at him, coolly.

'How could you?'

'What?'

'I saw you down there with your crossbow.'

'Only to chill my dad off. I went round the corner after it started and cotched down by the tracks. He's still mad at me for letting his rabbits go.'

'You didn't!'

'Yeah. Sprung 'em.' Ravi grinned. 'Just after you left he started givin' me some bullshit about being a man; basically wanted me to kill one. I ain't no bunny killer. Arsehole. I messaged you last week. Didn't they get thru?'

'No, they were all . . . weird and cut off. I really wanted to talk to you.'

'Oh, man, that's cos I had to borrow my mate's phone – and even then I could only get away for like a few seconds. Dad sent me to this carbon boot camp as punishment. It was hectic.' He frowned. 'Was it bad, then?'

'You could say that.'

'Got your postcard, though.'

'Did you?'

'Yeah, those ponies looked well evil.' He paused. 'Shit, it's been a mad summer . . .'

We stared at each other and then started to kiss dead

crazy, like we were drowning or something.

Dad's voice came from below. 'Laura, get down here!'

I went over to the window and leaned out.

'I'm not hungry.'

'I don't care if you're hungry or not, I want you to come out and help.'

'I'm not joining in this massacre party.'

'Then you'll stay in your room. No supper.'

'Fine!'

'Suit yourself. But send that boy down.'

'Who?'

He crossed his arms. 'Just send him down.'

I turned back to Ravi. 'He treats me like a kid, but I'm 16 . . .'

'Yeah, but it's all different now. After that rabbit thing I think I'd have just split before. But now where've I got to go? I can't survive on my points on my own. I *got* to stay at home and pass college – and there's no way I can afford to put myself thru uni on my own either. There's no jobs any more. I went round everywhere last week, looking. Everyone's getting fired. Even McD's, man. I know there's all the retraining schemes for wind farms and fitting Smart Meters and stuff, but I wanna go to uni.' Ravi walked over to the window. 'Anyway, I found this cool thing last week. There's this green college engineering scholarship – s'like A-levels but practical. I'm gonna apply for it. And you want to know the best part? It's in Germany. Far, far away.'

'Oh,' I said. All cold inside.

'Now, Laura! Don't make me come up there!' Dad bellowed from downstairs.

After Ravi left I sat in my room all night and glared down at the party below. Arthur dug a pit in the ground and started a fire. They set up a huge pot of water for corn and Shiva threaded a row of chickens and what looked dangerously like rabbit bodies along a metal pole. Not all of them escaped, evidently. Kids were roving around like *Lord of the Flies*. I tell you, there's no nut allergies now, no asthma inhalers, no over-protective mummies; these kids are fully survival-of-the-fittest animals.

After they'd gorged themselves, everyone sat down in a big circle. Loud Dad's children played a disgusting tune on recorders, and a group of men who I'd only ever seen washing their cars brought out a load of bongos and started to jam, their skinny white arms flashing in the moonlight. To finish they all did a hunt re-enactment, with Shiva in the middle, miming the fox.

I left a message for Mum. It's got to be better where she is.

Tues, Sept 8th

Yes! We got water back in the house today. I stood there at the bathroom sink for a minute, watching the water swish down the bowl like it was a miracle. Which I guess it is.

Weds, Sept 9th

I went to Camden market with Adi today. Told him about my grades.

He stopped dead. 'You gonna tell your parents?'

'Why would I do a stupid thing like that?'

'True.'

'I'm just going to have to fix up this term. For real. No more messing.'

We walked in silence for a bit.

'Adi, what are you going to do after college?'

'Dunno. I was gonna study Media at University, but my dad says there's no jobs in that now. He wants me to do Medicine. Like 1) that's ever going to happen with A-levels in English, History, Art and Media – and 2) I don't wanna be a doctor, I hate sick people.'

We paused in front of a row of sneakers. 'But rationing's not going to be this bad *for ever*,' I began. 'It's just super intense now, maybe for a decade . . . but then green engines and fuels'll sort us out.'

Adi picked up a trainer. 'Remember the Olympic stadium?'

I nodded.

'How it went 100 million over budget, wasn't ready till 6 days before the Games began and that poxy wind turbine collapsed on it?'

'Right.'

'So . . . that's like a few thousand tonnes of concrete and they messed it up. This is a total global fuel revolution.' He looked across at me. 'Better face it, this is at least our lifetime, maybe our kids' too.'

'Kids? You want to bring kids into this?'

'Sure. Someday. I don't know how it's gonna work any more than you do, but I'm not going to stop living my life just cos of some shitty greenhouse gas.'

I looked at him slyly. 'And what's Sarah say about kids?'

'Dunno, I don't talk about this shit with her.'

'But she's your girl, if you don't talk to her . . .'

He shrugged. 'Just don't is all.'

'All right, all right . . . but don't you get scared? I mean, what else is gonna go?'

'We'll adapt. I mean, what about the *angels*? We could really go somewhere now. Before we were just a bunch of losers with guitars – but now we're a bunch of losers with guitars with a message that people actually wanna hear.

Radical is becomin' mainstream, my friend.'

'You should go into politics, Adi.'

He gave a half-smile. 'Maybe I will.'

When I got home I found Dad asleep with his arm round the pig in a pool of sunshine, his trousers held up with bits of string. He is turning into an old tramp. I've started to do most of the cooking now; otherwise we'd all be living on cold beans and old bits of bread. Kim never helps. She's either in her room working or out at Carbon Dating nights.

Mum still hasn't got back to me.

Thurs, Sept 10th

Ravi knocked on my front door dead early.

'What?' I groaned.

'Coming?'

'Where?'

'Er, to finish your education so you can get the hell out of here . . .'

I slapped my forehead. 'Today?'

'Jump to it, girl.'

An hour later I was sitting in the main hall with the girls. I scanned the room; everyone looked bad – a long, hot summer all round. Bob Jenkins did a big welcome back speech from the stage; how proud he was of us and what an immense privilege for him it was to work with such a fantastic group of young people blah blah. And then he hit us with it. It turns out the college went way over rations last term and there'll be no heating until the spring term and no hot water. On the upside though, the air pollution in Greenwich is down by 22% and we're 6 times less likely to get run over in speeding traffic. He finished by saying our generation would be thanked by all those to come – it was us who finally made the choice to change our lives and save the planet. Loads of students clapped and cheered.

Er, excuse me, what choice? I ain't old enough to vote. I feel dead ashamed of myself, but right now I really hate rationing. I want my old life back. I can't tell the others, but I think I'm going dead right wing. Bob held up his hand. 'So, just as a little welcome back to all you students . . . I think the ladies amongst your tutors have prepared you some cookies and snacks.' He flashed his capped teeth at the miserable women teachers lining the back wall. 'Enjoy!'

'Ladies? *Puh-lease.*'

Bob looked up. 'Er, excuse me?'

Gwen Parry-Jones stepped forward. 'No, I won't. I haven't made a cookie since I was eight years old and I'm not going to start now, you sexist pig. You're not going to use rationing as an excuse to eradicate eighty years of female emancipation.'

Deep silence.

'Aha, ha. I'm sorry, I'm sure. I stand corrected.' Bob smiled, stepping off the podium and striding along the central aisle. Once he got alongside her I saw his lips form the words '*My office, now*.'

She just tossed her head. That woman's got a certain style.

Fri, Sept 11th

Lisa Bell got stuck straight into us today. She swanned into the room with her horrible teacher tan. (Joined-up freckles, blotches and strap marks.) 'Right! First assignment is going to be very topical. What I want you to do is come up with a personal account of rationing from the point of view of an American teenager.'

Well that's one homework done already. Just need to print off Amy's messages.

When I came out of the lesson, I saw Ravi talking to this strange-looking group outside the college gates. When I went over they immediately stopped talking and walked away. Ravi didn't even try and introduce me.

'Who were they?'

He shrugged. 'Just some people I know.'

'Why you being so mysterious?'

He flicked his hair back irritably. 'Why are you being so suspicious?'

Mum *finally* called me back tonight.

'Sorry hon, everything's been kind of unsettled.'

'Where are you? When can I come and see you?'

'Oh, soon! It's just . . .'

'Mum!' I took a deep breath. The shame: begging to see my own mother; the woman I would've 100% traded in for a set of bass strings 6 months ago.

'OK, OK, why don't you come and see me tomorrow, at my office? We can grab some dinner.'

Big news from Europe though. There's going to be an all-nation vote on rationing in October. I almost cried when I heard about it. Like all that fighting was for something.

Sat, Sept 12th

Met Mum at her office. I'd only been in there 10 minutes when her organiser beeped. She glanced at the screen and slapped her forehead. 'Damn. I totally forgot, I've got to go to this thing . . .'

I sighed.

She waved her hand. 'I know . . . but it's the first night of an intensive workshop course.'

'Fine!'

She picked up her phone. 'Look, I'll cancel it.'

'No, it's cool.'

'I know! Why don't you come? It'll be fun! But just one thing.'

'What?'

'You've got to promise not to laugh.'

'Why? What kind of workshop is it?'

'It's a women's skills group – in the old Co-op Building.'

'What, down by our house? Thought that place was dead.'

'No-o, I don't believe so. I think it's being renovated. Come! It'll be an adventure!' She pulled on her jacket.

20 minutes later we were picking our way thru a ring of trash surrounding the Co-op Building. I gazed up the stairs to the double steel doors. Mum stood beside me, hands on hips. 'This it? Where's the buzzer?'

'Try banging on that un-boarded bit of window.'

'Where?'

I pointed to a single dirty pane to the left of the door. She leaned across and rapped on the glass. Silence. She rapped again. Silence – and then suddenly a grille opened in the centre of the door. A pair of brown eyes and an eyebrow bolt appeared.

'Yeah?'

'Ah, hello . . . I'm . . . uh . . . here for the Women Moving Forward workshop?'

'Name?'

'Julia – Brown. This is my daughter, Laura Brown.'

'Let me check the list.'

'You never told me it was WMF,' I hissed. 'Mum, I can't believe you're going in there! Those women are—'

The door swung open and a tiny, nut-brown woman in karate pants and dirty vest stepped out. She waved a piece of paper at me.

'She ain't on the list.'

'Er, no,' said Mum, nervously. 'She's my guest.'

Nut Brown shook her head. 'Nah, mate. No name, no entry.'

'But . . .'

I nudged her. 'I don't wanna go in there anyway. Why are you doing this?'

'Oh, don't be so prejudiced.'

'In or out? Ain't got all day,' growled Nut Brown.

Mum kissed me. 'Look, I'm sorry. I'll definitely see you next week. Dinner. I promise.'

She turned and followed Nut Brown into the gloom

and the door shut behind them with a clang.

Well, so much for me staying with her.

Sun, Sept 13th

The whole street got together today to pick the veggies that survived thru the drought. Dad had me out there all day. I looked up at one point and honest to God I just thought *how is this London?* Actually, after a bit, I kind of liked it – and I've never seen Dad so happy. Ravi came out of his room and sat on the bench with me and we shelled peas all afternoon. The only bad thing was the way everyone kept hanging around the pig pen and drooling over Larkin. They are like a pack of vampires.

Later, when they'd all gone, I went over to his pen and found this pinned up! Bastards. Don't they have any heart at all?

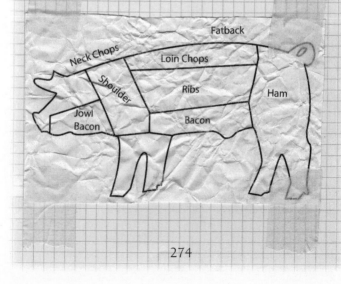

I reached between the bars of his pen and rubbed behind his ears.

'I'm not going let anyone hurt you,' I whispered.

He gave a great slurp of his tongue. I tell you, that pig understands every word I say.

Weds, Sept 16th

GPJ dragged us all into the main hall for a new Energy Saver thing at college. Something about picking cockles in Essex, like we haven't got enough to do. Anyway, just as I was walking in she pulled me to one side.

'I believe you came down to the warehouse with your mum,' she began, twirling a spanner in her hands. 'Sorry we couldn't let you in – it's just we need to do checks first, and nobody knew who you were. I guess it was a bit of a shock for you seeing your mum there, but don't be too quick to judge, she's—'

A sudden hot surge of anger flashed thru my brain.

'Don't you try and explain my mum to me! You haven't had 16 years of her,' I hissed. 'You're my tutor at college. I don't tell you what to do and you don't lecture me about my family. Clear?'

The spanner sat motionless in the palm of her hand. 'Clear.' She smiled. 'You're your mother's daughter all right.'

'Really?' I turned on my heel. 'Mostly it feels the other way round.'

Sat, Sept 19th

Claire's got us tickets to see the *hydro* again in December. I asked Ravi if he wanted to come, but he said no.

'College work,' he muttered. 'Gotta get that scholarship. There's only 30 places for the whole country and there's a chance they're gonna start it early. Maybe November.'

I went all cold inside again. Doesn't he care about me at all? And the horrible thing is the less he shows he likes me the more I like him.

Sun, Sept 20th

Women Moving Forward are now dead active in the area. They've started to patrol the streets in pairs, wearing big old tool belts and fixing things for people. Dad's gone all weird, like a dad in a perfect-dad training video. All this week he's insisted that we eat meals together and he keeps asking me how I am all the time. Breakfast is a nightmare; he's got me on porridge and *dis-gust-ing* goat milk. Mousy Woman got 2 goats over the summer. Curse her.

I want to go and see Mum again. Maybe she's calmed down a bit.

Weds, Sept 23rd

Adi came with me after college to see Mum, cos I couldn't face it on my own. When we got to the Co-op Building, Nut Brown swung the doors open.

'You again issit?'

I nodded.

'All right. Follow me.'

We walked behind her thru the empty corridors.

'D'you guys live here?' I asked, panting to keep up.

'Some do. Them what's in the collective, innit.'

'Shit!' Adi yelled. I spun around to see a huge rat leaping up the stairwell.

Nut Brown laughed. 'Ah – don't worry 'bout her, that's Killer. Prime lady.'

Suddenly the sound of weird chanting filled the corridor.

'Nearly there.'

'What the . . . ?' whispered Adi, but he had no time to finish cos Nut Brown yanked a heavy metal door open, to reveal a huge warehouse room, set up as a martial arts space. At least 30 sweat-drenched women were running laps around the wall.

A familiar voice shouted: 'Women! Moving . . .!'

All the women stopped dead, went into a tiger-style crouch and roared, 'Forward!' back at her. I didn't even have to look. Gwen Parry-Jones.

'No wonder she wouldn't do biscuits and tea for old Bob,' gurgled Adi, shoulders starting to shake.

'No laughing,' I hissed.

'S'too much.'

'Women, take a break!'

They all flopped down on mats in the centre.

'No, Julia. You've only done forty-nine – one more lap! No shirking.'

I looked over and there she was. Poor old mum lifted herself off her sweat mat and set off at a slow trot out towards the wall. She'd taken only a few paces when she came level with us. Our eyes met.

'Oh, hey, sweetie!' she drawled, coming to a stop. 'Howz it hanging? Wanna come and chill with the girls?'

I headed out the door.

'Laura! Come back!' Mum chased after me down the hallway, finally catching up by Killer's stairwell. 'Where are you going?'

'Out of here. This is just . . . not . . .'

She crossed her arms. 'And you are being so . . . judgemental.'

'Look at this place! It's a shit hole – and those women . . . Mum, you're in a cult.'

'WMF is not a cult . . . it's a valid expression of revolt

on behalf of disenfranchised women in the rationing era. We are rediscovering our female strength, power—'

At this point, Killer made a strike for female rodent power by leaping out from behind some boxes on to Mum's bare foot.

'Oh Jesus!' screamed Mum, leaping up the concrete stairs.

'Yeah, *Julia*, you're all about power!'

'You're such a goddamn teenager!' she shouted from the flight above. 'It's all right for you to be Straight X – but if anyone else wants to make a state—'

A bell rang. Suddenly the hallway was swarming with wimmin.

'What's that disgusting smell?' gasped Adi, catching up with us. 'S'like drains or something . . .'

Gwen Parry-Jones smiled as she walked past. 'Ah, Laura, Adisa – good to see you here. Grub's up – why don't you join us?'

'Lentils!' Adi spat. 'Mrs B, I applaud your radical stance an' all, but no good ever comes from lentils. Pulses corrupt. Trust me, I been there.'

'I appreciate your sharing that with me, Adisa – but I think I know what's best. I am a grown woman taking back her power.'

Adi shook his head sadly. 'Woman's blind. She'll have

to get burned before she can get out. Let's jet, Laura.'

I nodded. 'Mum, we're going!'

Mum took a step down towards us. 'Already?' she asked in a little-girl voice.

'Yup.'

'But when will I see you again?'

'Er . . . you know where I live.'

Her eyes hardened. 'You're not going to guilt-trip me, young lady. This is a very difficult time for us all.'

'I know, Mum. Enjoy your lunch!'

Adi leaned on the wall outside. 'Oh boy. I guess you got to hand it to your mum, she goes for it. I mean, those women are like banditos. They ain't taking things lying down.'

'I don't want a bandit for a mum. I just want someone normal.'

Adi blew his cheeks out. 'You always say that, but I reckon you secretly like it. I mean, it ain't never dull around yours, is it?'

Fri, Sept 25th

Lisa Bell slapped my American rationing homework down on my desk in Crit Thinking and waved Amy's emails at me.

'Is this some kind of joke? This teenager you've

fabricated is completely unbelievable. The father-figure is ridiculous. I was looking for genuine responses to rationing issues. Real-life people don't behave like this. Really, Laura, it's about time you took both your education *and* rationing seriously.' I didn't bother to answer, just stared into her googly eyes.

Anyway, I don't care. Going out with Rav tomorrow to the movies.

Sat, Sept 26th

Ravi blew me out! Said he was too busy with the scholarship. He's revising every night with a bunch of geeks from college. So that's who those boys were the other day. Basically it makes me dead sad to have my boyfriend snatched off me by a bloody greenhouse gas.

Tues, Sept 29th

Oh God. I've just found out it's parents' evening in 4 weeks' time. Got to keep them away; if they find out about my results it'll be instant death. Mind you it's not like they're noticing me at all. Mum's completely obsessed with her workshops and Dad's become desperate to get a job. He's gone right thru his redundancy pay.

He sat down with me and Kim at dinner. 'Don't worry,

we'll be fine. I've got an interview coming up for delivering fruit and veg.'

Kim put her fork down. 'What d'you have to do in the interview – juggle melons?'

Dad glanced up. 'Very funny. Actually this is a bit different – it's with a horse and—'

She cut in. 'Please. Enough. Anyway, *I'm* bringing in some money now, so I can help out.'

'You?'

'Yes, Dad. Me.'

'But I can't take money from—'

Kim snatched up her keys and turned to the door. 'Yes you can. See ya!'

I glanced across at him. He'd gone all pale. Poor old dad.

Anyway, all I need to do is get thru the resits in January, then everything'll be cool.

Weds, Sept 30th

Aargh, aargh, aargh. Got to focus on my Energy Saver homework, but all I do is think about Ravi. Got to stop giving him so much power. Miserable cold rainy weather. Can't even remember being warm any more.

Carbon Rations vote in Europe in 2 weeks. They better do it or I'll kill them.

October

Thurs, Oct 1st

Kim and Kier have taken over the whole upstairs of the house cos his flat is freezing after he's used so many points on travelling around London and running date nights. I squeezed past him on my way to the bathroom this morning.

'So, how's it going?'

Kieran waved a stack of paper. 'S'unbelievable. I think I might be on the verge of a nervous breakdown with it all – there's just so much to do. We're running three venues now on four different nights. We're turning into a . . .' he frowned, 'what's the word – a . . . a franchise.'

'Like Starbucks?'

'Don't get cute with me young lady, Carbon Dating is a vision, a tool of change.'

'Is that what these are all about?' I nodded towards a stack of books spread across Kim's floor. They had titles like *Mystic Money* and *Positive Dreamer*. The top one had a guy with an orange tan and a wig holding out a golden key. *Unlock the Dynamic You.*

'Nice wig,' I giggled.

'He makes a lot of sense.'

'He makes a lot of money.'

'Well, maybe *we're* going to make a lot of money – we're already Londonwide and looking to branch out to Manchester, Brighton, Birmingham . . .'

'Is that what you went into this for?'

'No,' replied Kieran, sulkily. 'You know why I did it – but it's nice to be . . . successful for once. Your sister's dead good at marketing and stuff, y'know? Please don't knock it.'

'OK.'

'Hmm. Anyway, how's it going with that cute boy?'

'Dunno.'

'What? I thought you were getting on really well.'

'To be honest, Kier, I've got so much else going on right now that Ravi Datta's not a real big deal.'

Kieran gave me a long look. 'You know best. Maybe you should get down to one of our nights – plenty of hot boys for you down there. Not that that's what it's all about,' he added quickly. 'It's just a safe space for people to explore their new identity— Ow!' He sucked his finger. 'Damn paper cut.'

I hung around and helped out for the rest of the morning, and the whole time Kieran was banging on about his plans and his great future. After he left I felt a bit sad, I think I don't like him half as much as when he was all skinny and sad and funny.

Dad got the horse and cart job.

Fri, Oct 2nd

I finally caught up with Ravi in college. I had to run after him down the link.

'Can you please tell me what's going on? You're acting like you don't know me.'

He glanced around the packed corridor. 'Look this ain't the time . . .'

'What's so bad you can't say it right now?'

'Fine. You wanna do this here?'

I took in a sharp breath. 'Are you breaking up with me?'

'No. C'mere . . .' He pushed open an empty classroom door and went inside. I followed and leaned against the door, completely cold.

'Laura, it's not you . . .'

'Oh Jesus! Please don't do that *it's not you* bullshit. Of course it's *me*. If you wanna finish, then at least be straight.'

He looked down. 'I *am* being straight. I got the scholarship.'

'That's so cool – but you're not going yet, right?'

'Well . . . they're doing an accelerated programme. I start in three weeks.'

'Three weeks? When were you gonna tell me?'

'I only just found out, Laur. But anyway, with everything that's going on it don't feel *right* to be kissing and holding hands and all that shit. What's the point . . . ? I mean, what future is there for any of us?'

'So you wanted to finish *anyway*? Cos there's no future? Give me a break!'

I gazed around the room, numb – and that's when I realised I was in the Food Technology room. Oh the shame, to be broken up with surrounded by aprons.

'You coward!'

A tray of cooling rock cakes caught my eye.

An hour later, I stood on the Greenway with Adi.

'What, the whole tray?' he asked.

'Yeah. One by one.'

He let out a low whistle. 'Nice work, girl. Those rock cakes are some solid shit.'

I kicked a Coke can into the nettles. 'Too right, Adi. What a loser.'

He looked at me for a long moment. 'I'm sorry.'

'Don't.' I held up a hand. 'Let's just change the subject.'

5 a.m. Can't sleep, been crying all night. I hate Ravi Datta so much. And you know why? Cos he's got no hope and now I'm scared I haven't got any either. That I'm just acting out a part and I know there's no future for any of us.

Sat, Oct 3rd

Got up early and clocked the college parents' evening invitation on the mat. Threw it straight into the bin. Dad started his new job today, delivering fruit and veg on a horse and cart around Blackheath. He came home this evening and they'd paid him with € 40 in cash and a box of cabbages.

I think it's better he stays away from college now he's turned into a simpleton.

Mon, Oct 5th

Band practice tonight and Claire had big news. An A&R guy from PoleCat Records has called her cos he's d-loaded *death to capitalist scum* and he loves it.

'Who?' asked Adi.

'PoleCat – they got Deadog, Slasher 6, Grrrrrr and Cheapgirl.'

Stace gasped. 'A deal?'

'Don't know yet.'

'When will you?'

'When he gets back. He said he was going on holiday and taking a bunch of music with him . . .'

We stared at each other in pure excitement.

'Oh my God,' cried Stace. 'We could really make it!'

But Claire shook her head. 'I can't let myself . . . it's too much.'

'I need something to keep me going.'

'Huh!' She punched me on the arm. 'You'll be over that loser in no time. You're a *dirty angel!*'

When I got home I lay in bed and played music for hours, my heart beating like a big drum. RD can go to hell.

Weds, Oct 7th

Mrs Datta has walked out on Mr Datta! They had this monster row in the street, which ended in her screaming: 'That's it, Mister. I quit!' and ten minutes later she was hauling a battered old suitcase out thru the front door. She caught me looking from the bedroom window.

'Men are all bastards, Laura!' There was a pause while someone said something from inside the house.

'Yes, that does include you, Ravi!' she shouted, setting off down the road.

God it was so good to listen to someone else's meltdown for a change.

Don't believe what's just happened – Adi just called and went: 'So what we doing?'

'Uh, when?'

'Tomorrow.'

'Tomorrow . . . nothing, why?'

'Cos it's your birthday an' all.'

'Jesus, Ad, I totally forgot.'

'Jesus is right. I'll call for you at 6.'

'But I haven't got anything left on my card to go out this month.'

'Then we'll go low.' He locked off.

I feel shaky. If you'd told me a year ago that I'd forget my own birthday I'd've just laughed in your face.

Thurs, Oct 8th

Happy birthday to me.

Mum took me out for lunch in some weird vegetarian canteen in Blackheath. She was *very*, *very* cheerful. Breakdown time, folks.

'Well, this is nice. Just me and you!' She laughed, waving a piece of tofu at me.

'Yeah, I guess.'

She squeezed my hand.

'It's going to be OK. I wish we were all celebrating together, but I think we just need some time apart. My therapist says I need time to centre myself before I can function again as a mother figure.'

I smiled.

I lay in bed all afternoon with the rain falling on the window, and felt dead sad. He didn't even try to call me or anything. When Adi came round, he took one look at my face and basically dragged my jacket on and marched me out of the house.

'Can't face anyone,' I mumbled.

We walked down to the river in the rain and sat and drank vodka; watching the Woolwich ferry come and go.

After a bit, Adi sighed. 'Well it makes two of us, anyway.'

'What d'you mean?'

'I've broken with Sarah.'

'But why? I thought you were so good together,' I gasped.

'Dunno. Just.'

I stared at him. 'That's it? 2 years and *dunno, just*?'

He clinked the vodka bottle against a bit of bridge.

'Yep. Move on.'

'Wow. I think it's gonna take me a long time to get over Rav, I mean—'

'Can you do me a favour and stop talking about that loser for one minute?'

I turned and caught a really strange expression on his

face – before he changed it to a smile. 'Happy birthday, Laura. Here's to changes . . .'

Fri, Oct 9th

Can't be definite, but thought I just saw Elise Penatata from the Carbon Dept go up the Leaders' stairwell. She's got some guts that woman.

Sat, Oct 10th

Our house is insane. Dad's got brochures for pig farms all over the kitchen, meanwhile the Carbon Dating stuff is spreading like a virus over the hallway, the stairs, the landing. You can't move for flyers and leaflets. I pushed past Kieran on the stairs and slipped on a pile of registration forms.

'Jesus, Kier. Can't you clean this shit up?'

He frowned. 'This is Kim's stuff actually, but I haven't seen her since yesterday.'

'Were you meant to?'

'Yeah, sure. We were supposed to hook up this morning but she didn't show . . . She said something last night about going to see her friend Fiona, said she needed a break.'

Sun, Oct 11th

This morning I found an envelope on the mat with my name on it. I tore it open and inside was a tiny angel wired up out of little bits of circuit and copper wire. I gasped – she was just so beautiful. There was a piece of ripped-up graph paper in the envelope. *Happy birthday. Sorry. I'm such a mess-up. R.*

Kim still not back, bit weird.

Mon, Oct 12th

I looked for Rav to say thanks but he wasn't in college.

Tues, Oct 13th

I'm worried about Kim. I guess she's fine, but it's just strange that she disappeared after that Elise Penatata went up to see the Leaders. I've called her about 5 times, but no answer. I wanna talk to Adi, but he's not picking up either.

Weds, Oct 14th

Still no Kim. Kieran's going mad, keeps mincing up and down the hallway muttering, 'We've got so much to do! What's she playing at?' He's so selfish sometimes. Doesn't even think that she might be in trouble.

I went for a long, long walk and worked out there was only one thing to do. So this evening I climbed up the estate stairwell and knocked on Tracey Leader's front door. After a few moments, Delaney stuck his head out of an upstairs window.

'Wot?'

'Is Tracey in?'

'Wossit to you?'

Suddenly the front door opened and Conrad stood there.

'C'min. My sister wants a word wiv ya.'

I took a deep breath, maybe my last ever, and followed Conrad thru into the kitchen. Talk about a Carbon Den of Sin. The place was massive, sort of 3 flats knocked into one – and they had like 5 PlayStations, a popcorn maker, 50 halogen spots, a massive projector TV, a movie surround system and a ski treadmill machine – all humming away at the same time. In the middle of it all sat 5 massive *Supersize-me* Leader girls eating kebabs on a curved black leather sofa. The treadmill was just for show, evidently.

Tracey turned.

'Ah, Laura innit . . . where's that sister of yours? I bin lookin' for her.'

I was so surprised I just stood there for a minute.

'But . . . that's what I came to ask you.'

Tracey frowned. 'Why would I know if you don't?'

'Because . . . y'know . . .'

She levered herself up out of the couch.

'Nah, I don't know as it 'appens. Why don't you tell me?'

I looked down at my trainers. 'I know about the carbon—'

Suddenly I was being pushed back on to the sofa. Fighting down panic, I kept my voice level. 'Look, I'm sorry, but I just want to know my sister's OK . . . I haven't said anything to anyone – and I'm not going—'

'Too right,' spat Tracey. 'I've already had that Government woman nosing around. I bet it was something to do wiv youse.' She lifted her fist.

'Look, leave it out, Trace!'

'Wot?'

'Leave 'er alone.'

Out of the corner of my eye I saw a size-24 Leader moving towards me.

Tracey whirled around. 'Are youse jokin', Chelsea? This little girl gotta learn who she's dealin' wiv.'

Chelsea shot up out of her seat. 'I says leave it, Trace. It's just nuffin' I s'pose, she prob'ly don't remember . . . but I was at school same time as Laura, 'fore I 'ad Clinton last year. Well, one lunch time, right, the Mackanallys has me cornered in the bogs and Laura 'ere comes in and . . . sticks up for me. Stopped Debby Mackanally from rubbin' chips in me 'air.'

All 5 sets of Leader eyebrows nearly flew upwards off their foreheads.

'Wot? *Wot?* You let a Mackanally do that to ya? Shame on you, girl,' growled Tracey. She turned back to me. 'Issis true?'

I looked up at Chelsea, trying to recognise her.

'Yeah, well, I remember, all right,' Chelsea continued. 'It was a couple of years ago an' I wos a bit finner in them days. You was proper good to me. So leave it out, eh, Trace?'

Tracey turned and gave me a long, low stare. 'All right, if you helped a Leader out we'll let it slide. But, no more questions – and when you see that sister of yours, send her down to see me. Know your way out, then?' Tracey's eyes flicked towards the door.

I nodded.

'Oi, Laura!'

I paused at the doorway.

'Is that your pig?'

'Well, yeah, I mean, he's Dad's.'

'Bleed like a waterfall when you kill 'em, pigs.'

The blood drained from my face. 'You wouldn't . . .'

Tracey smiled. 'Me? Wouldn't hurt a fly. See ya.'

I sat on our garden bench in the drizzle for ages, trying to figure it all out. I kind of believed Tracey when she said she hadn't seen Kim. Don't know why. But where *is* Kim? I can't wait much longer . . . And thru everything I kept getting this image of gallons of Larkin's blood oozing out into a big pool.

A torch beam flickered over the bench. Arthur's voice. 'Laura – is that you?'

I couldn't trust myself to look up at him. There was a long pause, and then he lowered himself gently on to the bench next to me.

He didn't say anything, just sat there quiet – much better than words.

'Sorry,' I sniffled.

He flipped open a pack of Senior Service and offered it to me. 'Very soothing.'

I took one and sparked up. It tasted like the inside of a cheap coffin.

'. . . It's my sister, Kim. I think she's in trouble . . . and I'm not sure what to do.'

He closed his eyes. 'Start from the beginning and tell me everything.'

And so I did.

'Hmmm,' said Arthur eventually.

'Say something, please!' I whispered. 'Is it that bad?'

'Well, this is a pretty pickle, and no mistake. I really think you should tell your parents.'

I shook my head. 'I don't know if that's the right thing . . . and then there's Lar—'

'Who?'

'Nobody.'

'Were you going to say Larkin?'

I nodded miserably. 'Tracey Leader's threatened to cut his throat if I tell anyone about what's been going on. She'll do it, too.'

'Good Lord, these Leaders are a rough crowd. They've got a certain style, though . . .' He narrowed his eyes appreciatively. 'How deeply is Kim involved, d'you think?'

'I don't know for sure. She's been trying to get out of it – and I think Tracey'd kept her kind of distant from the real dirty stuff. I reckon Kim was more of an introducer, y'know – a nice girl who could fix things up for you. But now Carbon Dating's really taking off I reckon Tracey's going mad cos Kim's getting away from her. But it seems weird that this all kicked off when Elise Penatata went to the estate.'

'Let's not rush in too fast. It could all be a coincidence. Did you *really* believe Tracey when she said she hadn't seen Kim?'

'I don't know. Maybe . . .' I started to lose it. 'It's

just . . . so . . . *hard*. I feel like I'm the only normal one left – and I'm only just holding it together. Arthur, I really messed my exams up, but I can't tell anyone. I'm trying to sort it out, but I'm so scared.'

He gave me a long, slow look. 'Don't be scared.'

'But I am—'

'Enough now, Laura. Enough. I'm going to help you. We give it one more day and then we'll have to go to the police. This is too big for us to deal with. Agreed?'

I nodded.

Thurs, Oct 15th

Kim's back! She sneaked into my room dead early this morning.

'Jesus, where've you been?' I cried. 'I've been so scared! Been calling and calling . . .'

She sat down heavily on the bed. 'I know, I'm sorry. It's just I saw that carbon policewoman coming out of Tracey's door last week and I . . . panicked. I just ran out the house, didn't even take my cell with me.'

'But where've you been?'

'Down at the Leopard. Always wanted to sleep at the pub.' She laughed, but it was pretty fake.

'Kim, are you all right? She hasn't hurt . . .'

'Who? Trace? Nah.'

'I went round there to see her.'

Kim turned to me in amazement. 'What? You went to the Leaders' house?'

'I didn't know where you were – and I didn't want to tell Dad. I promised you not to . . .'

She grabbed my hand and held it to her cheek. 'Oh, Laur – I'm so sorry . . .' Hot tears spilled on to my palm. 'I'm not giving in. I've found something I wanna do – and I can't let her . . . Even if it means I've got to stay down in Soho.' She squeezed my hand tight. 'I'm so scared, but please let me just ride it out a bit longer?'

I think I've just got my sister back, after 2 years. And all because of Tracey Leader. Unbelievable.

Arthur tapped on his living-room window when I went past.

'She's back. It's all right!' I whispered.

'Excellent! But now for the second stage,' he hissed, swishing back a corner of net curtain. 'What's the homework for this week?'

I sighed. 'I've got to do a report on the Carbon Vote.'
'When by?'
'Monday.'
'Come first thing Saturday and we'll do it together.'
'Arthur, you don't have to do this.'

'Toodle-pip!' He disappeared behind the net like some old posh spy out of James Bond.

Fri, Oct 16th

Voting begins tomorrow all over Europe at 6 a.m. for 2 whole days. The polls predict it will be 47% Yes to Rationing.

Sat, Oct 17th

I went round to Arthur's to watch. Millions of people are queuing for hours at the centres. But by the end of the day they're saying the No votes are ahead by 5%.

'But they've got to vote yes!' I shouted. 'People can't be that stupid.'

Arthur shook his head. 'Yes, they can.'

I sloshed home thru the soaking garden in a dead bad mood. I can't remember a day without rain.

Where's Adi gone? So weird.

Sun, Oct 18th

When the polls closed at 10 tonight, the Yes and No vote were equal. Each side thinks they've won. Won't know till 5 a.m. tomorrow.

Mon, Oct 19th

Dad shook me awake. 'Laura, we've won! By two per cent. Europe's going on rations!'

God, it feels so *good* not to be freaks any more.

Tues, Oct 20th

They tried to do these big celebrations across France, Germany, Holland and Belgium, but no one turned up. It's like celebrating poking yourself in the eye. My card's totally scaring me, another block's just gone. I've only got 2 left for the whole year.

Thurs, Oct 22nd

Ravi knocked on my door.

'I'm going tomorrow.'

Dead silence. Then we just lunged at each other, kissed for ages. And then just as quickly, we broke apart.

'Sorry. I really—' he began.

'Yeah, but not enough to stay.'

'Laura . . .'

I shook my head. 'Take care of yourself, Ravi.' And then I turned and came indoors. I'm in my room now and I feel different – it's like things have gone simpler for me. Basically, either someone is with you, or they're not.

Fri, Oct 23rd

Yes! I got an A for my European Vote essay, thanks to Arthur. It feels like I'm totally fixing up. I ran round to see him.

'Good girl,' he laughed. 'But there's still a long way to go. What's next?'

He is like one of those crazed Olympic athlete trainers.

I'm really starting to freak out about Adi. He says he just wants to be on his own for a bit, which is cool – but I keep seeing him out with other people. It's like he's avoiding me.

Sat, Oct 24th

Woke up and our porch was totally flooded so I spent the rest of the morning helping Dad clear leaves out of all the drains and gutters.

Dad sighed. 'I don't know how much longer we can keep going in this city. It's really time to think about moving out.'

'But where? This is our home!'

He blew out his cheeks. 'Can you start collecting bin liners and plastic bags? I think we're going to have to make up some sandbags.'

My heart sank. Not another disaster, please.

Sun, Oct 25th

Band practice and Adi a no-show.

'What's with that boy?' asked Stace.

'Yeah – I've been like totally stalking this A&R guy 24/7 and he can't even be arsed to come to practice,' Claire muttered.

'Any news on PoleCat?' I asked.

Claire shook her head. 'But it's only a matter of time till I hunt the man down and *destroy* him.'

'Did Adi try and call any of you?' I looked from one to the other.

'Not about tonight but, yeah, we've been talking most days,' said Stace.

'Really? He – he said he needed space to me.'

Stace glanced over for a second. 'Oh . . . I dunno then.'

I got home and found Kieran in the garden. 'Oh, Laura, thank God – I can't do anything with this pig.'

'Huh?'

He flipped his hands impatiently. 'It's nothing bad, it's just I've got this damn *Mail on Sunday* journalist coming over to do a feature. The shoot was supposed to be on my balcony, y'know – casual young entrepreneur at home type-thing – but that's not gonna happen in this rain. I've been going out of my mind trying to work on another angle – and then I saw the pig in the back garden, and I thought, *mud*! *Pig*! Make the rain *fun* – a strength, not a weakness!'

'Ha, ha.'

'*Pleeease*. It's our first national exposure. They're coming in half an hour, but Larkin won't let me near him.'

'So what're you going to do – nothing weird?'

'*No-o*, very tasteful actually. You can be in the shot too, it'd be great publicity for the *angels*. Did I tell you it was national?'

'Yeah. The *Mail on Sunday*. That's really gonna hit our fan-base.'

Kieran raised an eyebrow. 'Ah, that's where you're wrong. All those little straight edgers come from Middle-England suburbia. What d'you think made them so angry in the first place?'

I chewed my lip. 'All right, but just no weirdness. Larkin rocks.'

'Promise.'

And so half an hour later I was standing in the pig pen with these stuck-up guys from the *Mail*, Justin and Leo. Leo took one look at the garden, wrinkled his nose and went '*Jesus*' and started fussing around with lights and gels and angles while Kieran was being interviewed inside. Finally I couldn't take the drizzle any more and headed indoors.

It was nearly dark when Kieran popped his head into my room.

'Ready when you are!' he trilled in a strange, high voice.

I lifted my hands off the bass frets. 'You OK?'

'Yeah, course. Why shouldn't I be?'

'Look, maybe it's better that it's just you in the shot. It'll be cool – I've got to get this essay done.'

'No, you have to come. The pig still won't . . . *co-operate*.'

'The pig has a name. Larkin. So you've already tried to do it without me, anyway? What's going on, Kier?'

'Nothing!'

Oh, traitor, traitor. When I got down to Larkin's sty, they'd dressed him in these disgusting pink, heart-shaped shades and looped a string of pearls around his neck.

'What have you done?'

Leo rolled his eyes. 'Look, love – we needed an angle. It's an article about dating, so we can't just give the punters a picture of a pig. But a pig in pearls with a pretty girl, that's another thing.'

I crossed my arms. 'I'm not gonna be in that shot. You've stripped away all his dignity.'

Leo threw his hands up in the air. 'Right, that's it. Can't work under these conditions. Somebody sort her out.'

Kier grabbed me by the elbow and walked me down to the rabbit hutches.

'Oh, c'mon – where's your sense of fun?'

'This is bullshit.'

'I know. But if I don't give them the shot, there'll be no feature. This is a really big deal for us. Please, Laura,' he whined.

I gazed around the sodden garden.

'I really hate you sometimes. OK, I'll hold him, but they're gonna have to crop me out.'

He started to say something, but I held my hand up. 'Final offer.'

I think I may have started to find my inner power.

Mon, Oct 26th

Oh shit. I thought I'd got away with it, but no. I was crunching down a slice of toast this morning when Dad came into the kitchen.

'So what time shall I come tonight?'

My mind went blank.

'Parents' evening. I bumped into Louise Foster's old man down at the green centre. Weren't you going to tell me?'

'No need to come to that, Dad, I'm doing fine. It'd be really boring . . .'

Dad looked meaningfully into my eyes. 'No, I *want* to come, see how you're getting on. Not ashamed of me, are you?'

I glanced at him, raggedy garden trousers held up with bits of string.

'Course not. But honestly, there's no point.'

Dad smiled slyly. 'Hmm. She doth protest too much . . . I'm *definitely* coming down now. Be there at seven.'

That smile's so gonna be wiped off his stubbly face when he gets a sniff of my results.

At 6.50 I was standing in a big puddle outside the school gates, my only hope to manoeuvre Dad over to see Dave Beard (bribed to say good things with a box of Highland shortcake) then basically get him lost in the workshops until it's time to leave. And then I heard clopping hooves. Oh, God, he hadn't – but oh yes he had. A horse-drawn cart turned on to the street. And then I heard a voice behind me.

'Yoo-hoo, Laura!'

I swivelled round. Mum, on the other side of the road, waving at me from a hydro van with WOMEN MOVING FORWARD spray-painted down the side. I could hear a group of kids laughing behind me as she crossed the road. I shut my eyes. I am the child of carnival folk.

'Mum, what are you doing here?'

'Parents' evening, of course! I *am* still your mother, darling . . .' She smoothed my hair behind my ears. 'And Gwen invited me even if you didn't.'

I cursed the name, shape and form of Gwen Parry-Jones.

'Whoah!' The carriage pulled up alongside. Dad turned to a boy next to him on the seat. 'Look after her for half an hour, Johnny.'

Mother stared up at him. 'Good God, you've gone native.'

Dad glanced at her dungarees. 'Likewise.'

'At least brush the straw off your jumper.' She started plucking at bits of random hay on him. 'Your father was a complete bum when I first met him: wore the same shirt for six months. Hasn't taken you long to revert, has it?'

'You loved that shirt.'

'No, Nick.' She glanced at him shyly. 'I hated it – it was lime-green and too small in the arms. But *you* were so cute.'

Dad blushed.

'Right then!' I suddenly felt frantic to move this parental road-show on towards its hellish end.

And so 10 minutes later there we were, sitting in plastic chairs in front of Gwen Parry-Jones. One big happy family. GPJ stretched her lips into her most caring smile. Stoat of Death.

'So, I imagine you must be pretty disappointed in Laura's bad AS results, but I can assure you that all isn't lost—'

Mum frowned. 'Excuse me?'

Big pause. GPJ took in my burning face. 'You haven't told them?'

'Laura!' My mother. Dangerous.

GPJ held up her hand. 'Just before we all get overexcited, I think we should ask Laura for her explanation.'

I dug my nails into the palm of my hand, just willing myself not to cry. Silence.

Mum turned on Dad. 'Honestly, Nick, I can't believe you didn't know about this!'

'Me? At least I'm at home, not stuck up my own arse in a commune somewhere.' He leaned forward and took my hand. 'Laura, love, why didn't you say?'

I stared back at him, so angry. What was I gonna say? Cos you and Mum are so messed up it's like I'm your parents right now?

GPJ picked up my results sheet. 'Maybe we should focus on the grades and move away from these personal issues. Hmm, an E in Design Tech. It seems that practical skills are not a strong point in the family, Julia.'

'And what's that supposed to mean? You know I've been working really hard in the skills sessions, Gwen.' Mum's bottom lip began to tremble.

'Oh, Jesus,' cut in Dad. 'This is about Laura, not you.'

'Really? Well, you don't seem to have been taking much notice of her in the past few months if you've let this slip. What, are you having some little affair?'

Dad blushed. 'Of course not.'

I stood up so sharply that my chair skidded across the room. 'Stop it. Both of you. Why do you *think* I didn't say anything? Like there's any point! And Arthur's been helping me. He – he – *listens*.'

Now it was their turn to be silent.

I overheard Dad and Arthur in the garden this evening. Dad asked Arthur why he hadn't said anything. For the first time ever, I heard Arthur sounding sharp.

'Because Laura asked me not to. And I would *never* betray a trust,' he said, before marching off stiffly between the bean poles, like the old soldier he is.

Tues, Oct 27th

Dad came into my room this morning and put his head in his hands.

'It will get better, Laura. I promise.'

Poor man. Who's he trying to kid?

Fri, Oct 30th

College stank today. I sat in the back of Design Tech with a scarf round my nose. Dave Beard came in, looking sick.

'What's going on, sir?'

'The sewers are backed up.'

'What exactly *are* sewers?' Claire muttered.

I shrugged. Dave looked over.

'They're pipelines that connect buildings to drainage pipes underground – which connect eventually to sewage treatment plants.'

'Yeah, but what's *in* them? I mean, I know about . . . *waste* from the house, but what about rain and that? Does it all just get mixed up?'

'In London, yes.'

'So we've got miles of shit running underneath us all the time?'

Dave nodded. 'Not so far underneath right now.'

November

Sun, Nov 1st

Shame, shame.

Just 'Larkin' around!

Justin Giles

The hugely successful new c0 d8 Agency has a new public face - all 85 kilos of him - but this is no gorgeous human hunk - it's a prime piece of pig!

'He's a beauty!' beamed Kieran Maclean, co-founder of the popular dating agency.

'We love him here at c0 d8... Larkin really sums us up - he's cool, he's different - and he's not afraid to get down and dirty!'

The Agency, which was founded only four months ago, has made a real impact on the London dating scene, boasting two thousand members and four regular venues around the city. So what does Kieran put his success down to?

'I just saw that there was a real need in society for meeting people in different ways under the new rationing system. Our ethos is to kind of take it slow and get back to

Larkin with proud owner, Laura Brown

dating basics. We run loads of workshops as well - it's not just about romance, it's about learning new skills, basically finding yourself in the new environment.'

And Larkin - would he be welcome on one of your nights?

'Sure he would,' grinned Kieran, 35, 'at c0 d8 it's all about who you are inside!'

Dad is so proud. It is like Larkin is his own child.

Tues, Nov 3rd

The whole country's gone nuts about Bonfire Night. Everyone's going on about *this threat to our national way of life*. Classic British – you can take away our cars, holidays, freedom of choice, future – but back off our right to stand in a muddy field, clutching a sparkler and a burnt jacket potato smeared in Utterly Butterly. Who cares? I guess we'll all just have to find another way to celebrate the murder of a 400-year-old Catholic.

Thurs, Nov 5th

The council called off the bonfire in Greenwich Park because a bunch of people stood around the unlit fire in the rain thru the night. Like that is going to save the planet. Anyway, Arthur's invited Dad and me round for indoor fireworks. I haven't seen Dad for days; he's shut himself away in the cellar making homebrew. I banged on the cellar door and had to wait for ages for him to open up. He stood there, blinking into the light like a mad scientist.

'Are you coming to Arthur's?'

'Can't, I'm afraid. At a very delicate point with the yeast. And the parsnips. But you go.'

So I went next door to see my needy person. Ha, ha. As soon as I walked in he ladled me out a tin mug of lethal rum punch.

'Marvellous. Now we can get this show on the road. Fireworks for ever!' He took down a box of matches from a shelf above the cooker and set fire to a tiny Catherine Wheel on the wall. We watched in silence as it began a jerky spin, flinging off a total of about 6 sparks – while spurting out what looked like dog poo into Arthur's bacon-frying pan. Arthur cleared his throat.

'Of course, I remember rationing in the war. We were out in the country, before I enlisted, so things weren't so bad. You could always bag a rabbit or a rook for the pot . . .'

I tried to do the sum in my head.

'How old were you when you joined up?'

'Ah, umm, seventeen?'

'What year?'

'Oof. Nineteen for-ty . . . ah – three.'

'So that must make you . . . 89?'

He opened his eyes wide. 'Suppose it must. Time rather flies when you're having fun.'

'You call this fun?'

'Hmm, well the trick is, to make it all into an adventure . . .'

'But what if you don't know how to?'

Arthur lowered his voice to a whisper. 'You use your imagination. You've got one of those, haven't you?'

I shrugged.

'Oh I think you do, so you're off to a flying start. The thing about rationing I remember most clearly was that everyone did their damndest to carry on as if it were normal. And soon it *was*. I know it's a dreadfully dull thing to say, but in a way they were very happy times – all pulling together, knowing we were doing something good for the country. And that's how it'll be with this generation. Carbon rationing won't last for ever. If we do it properly it won't be long before alternative thingumajigs fill the gap and we'll be flying around the globe and what have you again.' He took a swig of punch. 'But Laura, these years, when we all said *No, enough!* – those who come after us may well view us all as heroes.'

The thing is though, it's all right for him to bang on like Churchill – he's gonna drop dead soon. And what's a rook, anyway?

Fri, Nov 6th

Rain, rain, rain. Leicester Square is flooded cos – this is so disgusting – a 120-metre block of solid cooking fat is blocking the sewerage tunnel underneath. It's built up from the restaurants and cafés sending all their oil and grease down the plughole. Thames Water is pleading for help from the public with pickaxes.

I bumped into Adi in the Yard, asked him if he was going. He spat on the ground.

'Like they helped us in the summer. But anyway, I can't, Laura, that fat's bare raw.' He shuddered. 'Have you seen it? It's all white like a dead body.'

'D'you want to come to mine later? I've saved up 2 extra points for downloads this week.'

He shook his head. 'Nah, can't make it. I'll bell you when I got some free time.'

'Adi. What's wrong? Are you mad with me?'

'No. Why should I be mad with you?'

I was gonna say something back, but I dunno, maybe Stace is right, I've got to back off and let him have his space. God, I'm talking like he's my boyfriend or something.

Sat, Nov 7th

Historic band practice. Claire ran down the garden, leaned against Adi's garage door and gasped, 'PoleCat's just offered us a track on their New Wave download! They're booking us into a pro studio on December 6th for a whole day!'

'Oh my God!' screamed Stace, throwing her sticks into the air.

Adi got Claire in a big hug and then he ran over and lifted Stace clean off the ground – and then just nodded at me. I walked outside and sat on the garden wall.

Suddenly Adi was there beside me.

I turned. 'I've had enough. You're treating me like a total stranger.'

'Yeah, well, maybe I've just got sick of being your little friend. Y'know, the one who always lifts you up. What about me? I got feelings too, man.'

'You guys, come on! We've got beer!' Stace yelled.

Adi turned and went inside. I followed him and joined in blah blah blah but I hated it. I don't wanna be in this band if Adi's not my best mate any more.

Sun, Nov 8th

The sewers can't cope with all the rain so Thames Water pumped 800,000 tons of shit into the river. Good day for the fish.

Tues, Nov 10th

Central London is disgusting. The whole place pongs like mad. They're calling it the Second Great Stink cos there was one before, in the 19th century, back in the days

317

before drains. But the worst thing is the rats. They're running around all over the place cos their little homes are all washed out.

Weds, Nov 11th

A wave of sewage swept down Oxford Street today and Kim got caught up to her knees on Wardour Street. She dragged herself back home for the first time in weeks. Mum was round picking up some clothes. She saw Kim, went, 'Jesus' and pushed her into the bathroom and made her stay in there for 3 hours.

'I wanna get in there, Mum. She's been ages,' I whined.

Mum looked up from the laptop screen in the office. 'Well, you'll have to wait. I've been doing research and that water's filthy – full of salmonella, cryptosporidium, giardia, norovirus, cholera . . . All of them are killers given half the chance.'

I rolled my eyes.

Mum grinned. 'Ooh, and listen to this – an eighteenth-century flood, as described by Jonathan Swift . . .' She clicked on a page.

'Seepings from butchers' stalls, dung, guts and blood,
Drown'd puppies, stinking sprats, all drenched in mud,
Dead cats and turnip-tops, come tumbling down the flood.'

I went to my room and shut the door. It's weird when Mum comes round, like everything's normal again.

Thurs, Nov 12th

Kim stayed the night. Her and Kier are mad cos they've had to cancel a big event on the South Bank this weekend.

'What happened to global warming?' Kieran growled. 'We're just going to have to rethink the whole thing now that London's turning into a big river. Oooh . . . rivers, canals – what about taking to the water . . . a gondola event! The – the *reflective streets of beauty*. That'll get the punters.'

'Punters?'

He gave me a sideways glance. 'Sorry, Date members. They're like a family to me.'

Ever since parents' evening, Dad's been in manic overdrive. He spends his whole life either in the cellar making homebrew or outside with the pig. Seeing Mum just makes him crazy. There are 2 possible reasons for this.

a) He hates my mother's guts.

b) He is still in love with her.

Larkin spends all day in his sty looking miserable. He is one big pig.

Fri, Nov 13th

It took me 40 minutes to get to college this morning cos Lee Road's all flooded. When I finally turned into the gates, site staff were setting up sandbags around the walls of the building. Everyone looked kind of scared but trying not to show it.

I went to my Design Tech session, but we could hardly hear Dave Beard over the rain crashing down on to the plastic roof of the technology room. Suddenly a piece of pipe broke away from outside and sent a stream of dirty water gushing across the roof and walls. It was like being inside a car wash.

Phil Dixon, this dweeby kid in high-waister tracksuit pants, put his hand up and asked the question we all secretly wanted to ask.

'Is London going to flood, sir?'

This was met with a chorus of *shut up, idiot, duh* from all of us and the kid next to him mock-cuffed him round the ear. Dave Beard held up his hand for silence.

'No, we're going to be fine. London's got the Thames Barrier to protect her.'

We all stared at him.

'You know what that is, don't you?'

Silence.

Dave sighed heavily and turned to the smart board and began to draw. 'Watch. Thames Barrier, opened in May 1984, consists of a line of reinforced concrete piers spanning the river at Woolwich Reach. Their foundations are sunk seventeen metres into the chalk.' He flashed a small smile. 'That's pretty deep, ladies and gentlemen.' When we didn't smile back, he blushed and plunged back into his explanation. I don't think anyone's ever listened to him like this before.

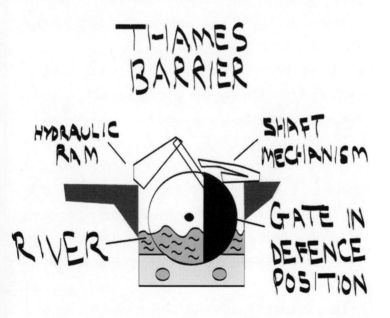

'Right, there are four main gates to allow for the free flow of the Thames through the barrier. Normally the rising gates lie on the riverbed to allow boats to move, but when the tide is high – due to flooding, tide or surges – the gates can be put into flood defence position with hydraulic rams, which are controlled by a tower on the south bank. That's what I've drawn here. Is that clear?'

'Who takes the decision to close them, sir?'

Dave frowned. 'Er, not sure. The Mayor, maybe? It used to be that individual boroughs had their own emergency plans, but since the barrier was built the whole system's been centralised. The decision is taken on the basis of data from the Met Office – and then they close the gate four or five hours before high tide.'

'But, sir,' Nathan raised his hand, 'the weatherman, he don't know shit. He say rain and the sun shines, he say sun shine and it rains.'

Everyone nodded.

'And another thing – you say the Mayor takes the decision? Last night I watched *Jaws* with my little bro, man. Y'know when the mayor and the money men won't close the beach even though Inspector Brody's seen the shark with his own eyes? I ain't got no faith in no white mayor.'

Dave shook his head sadly. 'Well, Nathan, be that as it

may, if this rain continues to fall, or we're hit by a bad storm on the east coast, the Thames Barrier system is what's standing between us and disaster.'

Suddenly the bell started to ring even though it wasn't the end of the lesson. Dave jumped up and went out into the corridor. When he came back in, he looked pretty white. 'All right, everyone to the main hall. *Quietly*.' But no one was talking anyway. We all knew what it was about.

Bob was already on the stage when we got in there. I dunno, there's something about that guy; the more he tries to look like he's in charge, the less you believe in him. He got straight to the point. 'As you are all no doubt aware, the rainwater is rising to a dangerous level. Today's storm has, I feel, taken this to an unacceptable point – and therefore I have made the decision to suspend college until conditions improve. Which of course, they will. Any questions?'

The hall exploded with voices. Bob held up his hand for quiet. 'I understand you have a lot of questions so now I'd like to ask our energy specialist, Ms Parry-Jones, to come up to deliver a short lecture on flood preparation procedures – and to answer any of your queries.'

GPJ leaped on to the stage, looking like a woman whose hour had come. 'First point on the agenda –

sandbagging,' she began, eyes sparkling like sapphires. 'If you act early enough, sandbags will help to keep water out of your home. They are available at places like B&Q and other DIY stores, but you can make them yourselves from plastic bags or pillow cases. The important thing is not to overfill the bags with sand or earth – otherwise they won't sit on top of each other properly and water will seep through the gaps.' A student carried a sandbag on to the stage and demonstrated filling it with soil.

I sat there, numb, as she droned on about turning off gas and electricity, filling baths with drinking water, getting mops and buckets ready, moving supplies of food, clothes, blankets and pets upstairs. An image of Larkin romping around on the landing flashed into my head. 'And finally, do not go out in a flood – even twenty centimetres of water can suck off manhole covers, uproot paving stones and knock an adult off his . . .' her eye briefly met mine, 'or *her*, feet.'

Sandbags? Give me a break.

When I got home Dad was staring out the kitchen window at the ruined garden. It's just a big churned-up mass of mud and water.

'It's time to get out of this city,' he muttered.

I can't believe it. We just go from one crisis to the next. I'm so lonely without Adi.

Sun, Nov 15th

Loads of neighbours met in our kitchen today. When I walked in, Shiva was going, 'But surely this Thames Barrier is enough? The British Government would never leave London unprotected . . .'

Loud Dad snorted. 'Yeah, right. I've worked in the Environment Department for fifteen long years and—'

'And what?'

'Well, basically, the Barrier's too small. And they know it. The thing was built in the first place because of the storm of 1953. Y'see the real danger to London isn't all this rain, it's a storm surge, and that's what happened then. Ten thousand people had to be evacuated. The Docklands was flooded, but that time Central London was spared.'

'Yes, I remember it well,' said Arthur. 'Awful business – the East End was a total disaster. One minute we were safe and dry and then this huge roaring wall of filthy water swept everything up in its path.'

I glanced over at Arthur. Honestly, he's like Forrest Gump – he's been at every single major event of the last century as far as I can see.

Dad held up his hand. 'Sorry. What's a storm surge?'

'Roughly speaking it's a big hump of water that rises off the Grand Banks of Canada and sweeps across the Atlantic, becoming more dangerous as it travels onwards. Surges happen all the time and mostly they sweep away north once they reach Iceland but, sometimes, if the wind is blowing the wrong way, the hump is forced down the North Sea and into the Thames Estuary. You can imagine the sort of force we're looking at.'

'Plus the Estuary's shaped like a trumpet,' said Mousy Woman, shyly.

Arthur turned to her. 'A what?'

'A trumpet. I – I looked it up. The shape makes the surge travel even faster. But mostly it's all right – as long as the surge doesn't happen at the same time as high water. And it almost never does, it's called the – the . . .' she pulled a sheet of paper out of her bag, '. . . the surge-tide interaction! That means that the surge nearly always happens four hours *after* high water – and so the Barrier can cope with the water levels.'

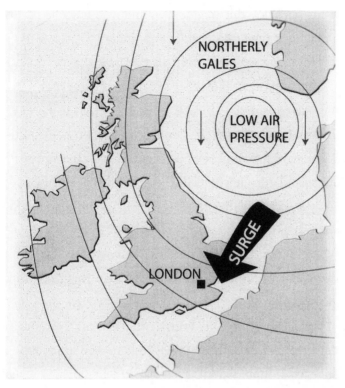

Loud Dad reached for the sheet and traced his finger over London. 'And that's where the politics comes in. They don't want to put any more money in – the current barrier ran seventy-five per cent over budget so the Government line is that surge-tide interaction is a proven fact – that it's *impossible* for a surge to happen at the same time as high tide.' He shook his head. 'But it's not impossible, it's just *unlikely*. And if it *does* happen, the Barrier's too small. Add to that all this damn rain and rising sea levels due to global warming – I tell you, it's just a matter of time till London goes under.'

'How long would it take?' asked Dad.

Mousy Woman looked at her paper again. 'High water only takes an hour to travel from the Barrier to Putney – Central London could be flooded within two hours of the Barrier overtopping. How deep depends on the size of the surge and the height of the embankment walls. But in Central London they're not that high – only about five and a half metres.'

'But surely there are systems – emergency services, a plan?' cut in Shiva. 'I do not believe all this doom and gloom talking.'

Loud Dad shook his head. 'I don't mean to sound so negative, but the Barrier has given London a false sense of security. Councils don't even have maps any more that show where in their borough is likely to flood and where's safe. You've no idea of the power of moving water – once it rises above exhaust-pipe level, that's the whole emergency ground force knocked out – fire brigade, police, ambulances. Then you're relying on river and air rescue. Rescue from the river is a joke – all we've got is a few tugs and barges – and d'you know how long it takes to evacuate people by air?'

The room went dead quiet.

Arthur cleared his throat. 'Well, it's good to look the devil in his face – but let's remember that this is all very unlikely.'

Loud Dad sucked in air between his teeth, but said nothing.

Mon, Nov 16th
It's stopped raining!

Weds, Nov 18th
Still stopped. God, I was just looking back in the diary to the summer when I was praying for rain. Now I'm praying for none. We're messed up.

Thurs, Nov 19th
Still stopped and the water levels have dropped fast cos the summer was so dry – the ground's just sucking it up. Maybe we're not so messed up. Like there's a new balance.

Sat, Nov 21st
Still stopped. The Met Office forecasts dry weather for the week.

Sun, Nov 22nd
I woke up to a disgusting burning smell in the house. I

legged it down to the kitchen and found Dad, standing over the grill. I could only just see him thru the smoke, scooping a blackened pancake on to a plate.

'Ah, Laura. There's my girl! Hungry?'

What, now? I've never seen him cook a pancake in his life. He came and sat down next to me.

'Wondered how you felt about having this place to yourself for a few days? I want to get away – and the Met Office say the worst is probably over.'

'Where are you going?'

He fiddled with his fork. 'Er, well, I want to take a look at a couple of market garden farms in the country.'

'But Dad, I don't want to move . . .'

'It's only research. I want to explore growing under glass – we could extend our crop life out in the garden here all year . . . even grow some exotics.'

'Oh come off it, I'm not a kid.'

'All right. I know you don't want to leave, but I don't know how much longer London's going to be safe.'

'We've been fine this year. Nothing bad's happened.'

He poked at a pancake. 'That's not true, and you know it . . . and anyway, how long—'

'But this is where I wanna be. I've got a life here, the band. All you're thinking about is you.' I watched him sawing at his pancake. 'And you're gonna need a chainsaw to get thru *that*, it's radioactive.'

He threw his fork down. 'I don't know how much choice we've got any more.'

Tues, Nov 24th

Dad went today. He came into my room early this morning.

'Will you be all right? I mean, I won't go if you don't want me to.'

'I'll be fine. Mum and Kim are around if I need them.'

'Sure?'

I nodded.

'Well then, I'll see you in a few days. No mad parties, OK?'

Spent the rest of the day completely alone. Claire and Stace are on a college trip. I'm too proud to call Adi.

Weds, Nov 25th

Did nothing. Spoke to no one.

Thurs, Nov 26th

I called Kim, but she had about 6 call waitings just in the 30 seconds I spoke to her.

'Look, it's not a good time, Laur. Now the floods have

started to go down everyone wants to get out . . . The
flower delivery's late and I'm having a . . . No! Not there
– in the freezer! Look, I'll call you later.'

So basically I've talked to no one for 48 hours. Marooned.

Sat, Nov 28th

I got so desperate I went down the Co-op to look for
Mum. I banged on the doors for ages, but no one there.
Just this poster pasted up on the gates.

I couldn't stand it any more. I called Adi. All I said was hi and he knew I was bad.

He sighed. 'Hold on, I'm coming over.'

It was *so* good to see him. We talked and talked and talked till dawn. Don't even know what about. Fell asleep on the sofa.

Sun, Nov 29th

'Laura! Laura!'

Adi shaking me.

'Wake up, it's 4 in the afternoon! Look at the news – there's a storm coming.'

'What?'

'A storm! An offshore wind-generating site's been destroyed, and a ferry's sunk off Scotland – 52 dead – and it's heading right for us.'

I struggled upright on the sofa and stared at the TV. They kept repeating the same Met Office warning over and over again.

The light was flashing on the answering machine. It was from Mum, she must have called while I was asleep this afternoon.

'Just checking in on you all. I'm out with WMF but, Nick, can you call me? I've just heard about the storm – take the girls down to the Co-op Building. They'll be safe

SEVERE GALE WARNING

Issued by the Met Office, London
3 AM GMT Nov 30 2015

Severe Gale and Flood warning for UK
Eastern Coastal and North Sea regions

Winds are expected of up to 100 mph, waves of
10 metres and rising. Severe breaches of East
coast sea walls predicted. Power failure is predicted
throughout the affected areas for several days.
Access to shelter and water will be limited. Massive
destruction of agricultural land and livestock expected.

The government has issued an advisory evacuation
warning for the population of the affected area.
If you choose not to evacuate you must remain within
the confines of your property at all times.
DO NOT, we repeat, DO NOT venture outside.

there. Call me. OK?'

I dialled her number but no answer. Tried Dad, Kim, but nothing. No connection on Adi's mobile either. The network must've been down. I didn't know what to do. Adi wanted to take me to his place, but I wanted to wait here for the others.

He jumped up. 'All right. I've got to go home to tell my

family what I'm doing, then I'm coming back. I won't be long, I promise.'

The door slammed behind him and all the lights flickered in the house. I'm scared.

Mon, Nov 30th

6 a.m. Woke up again on the sofa. It's bad. At 1 a.m. the first sea walls on the Northumberland coast collapsed. Gigantic waves smashing homes into rubble. 12 dead in a town called Alnwick. As the storm came down the coast, the waves just kept getting bigger and bigger. Scarborough, 27 dead; Grimsby, 38 dead; Cromer, 40 dead; Lowestoft, 52 dead. It's on its way to Southend – and then it's the Thames Estuary. Us. The sea's pouring in everywhere. All the poor animals drowned, thousands and thousands of them. The army's evacuating Canvey Island now. I don't know what to do.

'Laura!' The sound of footsteps coming down the hallway. Dad! He ran into the room.

'Oh, thank God. Couldn't get through to you. Where's Kim and your mum?'

'I . . . don't know, I can't get thru either. Mum's with the WMF . . . but Kim, I don't know. She's been down in Soho for days.'

'Stupid girl. Is she with Kieran at least?'

'Think so.'

Dad let out a deep breath. 'I'll have to go down there if she's not back by tonight. But first we've got to work to do . . .'

When we got outside, we could hardly stand up in the wind and driving rain.

'Jesus,' he shouted. 'The storm hasn't even got here yet.'

There were about 20 people gathered in the street – and more streaming out of their houses the whole time. Loud Dad stood at the centre of the group.

'People! If you wanted to leave, you should have done it by now. I warn you, the roads will be hell, with no guarantee of safety at the end. This storm will be on us in a few hours. If there's a surge there's no telling if the Thames Barrier will hold. I reckon the safest thing is to stay, and if you believe that too, then we've got two main jobs. Number one: we've got to move everything important upstairs – food, water, blankets – we may need to live up there for a while. Number two: we've got to sandbag the whole street. Bring out every sack, bag, bin-liner – anything you've got. And then get digging. We've got to fill them all.'

At midday the storm hit. I was part of a digging group down by the railway tracks. We could hardly move, the wind was so fierce. And then suddenly there was a sound

336

like a shotgun and a massive branch slammed down on to the line.

At 3, Mr Datta ran out to tell us the electricity was down. 'Now I miss Hyderabad,' he cried. 'It stinks, but you can trust to cow shit to keep the lights on.'

Arthur wiped the rain out of his eyes and peered at his watch. 'High tide in thirty minutes. If we can get through that, we might be all right. Can someone get a radio up and running?'

At 5 the first reports came thru. The Barrier held! But bad flooding all over Docklands – half the Olympic Village is underwater. It was so close though, the river rose right to the top of the embankments in Victoria and Chelsea.

Everybody shouted and cheered and hugged each other.

'Don't stop now,' shouted Loud Dad. 'It's not over till the storm's blown itself out.'

As if to prove the truth of his words, a wicked burst of wind ripped a chimney stack off Arthur's roof and sent a pile of bricks crashing to the ground.

1 a.m. Dad's gone down to Soho and I'm sitting cross-legged on my bed. It's the only space left – everywhere's stacked up with tins, blankets, boxes, medicine. I can hardly write, my hands are all cut and trembling. But we've done it – the whole street, wall after wall, is lined with half a metre of sandbags. Mum left a message pinned to the front door, saying she's helping out and for us to go down to the warehouse if there's any trouble. I'm so tired, I can't stay awake any more. Hope Adi's OK. I guess he's decided to stay at home.

I had the weirdest dream about Kim last night. It wasn't a nightmare, but it was sad. There was this messed-up bird fluttering and banging into glass. I don't even know why I know it was about her.

Winter. December

Tues, Dec 1st

7 a.m. I woke up with my heart pounding. Something wrong. The storm was still battering outside, but it wasn't that. I went over to the window and peered out. My heart went cold. A wall of swirling, dirty water was starting to spill over the sandbags at the end of the street. A few people had come outside, but they weren't doing anything, just standing still and looking shocked, like toy people.

I ran downstairs, calling out for Dad, looked in every room, but he wasn't there. I ran back upstairs and when I looked out at the street again, the water was already pouring down the road and rising, fast.

A car was moving thru the flood down at the far end, towards where the water was rising most quickly – and then it stalled. I watched it for a minute, but no one got out. The car just sat there, water ripping past its doors. Then this woman's head appeared out of the sun roof and she started screaming for help. I flung the window open and shouted for people to help her, but no one heard me. Everything in the room went dead. For a long frozen minute I couldn't move . . . and then suddenly I came back to life and ran down the stairs as fast as I could go.

The front door was jammed shut with sandbags, so I went into the study and threw the window open. I sat there on the sill for a moment, trying to work out the best move cos by now there was at least half a metre of water rushing past. Then I saw how to do it – by jumping along the parked cars. I climbed on to the window-sill, sucked in a big breath and jumped on to the bonnet of Loud Dad's electro car. So far so good. I crawled over the roof and on to the bonnet and then sized up my next move – a metre to a red Sierra. Though I was shaking I still made myself jump, but this time I slipped when I landed and my legs wound up in the flooding water. Man, the current was unbelievable, it sucked and dragged at my boots like a crazy dog.

The trapped woman was totally mental by now. I stood up and waved my hands, shouted to her that I was coming. She turned. 'Oh my God, I'm gonna drown! I can't open the door! I can't swim.'

And that's when the adrenalin *really* kicked in. I jumped car to car down that street until I was finally alongside her. The woman didn't stop screaming even though she could see I was there. She was trying to punch out the sunroof.

'Hold on,' I shouted, pulling back as a wheelie bin crashed into the side of my car. I looked down into the water. There was nothing else for it, I'd have to make it across the gap. I started to slide down the bumper, planted one foot into the water – and immediately *slipped*. Panicking, I grabbed the side mirror, and used it to pull myself up again. I was shaking. For the first time, it hit me I was in trouble myself.

'Use your mobile! Call for help,' she shouted. 'Somebody's got to get these doors open.'

I scrabbled in my pocket for my phone, jammed in 999. Nothing. I looked at the screen – no network connection. Hands shaking, I tried again – and again. Nothing.

The woman had gone quiet; she was lying against the back seat, desperately kicking the inside of the doors. The water had risen up to the level of the window. It was like a dream. And then suddenly she threw up her arm, pointed. I turned, and saw maybe the best thing ever – Gwen Parry-Jones in a canoe, sliding along in the current

341

towards us. It was so damn good I turned and took a photo on my mobile.

'Hold on!' yelled GPJ, paddle-blade flashing in her hands. The current was so fast she nearly overshot us. 'Grab the side, Laura!'

I flung out my arm and grabbed the boat with both hands, and then nearly fainted with pain. The fibreglass had ripped across my palm, opening up a huge slice of flesh.

'Hold it!' shouted GPJ.

I dragged the boat close to my chest.

'Good! Now, get in, but keep hold of the car, or we'll be swept away.'

I transferred my grip from boat to wheel arch as I slid down the bonnet and into her canoe.

'Good,' she shouted. 'Door won't open, right?' She reached behind her, and pulled out a hammer from under a tarpaulin. 'You'll have to smash the window. Carefully let go of the car then take this. You'll have to move quickly, I'll only be able to hold us against the current for a few seconds. Got it?'

I nodded. 'Now?'

'Yes!'

I released my grip and the canoe flew across the space and smashed hard against the stalled car.

'Break it!'

I grabbed the hammer and smashed it against the rear-side window. A crack appeared across the pane.

GPJ paddled like crazy against the straining current. 'Again!'

With a cry of pain, I swung the hammer again – and this time, the window shattered. The trapped woman punched her fist against the remaining glass shards.

'Get the door open, Laura!'

I leaned across and put my arm inside the door and yanked it with all my strength, while the woman pushed from inside with her shoulder – until it opened enough for her to squeeze thru. I grabbed on to her and, bit by bit, dragged her into the boat. She lay there gasping.

'Oh, my God, what's happening?'

'Barrier went under at five this morning. London's flooded.' GPJ lifted her paddle out of the water. The canoe spun violently down the street, back toward my house.

'I'm taking you to the Co-op Building – we've set up a rescue centre. Four floors – you'll be safe there.' She glanced at me. 'Are you OK? You look pretty white.'

I winced with pain. 'Have you seen my mum?'

'Yes, she's gone with a party of WMF to sort out an old folks' home. She'll be back soon.'

'What about Arthur?'

She leaned over and lifted my sleeve, uncovering my hand. 'Oh, Laura, that's bad. Why didn't you say? Yes, I'm pretty certain we've got everyone on your street. Jesus, now what?' She rested her oars on the side of the canoe. We'd come alongside the Dattas' house, where there was another WMF rescue boat, already full with people. There was some kind of row going on with Mrs Datta standing in the driving rain in front of the rocking boat, waving her arms. Mr Datta was shaking his fist out of the top-floor window.

'No, Varshana. Never!'

Mrs Datta waved her arms crazily. 'Come, please!'

'No, it is too shameful. I will be fine in this attic. The rabbits are with me.'

'Shiva, we do not have time – please come.'

'No!' His face red with anger. 'I will not be rescued by my own wife. It is not the natural—'

The rest of his words were cut short by a crossbow dart thudding into the window-sill, missing his head by centimetres.

'Jai Rama,' he gasped. 'You nearly kill me!'

Everyone turned to look at Mrs Datta, slipping another dart in her crossbow. 'Bloody right. Get down here, you damn fool!'

'But Varshana!'

'Don't *Varshana* me. Twenty-two years of nonsense. You must come down to me, you silly little man. I love you.'

They stared at each other for a moment, tears in their eyes.

'Hold on, darling, I am coming!' cried Shiva – and 30 seconds later, he appeared at a downstairs window and scrambled into the rescue kayak, into the arms of Varshana Datta.

And then it hit me. 'Larkin!'

GPJ whirled around. 'Who?'

'Our pig, Larkin.'

'Sorry, Laura, no. People first.'

'But he'll drown . . .'

'Sorry. No. Got to get you safe.' She began to paddle away from the house.

There was nothing I could do. If I'd gotten out of that boat, I'd have just been swept away. I squeezed my eyes shut as we floated past the corner of our street.

When I got to the Co-op, Mum was standing on the steps. I threw myself into her arms.

'Oh, sweetheart, are you hurt? Where're the others?'

'I don't know. Dad went to Soho to try and find Kim.'

Her face went white. 'Soho? But that's completely flooded now.'

'Julia!' A woman jerked her thumb towards the exit. 'Got to get going again.'

Mum turned to me. 'I'll be back as soon as I can.' She ran her fingers thru her hair. 'Don't worry, they know how to look after themselves.'

When Mum left I started to search the building for Arthur. Everyone was up on the fourth floor, which was a kind of gigantic open-plan office. They'd dragged up wooden pallets and boxes and put them all around the edges and down the sides of the gangways. It was nearly dark, cos most of the windows were boarded up, but here and there were paraffin lamps and torches giving out bits of light and showing all the pale, strained faces. But no sign of Arthur anywhere.

By evening I was going out of my mind. I'd waited on the steps the whole day, watching boat after boat bring in survivors. There's hundreds of us now. Some people are really bad. And then suddenly Adi was there in front of me.

'Is it you?' I whispered.

'Sorry it took so long. I got trapped at my place.'

'Are your family OK?'

'Yeah. Yours?'

I choked. 'I don't know . . .' I buried my face in his shoulder. 'I . . . can't believe you came back.'

'I promised.'

Silence for a long moment. We held each other so tight. Then I pulled away.

'Arthur's not here. I've got a really bad feeling. We've got to go and check his house.'

'But there's no boats now, could be ages before they're back.'

'We've got to do something.'

He frowned. 'Come on. I've got an idea.'

I followed him down the rear stairs of the building and into a wide corridor stacked with wooden pallets.

'I saw these before when we came to see your mum. It's

the best we got right now. I'll drag one to the door, you use your foot to break one of those planks in half for a paddle.'

Once I'd split the wood I joined Adi, who'd got the pallet to the edge of the front steps. He shone a torch downwards. Flood water, raw sewage, dragged and sucked just below.

'Oh man,' said Adi. 'You really sure? This ain't no boat.'

'Adi, we've got to.'

He jutted his jaw out. 'Drop it in the water. Then can you get on and hold it against the side for me?'

I scrambled on to the rough wood, lay down, and plunged my hands into the freezing water so I could grip the steps. The pallet tipped like crazy when Adi jumped on.

'Let go!'

I released my grip and we spun out into the darkness. For a minute it was total madness – us smashing into walls, cars, beating away huge floating things – and then Adi shouted, 'When I say row, row. We've got to get in time! And go along the edge. It's not so fast. Now, row!'

I plunged my paddle into the water, again and again and again. For the longest time it felt like we were standing still while the world roared and frothed around us, but then the beam of Adi's torch swept over the top of Arthur's front door.

'Stop!' I shouted. 'We're here!' Together we drove the pallet up against the door. Adi passed a piece of rope down to me. 'Tie us on.' I lay flat on my stomach and groped forward until I reached the door and then knotted the rope around the handle.

'Keep still, Laur, I'm gonna break the window.'

The pallet rocked as he scrambled forward. The sound of breaking glass.

'Shit!'

'What?'

'Dropped the torch.'

I groped my way on to the window-sill behind him. For a moment we both sat on the ledge, no breath left between us.

'Jesus,' he gasped, wiping his face.

I cupped my hands around my mouth. 'Arthur!'

Nothing.

'All right, let's go in. D'you wanna go first? You know the house better.'

I plunged waist-high into the icy cold and slowly led the way into the pitch-black hall, calling out Arthur's name. We went thru to the kitchen and then the living room. Nothing.

'He ain't here,' muttered Adi. 'Upstairs?'

I held up my hand. 'Wait.'

'What?'

'Thought I heard something.'

We stood completely silent.

'Nothing, I guess.' I moved towards the hall stairs. And then I heard it again – coming from the kitchen. 'Over here!' I turned back into the kitchen, pots and pans bumping around me. 'Arthur! Where are you?' And then I remembered the box of matches he kept on the top shelf above the cooker. I felt my way along the wall till I reached the shelf, praying it was gonna be there. My fingers rubbed up against the cardboard. Yes! I grabbed the box, struck once, twice. The match flared up, I caught a glimpse of Adi's eyes, massive in his face, before sweeping the flame around the room. And then right in front of me there was a hand. I dropped the match.

'Adi. He's here!'

'Light another one.'

'I . . . can't.'

He waded over. 'Give me the box.'

The match struck, flared. I turned like a girl in a horror movie to see Arthur trapped under a pile of debris, up to his neck in water.

'Oh God,' I choked.

Adi reached out a trembling hand.

'Arthur?'

Nothing.

'He's trapped under this beam. We've got to lift it clear.'

'Is he . . . ?'

The match burned out, plunging us into darkness again.

'Light another.'

As the light came again I bent down over the old man and gently took his head in my hands.

'Arthur, please. We're going to get you out of here.' I scanned his face. Nothing. I tightened my grip. 'Oh, God, come on. Don't die on me, Arthur! Please!'

And then he smiled and whispered, 'Lau-r marv'l . . .' before fainting away again.

It felt like an electric shock passing right thru me.

'Adi! Adi! He's alive!'

'Right, hold him there. I'm gonna lift this beam off.'

I cradled Arthur in my arms while Adi slowly moved the wood to one side and then between us we dragged him out along the hallway to the door. If you ask me now how we got him on the pallet or back to the Co-op I don't know, but we did. I think Adi did most of it. Mostly I just remember Arthur's face, so old and frail.

When we got back to the centre they took him to a corner of the floor they'd set up for first aid.

'Is he gonna be OK?'

The woman gave a tired smile. 'We'll do the best we can for him. He needs to go to hospital, but . . .'

She let the rest of the sentence hang. We don't even know if there *are* any hospitals right now.

Midnight and still waiting. Adi sat with me for ages, but in the end I had to be alone. I went out on to the steps. After a while Mrs Datta came out with a waterproof.

'You're getting soaked,' she whispered. 'They'll be back soon.'

'When?'

'Soon.'

'But what if . . . ?'

She looked at the ground. 'They'll be back.' Adding quietly, 'Thank God my boy is away from all this.'

I didn't want to talk any more, then. Her quick look down was enough for me. After a bit I felt something wet on my arm. I lifted it, curious – to see I'd opened up the cut on my hand and blood was oozing out. But I couldn't feel it, it was like I was a thousand miles from everywhere. I tell you. You never think it's gonna happen to you, but all that pollution and dirty fumes and flights and factories and shit we don't need and suddenly there you are, a stupid girl sitting alone on some steps, waiting to see if your family is ever coming back.

Suddenly, a sound broke thru the storm. I froze. Something coming towards me? I couldn't even cry out. And then a boat came out of the blackness. And then I saw Mum. She was bent over someone – my heart went like ice. And then I saw Dad. Lying still. The boat pulled up to the steps. Mum cried out.

'Quick, get help. We found him floating in the water! But he's alive!'

2 a.m. Up on the 4th floor. It's freezing. We've wrapped Dad and Arthur up in like a hundred blankets. Arthur's sleeping peacefully, tough old bird, but Dad's out cold, shivering the whole time. Mum's cradling his head on her lap. Gwen Parry-Jones came and felt his pulse.

'Hopefully, it's just concussion,' she muttered. 'I'm so sorry, Julia. Wish I could do more.'

Mum smoothed the hair back from his face. 'I know, but I'll manage. I've been looking after this man for twenty years.' Then her face collapsed. 'But Gwen, my girl's out there. Why didn't he bring her back?'

Weds, Dec 2nd

A chopper came overhead early this morning. People ran on to the roof and waved, but it just circled around us a couple of times then shot off over the city. That was 4 hours ago. So much for air rescue. Adi is a total hero, though – he worked all thru the night to get a TV hooked up to an aerial and a battery.

'OK, people – we've got a TV working, gather round,' yelled GPJ. Everybody struggled up in their blankets and layers of clothing as the screen flickered into life. An American Sky presenter covered in make-up appeared onscreen.

'. . . London – a city on the brink of disaster. Can she hold on? The death toll is two thousand and climbing, but the *good* news is that so far today, the water level has not risen. However, the storm still shows no sign of blowing out – and what will happen at the *next* high tide?'

She turned sharply for a different camera angle, face full of fake concern. The screen filled with a map of London.

'This is the current status of flooding in the capital. The darkest sections represent five metres or more of flooding. When an embankment caves in under the strain of flood water, the collapse unleashes a *deadly* wall of water . . .' She raised an eyebrow as far as her Botox would allow. '. . . This acts like a battering ram, carrying *all* in its path.'

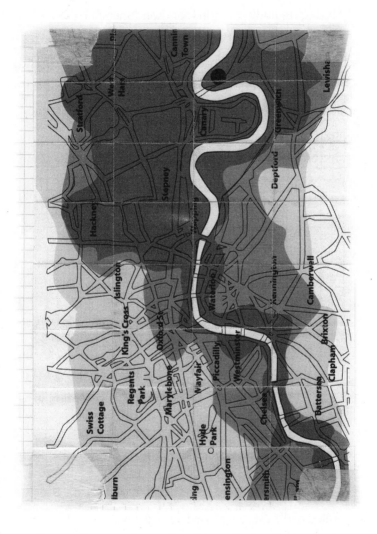

Cut to footage from the Olympic Stadium. A giant

crane floating in the main arena, smashing up against the stands.

'Today, literally millions of Londoners are stranded without electricity and with no access to phone networks. All hospitals have been badly hit – in particular, Guys and St Thomas', both close to the river. All over the capital, roads are impassable, cluttered with debris and abandoned vehicles . . .'

Cut to aerial shots of the Blackwall Tunnel – miles and miles of gridlocked, half-sunk cars.

'London Underground has been severely hit; specifically, the central zones and lines east of the river, which have experienced substantial flooding.'

Another cut to an aerial shot of Victoria Station, train tracks glinting underwater.

'The Prime Minister has convened the Civil Contingency Committee – or the Triple-C – at the Cabinet Office in Whitehall. An announcement is expected today as to whether a full-scale evacuation is to take place. Much depends on the next high tide at six p.m. If the barrier is over-topped again, every major governmental and rescue department will be forced to evacuate. Chaos will ensue. London waits.'

And so the hours passed and we waited. At 5 they switched the TV set on again. Complete silence, watching our own city fight for her life. All focus on the Barrier. The dirty, swirling Thames spreading out over the city. High tide. Aerial shots. Water sliding over the embankment walls. Tension. Minutes going by like hours. Flood water creeping up to the top of the Barrier. Climbing, falling, climbing, falling . . . and then, finally falling, falling – the Barrier had held! All of us crying, sobbing, grabbing at each other. Hundreds of dirty, lost souls.

8 p.m. Dad's still unconscious. Mum keeps calling and calling Kim's mobile, but there's no network anywhere. Please let her not be alone.

Midnight I couldn't sleep, so I went up to the roof and looked out over the black city. Suddenly I felt a hand on my shoulder. I knew it was him. Without a word I turned and we kissed, deep. We sank to the floor. Both of us the same. It was perfect. Me and Adi and the black water rushing all around us.

Thurs, Dec 3rd

I woke up with Adi next to me. I sneaked away without waking him and went to my parents. Dad's starting to scare me, he's totally burning up and keeps tossing and turning and muttering Kim's name. Adi came down and joined me and we held hands under the blankets. Didn't speak, nothing to say, nowhere to go, nothing to do. The power came on for a few minutes in the afternoon – the TV flickered on: the Prime Minister pleading for calm. The batteries are dead now. When will they come and rescue us?

Such a strange silence in the semi-darkness. Sometimes there's weird thuds and the sound of rushing water from outside. Some people talk and laugh, some just stay completely quiet. In a corner a woman's been singing quietly to herself all day. Over everything there's this strange tone that you can almost feel. Every now and again someone asks the time, 10 to 7, half past 12, quarter to 6 – but it all feels the same. People are lying asleep everywhere. They look like little children.

I woke up in the night to the sound of Mum sobbing. I didn't have any words, just held her hand.

Fri, Dec 4th

2 a.m. A miracle! My mobile buzzed. I snatched it up. Kieran.

I couldn't hear anything for ages, just static, then . . .

'Laur . . . me? . . . here . . . Kim's OK . . . but . . . can't get through . . .'

The network crashed again. We tried for hours to get thru again, nothing.

But she's alive!

Sat, Dec 5th

A chopper came overhead and dropped emergency food and water supplies on the roof. They dropped news flyers too. Thousands of army and UN soldiers are here. They're working 24/7 to pump the flood water out and set up rescue and medical centres across the city. The Mayor's ordered a complete ban on civilian movement unless it's an emergency. Duh.

Dad's fever is going down at last, he's finally stopped shivering like a dog. This afternoon he even drank a little water and sat up. 'I couldn't get to her, Ju. I went into Soho, to that Leopard place but she wasn't there. I walked the streets for hours, went in every bar. Nothing . . . I had to get back to Laura.' He put his head in his hands. 'I didn't know what to do, didn't mean to leave her . . .'

Mum stroked his shoulder. 'It's all right, Nick, she's with Kieran now. We'll go and get her together.'

He nodded. 'I'd got all the way to Greenwich when it started to flood. I ran and ran, thought I was going to make it, then on the corner of the High Street I just got knocked off my feet. Big wall of water . . . I . . . can't remember anything else . . .' He started to cough.

Mum eased him down on the pillow. 'Enough, now . . .' She turned to me. 'I can't believe we found him, Laura. We're so goddamn lucky.'

Sun, Dec 6th

Finally, finally some of the phone network is back, but all the emergency service numbers are jammed. I stood up on the roof with Adi while he spoke with his family. They're safe, but scared – they had to go to the 3rd floor of their building with 20 others. He hung up and stood there for a moment looking out over the streets.

'Y'know today was supposed to be our recording session?'

I ran my hands thru my hair. 'Oh God, yeah.'

He sighed. 'Feels like another life. It *was* another life.'

I reached out and took his hand. 'Adi, when did you know?'

''Bout you?' He paused, then broke into a grin. 'Dunno. I think it just crept up. This year's changed a lot of stuff, it's like I couldn't see before what was right in front of me . . . Plus I never thought I had a chance. I was way too normal – I mean, I actually *like* you.'

I laughed. 'All right . . . but I've changed too. Things are . . . clearer, somehow.'

I looked out across the devastation, hand in hand with my lovely boy, and I know this is weird, but I just felt so, so . . . *lucky*.

Mum can't get thru to Kim, though. She's been trying all day, but nothing. Suddenly this afternoon the power came on for 2 whole hours and all the lights and the TV monitor came to life. A huge evacuation is happening by the docks, but the rest of London is safe, even though 40% was flooded. The east has been hit the worst. The army found thousands of people wandering up and down the shattered A2, just past the Blackwall Tunnel – pushing shopping carts, laundry racks, anything they could find to carry their stuff away. Crowds were trapped on the other side of the tunnel. They waved up at the helicopter rescue teams with empty water jugs, begging for help.

Oh man, but the most disgusting thing ever is the rats. They've swarmed into the Olympic Stadium to escape the water. Millions of them, covering the stands like a sick, filthy, living, breathing carpet.

Bet that wasn't in the Olympic bid.

Mon, Dec 7th

Urggh. Can't move – it's like I've been punched in the head.

GPJ took one look at me. 'Flu. Lot of it around. Rest up.'

Adi came over just as I was vomiting into a bucket.

Tues, Dec 8th

Vomit, sleep, vomit, sleep. Woke up for a minute and overheard Mum talking to Kieran. He's got Kim down to an emergency treatment centre. She's got a fever and broken her arm. Mum wants to go straight down there, but Kieran said to wait. 'Julia, you don't know how crazy Soho is right now. There's no civilian movement yet. You'd never get thru . . . I'm looking after her the best I can.'

Weds, Dec 9th

The water's nearly drained away around Charlton. The army are going to let people move again tomorrow, but only for medical reasons. The Prime Minister's been all over London. He did that thing leaders do when they jump out of helicopters in shirt sleeves and talk about the human spirit. I keep falling into a flu stupor, can't move, just drift in and out of stuff going on around me. I woke up to this one, though.

'So what are we going to do about the rats when we get outside? Poison?'

'What sort of numbers are we looking at?'

'I read four thousand rats are born every hour in London.'

Gwen Parry-Jones cut in. 'Well, we'll just have to clear them out – one by one, if we have to. I'm not really sure how to do it, though. Anybody here got any experience?'

'I do. I was in New Orleans after Hurricane Katrina in '05. Got caught on holiday.'

I lifted my head from the pillow. A guy I recognised from up the street was talking, candlelight flickering across his exhausted face.

'First, we kill as many as we can by hand, but we've got to be really careful.' He nodded towards a crowbar leaning against the wall. 'Carry something like that, and a torch, and then you got to go through *everything* – furniture, drawers, mattresses, clothes, paper, appliances, dark corners, attics, cellars . . .'

An old woman raised her hand. 'They . . . don't really attack you, do they?'

'I'm not going to lie to you. Rats can be pretty ferocious. Go prepared.'

'What if you get bitten?'

The man looked down. 'Hospital and . . . the vet – to check the rat that bit you for rabies.'

Everyone looked sick.

'I know . . . it's horrible – but after we've killed as many as we can then we go on to using poison. Lots of it.'

'But what about the children?'

'Keep them home.'

GPJ frowned. 'And what about rubbish?'

'Yeah, very important. We've got to get rid of all food waste. Lift the bins high off the ground – on trees, on hooks, whatever.' He looked around at us all. 'And after that we keep up a daily patrol till the job's done.'

'How long?'

'Days, weeks, months.'

'How do we know?'

'When there's no more rats crawling over your feet at night.'

Arthur closed his eyes. He looked like he was shaking. I hope he's not getting sick and not telling anyone.

Later on at supper, I noticed Arthur was missing. I dragged myself out of my blankets and finally tracked him down on the stairs. I only clocked him cos of his lit cigarette tip. God knows where he'd got a smoke from.

'Arthur?'

No reply.

I climbed up, touched his arm. 'What's wrong?'

Silence while he took in a long drag. 'I was seventeen years old, on patrol. In the Ruhr Valley. There'd been running battles for days and they hadn't had time to clear away the bodies. So there I was, a skinny young boy with a rifle and a torch I could barely keep in my hand I was trembling so much. I was walking along a section of riverbank near a bridge and my torchlight picked out something up ahead. I . . . forced myself to go forward . . .' Arthur took another deep pull on his cigarette. '. . . And I saw three dead men lying on the ground, almost as if they'd fallen asleep – except . . . rats were running from under their coats, enormous rats, Laura, fat with human flesh. I bent down over the nearest man. His helmet rolled off . . . his face was stripped of flesh, the eyes devoured. Then from where his mouth was a . . . rat . . . leaped out.'

When I went down to the main hall, the stink hit me. I looked around – everybody's finished off. Dad looks like an old man.

Thurs, Dec 10th

Nut Brown dragged open the big steel front doors of the Co-op this morning and everyone went out on the front steps of the building, like we were posing for some totally messed-up wedding photo. Nothing to see but sewage and slime. And then the sun came out. Everybody gazed out in silence, dazzled by the play of sun on mud and swamp water.

'Now I know how Noah felt,' muttered Loud Dad, tears in his eyes.

Mum set off to find Kim straight away. She won't let Dad go.

'You're not well enough, Nicky. I'll be back before you know it.'

Dad sighed. 'No dramatics now – just stay out of trouble . . . please?'

'I promise.'

And then me and Dad stood on the steps and watched her walk down the filthy street till she turned the corner. Adi's gone too – to his family. It's only been a few hours and I'm already so lonely without him.

Mum got back just before dark. 'I couldn't make it past the Soho checkpoint without ID.' Her mouth was grim. 'ID for my own city. I can't believe it.'

'What'll you do?' asked Arthur.

'Go to the house tomorrow and find my goddamn passport.'

'What's the city like?'

'Don't ask . . . The army crews are still searching over the last bits of flooded area for the dead. They say the death toll's at two thousand, four hundred and fifty.'

There's a rumour going round that cholera's broken out in the east. It can't be true. That's like, so medieval.

Fri, Dec 11th

Every day gets stranger and stranger. Like Alice in Wonderland, cept it's real. Mum's finally with Kim, she called us from the medical centre in tears. Kim's got a bad fever and can't be moved. I could hear Mum crying down the phone. 'But this place is making her worse, Nick – it's nothing but filthy tents and dead bodies. I've got to get her out of here.'

It's been confirmed. There's an outbreak of cholera in Canning Town.

'Cholera?' cried Mousy Woman. 'Oh, you've got to be joking. Which world are we living in?'

'The third world now,' GPJ muttered. The room was suddenly full of people shouting.

The woman who ran the sick bay got to her feet and held up her hand. 'I'll tell you as much as I know. Cholera is an acute intestinal infection and it's spread mostly by contaminated water.'

'What are the symptoms?'

She checked off her fingers. 'Acute diarrhoea, vomiting, massive fluid loss. If it goes too far the body goes into shock, coma and . . . But mostly it's treatable. You've just got to get fluids back into the patient – in severe cases, intravenously. The trouble is that a lot of the time cholera's spread by infected people who don't look sick.'

GPJ cleared her throat. 'What can we do here?'

'OK, we've got to be really strict about food and personal hygiene – particularly about making sure the drinking water's clean. Then we've got to stay away from other people. Healthy-looking carriers and big groups of people are the fastest way to spread the disease.'

Dad raised his arm. 'But we can't do that. We've got to bring our daughter home.'

The nurse sighed. 'Then you can't bring her here. You'll have to set up a quarantine area in your own place.'

GPJ looked around at us all. Dirty and exhausted. 'I guess we've got two choices now – either we wait for the authorities to come, or we start sorting this mess out ourselves. I say sod waiting – where were they when we needed them before? We've proved we can look after ourselves once – and we can do it again now. What do you say, home for Christmas?'

A great murmur swept across the hall. People struggling out of blankets, standing up, grabbing each other's hands. GPJ laughed and raised her fist. 'Let's do it!'

You gotta hand it to that woman. She is some kind of hero.

Sat, Dec 12th

There's looting across the city, and it's spreading. The Mayor's ordered loads of police to stop search-and-rescue and get back to the streets to stop the raiding. The cholera's spread out from Canning Town. 5 dead overnight and 105 hospitalised today from Beckton and Silvertown. All water's been cut off in the east to stop people even *washing* with contaminated supply. The only way they can get water is from UN tankers. The army's set up a cordon around the area and soldiers are guarding the perimeter wearing those bio-chemical white boiler suits and masks.

Mum's gone back to Soho and Dad and me went over to our house this morning to start getting it ready for Kim. When we got there, we just stopped dead and stared at the mess. The water's all gone, but it's left behind the most massive, grossest, stinking pile of mud. Dad swayed on his feet, he's still so weak. 'Right, we'll just have to live upstairs to begin with.'

I looked at him. I think I finally understand about pretending everything is normal. If we don't we'll go under.

Sun, Dec 13th

There's talk that Soho's going to be cordoned off too. Queen Elizabeth Hospital down the road has opened up again to take in cholera cases from across the river. They're setting up an exclusive diarrhoea ward. Puke. I overheard Mum and Dad rowing about it. Dad wants to take Kim down there.

'No way!' shouted Mum. 'She's coming home.'

'But we don't know how to care for her properly, Julia.'

'You haven't seen these places. I have. They're where people go to die.'

Dad dragged his hand across his face. 'Don't say that . . .'

Mum sighed. 'I want her home.'

He nodded.

Weds, Dec 16th

Our street. For days now it's been nothing but work, work, work. Everywhere you look there's people zooming about with wheelbarrows, chopping, digging, clearing, slinging sandbags. We look like medieval peasants . . .

and the strange thing is everyone keeps throwing back their heads and laughing. Adi came round with Claire and Stace. We screamed when we saw each other, couldn't even speak. We are the *dirty angels*, yeah!

Loads of people have helped us cos of Kim. The whole street's pooled all their carbon points to power up saws, drills, water pumps, and whenever the grid powers back up they jump into life. We moved back to the top floor of our house at midnight – and only just in time. Mum and Kieran are gonna smuggle Kim out of the ward tomorrow. I was clearing the stairs this afternoon when Dad yelled from the bathroom. I ran up.

'Look!' he cried, pointing at the running tap. 'Water!'

The other good news is the looting's under control. But not before they shot 20 people. 4 shops have opened up on Lee Road. All the children on the street have gone down to get food for everyone, if there is any.

Thurs, Dec 17th

Finally, finally my sister's home! Between them, Mum and Kieran carried her into the hall and when I caught sight of her face, I nearly threw up. She's bad. Kieran's in my room now. I took him in some soup, but he pushed it to one side.

'We just sat there for days. Sometimes a body floated

past. I wanted to wade in and tie it down, *something . . .* but I can't swim.' He turned to face the wall. 'I see it every time I close my eyes.'

Sat, Dec 19th

I've queued for 2 days at the hospital for antibiotics for Kim. They've cleared out the reception, turned it into an emergency room and there's tents set up all over the car park. It was so horrible. At one point they wheeled in this little kid. He was curled up on a bed and he kept groaning, 'Please don't inject me,' but the doctor pushed a syringe into his skull and began to stitch up a deep cut in the back of his head. A man sat next to the boy, holding his hand so tight.

'I waited and waited for help, but no one came. No one came for my son.'

The doctor glanced up, but kept on stitching. Then 2 new patients were rushed in. A girl cried out in pain. The doctor rushed off to help.

I got chlorine tablets, but no antibiotics for my sister. We've got to pray she's not got cholera. I feel so useless.

Sun, Dec 20th

Kim keeps throwing up again and again. She's dead cold,

but her sheets are soaked in sweat. The army shot 6 people for trying to escape from Canning Town. 11 more people died overnight.

Mon, Dec 21st

Mum's birthday. She heard about antibiotics being given out in a UN emergency centre in Crystal Palace on the radio and jumped straight on my bike, cycled 15 Ks, queued all day and then cycled home. She nearly collapsed when she came thru the door, but she reached into her pocket and pulled out a packet.

'Laura, look! I've got doxycycline for Kim. Seven days' supply.'

She dropped the pack, her hand was trembling so much.

I gave her a Shiseido moisturiser sachet that I'd found round the back of the pig pen. She took it in her shaky, gnarled hands and then burst into tears.

Kim's got to start getting better now.

Tues, Dec 22nd

Unbelievable! I was washing pans out the back when I heard Arthur calling my name from the street.

'Laura! He's here! He's back! Laura, come now!' I threw down my rag and ran thru the house – out on to the street

– and there he was . . . Larkin! I ran over and just flung my arms around his neck and he threw his head back and squealed with joy. Wonderpig!

The whole neighbourhood threw their tools down and gathered round as I took him back to his pen. When I closed the latch, everybody cheered. I tell you, that pig is so cool. He's like the Red Indian totem spirit of the street.

Weds, Dec 23rd

When is Kim going to get better? The antibiotics should be kicking in by now. It's too dangerous to move her and we can't get a doctor to come out. The scariest thing is her nails and fingertips. They're starting to turn blue.

Adi came round and I buried my head on his shoulder and cried and cried and cried.

He whispered, 'You've got to hold on.'

'Why?'

'Because . . . is all.'

I burst into tears again. 'I can't go on like this, Adi . . . what's going to happen—'

He stopped me. 'Don't. Day by day is all. And tomorrow's Christmas Eve.'

I stared at him. 'Christmas? You're joking, right?'

'Nah, mate. Leave me out of it – that's God's joke, that one.'

Thurs, Dec 24th

2 a.m. I found Mum slumped asleep by Kim's side. I shook her shoulder. 'Mum, go and lie down. I'll watch her.'

She ran her hands thru her filthy hair. 'OK, but call me, if . . . if anything . . .'

'I will.'

So I'm here with my sister now. I watch her chest rise and fall, terrified the next breath will be the last. It's dark outside, but there's a new moon shining thru the window. I've never felt so powerless. I lean forward and grab Kim's arm, suddenly furious.

'Come on, you bitch. Fight.'

I look down at her pale, thin face, so different . . . and then the most amazing thing happens. She takes in a long, deep, shuddering breath – and a red flush sweeps across her cheek and neck. It's impossible, but it's happening right in front of me. Life is flooding back into my sister.

'*Kim . . . Kim!*'

She opens her eyes for a moment. Recognises me. I squeeze her hand. She squeezes back and then falls asleep again.

Fri, Dec 25th

I've never had such a beautiful day. It's our own miracle. It's evening now and we're all in Kim's room. The candle's nearly finished so I'm taking everything in before the light dies. It flickers over Dad's face, makes him look about 20 years old. He's got tight hold of Kim's hand. Mum's leaning back against the wall, silent, but she's got this tiny little smile playing around the corners of her mouth as she gazes at my sleeping sister, breathing peacefully.

Sat, Dec 26th

Adi and me went round to Arthur's this afternoon. When he saw us he held up a finger and dashed out of the kitchen, reappearing a moment later with a bottle of rum and 3 glasses.

'Always keep a secret stash, that's what I say!' He lowered himself down on to a chair and sat a moment, with the low winter sun falling across his face.

'Ah, it feels good to be alive!'

He took both our hands in his. 'This is what it felt like in the war. Every day I was just so grateful to still be here.'

Mon, Dec 28th

Kim's definitely getting better. She even had a scrap with Mum this afternoon. Talk about music to my ears.

Looked at my carbon card this afternoon – I made it, still got half a block left. Unbelievable.

Tues, Dec 29th

They think they've controlled the cholera outbreak. No one died last night.

Weds, Dec 30th

All clear, again.

Thurs, Dec 31st

Everyone's still working like dogs cos there are loads of families not back home yet. But something big happened today. Tracey Leader gunned her Jeep down the street. God knows where she's been. She parked up, got out, lit up a fag and looked up and down the road. It was like she was laughing at us. Everything went dead silent. Mops, brushes, hammers, drills all suddenly still. And then Mousy Woman – of all people – stepped forward.

'No,' she said.

Tracey looked her up and down.

'You *wot*?'

'No more Jeep, no more black market. We know . . .'

Tracey snorted. 'Course you know. It's youse lot buying off me.'

'No. You're wrong. *Not* us lot.' Mousy shoved past Tracey, lifted her arm high and smashed her hammer on the boot of the Jeep.

Tracey went to drag her away, but suddenly Loud Dad was there. He pushed Tracey to the ground and dragged his chainsaw across the Jeep door, spraying sparks everywhere. And then a crossbow dart thudded into the front tyre. In 30 seconds the Jeep was *covered* in crazed neighbours, jumping all over it like a gang of jackals – smashing, bending, ripping and rocking – until, with a huge shove, they flipped the Jeep over on its roof.

Mousy Woman turned to Tracey. 'Tracey Leader,' she gasped. 'The law might not be able to touch you, but we can. Now clean up or piss off!'

It was about the best thing I've seen all year.

So, it's the last day. I wish I had some big words to finish, but I've got nothing. I made it thru – but my family, the *angels*, college, the future . . . I don't know. Like Adi says, it's just one day at a time from now on. That's the only thing I got left.

ISBN-13: 978 0 340 97015 7

Typeset in Berkeley by Avon DataSet Ltd,
Bidford on Avon, Warwickshire

Printed and bound in Great Britain by
TJ International Ltd, Padstow, Cornwall

The paper and board used in this paperback by Hodder Children's Books
are made from 100% recycled material. The manufacturing processes
conform to the environmental regulations of the country of origin.

Hodder Children's Books
a division of Hachette Children's Books
338 Euston Road, London NW1 3BH
An Hachette Livre UK Company

THE CARBON DIARIES 2015

SACI LLOYD

Hodder
Children's
Books

A division of Hachette Children's Books

For my mother